THE HAY PATROLLERS

Book Two

Another Juvenile Crime-Prevention Story

By Brian Montgomery

"EVERY COMMUNITY SHOULD 'AVE 'EM!"

Version 1.0
ISBN 978-1-9993151-3-9
www.dhconsulting.me.uk

I once heard a politician say, "Parents are losing control of their kids." That same politician also blamed parents for the increase in juvenile gang-related crime within our communities. Are parents really to blame or is it society in general? I will let you decide.

Having already completed my first crime-prevention novel: *Degsy Hay, A Juvenile Redeemed*, I knew the importance of completing book two in the series: *Degsy Hay, The Hay Patrollers*. Not only have I been inspired by everyone that has been part of my team, 'The Hay Promoters', which went on to become a reality Down Under in Perth, Western Australia, but I wanted to create a platform to show how valuable these types of juvenile crime-prevention programmes are and how they can make a difference if they are given more recognition and long-term support to work within the community.

ACKNOWLEDGEMENTS

I would like to thank my mentor and editor, Hayley Sherman, from Whoosh! Editing.
www.whoosh-editing.com

Rathamani, Aneesha and Benjamin, who have been there for me from the start.

Olly and More-Visual, for assisting me again with an excellent cover design.

Monique Monks, my website designer
www.walkinwebshop.co.uk

A special thank you to the Hay Promoters team (you know who you are), who not only joined up but also turned it into a huge success.

CONTENTS

1 DO YOU SMELL BURNING?

I must have been out of it when the fire started because it crept up on me in my dream – nar'mean? Like when you dream you're out walking the street, minding your own business, and all the car alarms start screeching, and then you realise it's your alarm going off and it's time to get up. Only, I wasn't dreaming about streets or car alarms. I was dreaming about Gabby like I always did. We were on a beach together, lying on those sunbed things, reaching across to each other, looking into each other's eyes. The dogs were skipping beside us, and then Sadface jumped up on me, landing me square in the nuts, but we all laughed because in this dream they're still alive and we're a family on holiday.

"Bloody hot!" she said to me. It wasn't the most romantic thing to say. And we couldn't complain about the heat anyway; made a change from being on the frozen streets of London together, sleeping on a bench with only hooch and weed to keep us warm, but that was all in the past now, and this was a dream anyway. "Why's it so bloody hot?" she asked.

I could feel it then, the heat, and when I turned to her, I could see she was bright red and sweating like a guilty geezer in the stands. I could feel it too. It was flipping hot. I knew this was a dream beach, but I didn't fancy getting roasted.

"And what's that noise?" she said, looking around and out to sea.

I could hear it too. It sounded like the sea was raging, screaming out, scrapping with itself, but when I looked across, it was still. Then a crashing noise. There was nothing around us but sand and sea, though.

I got up off the sunbed. The noises were getting louder and stranger and although I only had these little shorts on, I was so hot I wanted to rip my skin off.

"Don't worry," I told Gabby, but when I turned back to her, she'd gone. I should've got used to losing her by now, cos it happened every night in every dream (she's there and then she isn't – just how it happened in real life), but it still surprised me. "Gabby!" I'm calling. "Gabby!"

And then – Crash!

And I was awake and back in the house, in my bedroom, back to reality. And before my eyes were even open properly, I was up and off the bed. Something was seriously wrong. The dream was over, but the heat, the noise, the crashing, it was all still going on, and the room was tinged with orange, lit up in a way that might have been relaxing if I hadn't been hacking my guts up from the smoke creeping in under the door.

I heard a shout from the hallway. "Degsy! Winston! Degsy!" They were shouting it together, Mya and Sheila. At least they were okay, but I didn't know what to do. The flipping house was on fire, and I was standing there in my boxers, too shocked to do anything. Then I got over myself and sprang into action. I whipped the duvet off the bed and wrapped it around me. I'd seen geezers do that in films. Then I realised they do it with wet blankets and towels, not duvets, and I'd turned myself into a great big, flammable marshmallow, so I flicked it off again, ran over to the door and pulled it open. My heart was pure drum and bass, but it wasn't as bad as I thought. I couldn't see much of anything because of the smoke, no flames, but that orangey glow was still there, and I didn't like the look of it, so I breathed into my arm and ran down the stairs. I'd run down the stairs a hundred times since we all moved into that house, but now none of it was familiar or safe. With every step, I was bricking it, thinking the stairs would collapse or a wave of flames would lick out over the bannister and torch me, but I kept going, blinded by smoke now, my lungs black and useless, coughing out razor blades. And then the outside was in sight – the streetlamps and cars and pavement and maybe even some stars. The front door was wide open, and just a few more steps would take me out into the night, where the air was breathable, and I had a chance to live again. A few more steps and I made it. I dropped down to my hands and knees, retching and hacking lumps onto the pavement, then dropped down and rolled onto my back, letting the freezing cold pavement put out the fires on my flesh. As you know, lying down in the streets ain't my thing, so this was a first.

"Shit! You okay, Degs?"

Sheila and Mya were both standing over me in their dressing gowns, looking red but unhurt. I leapt up just to make sure.

"You okay? What happened? You ain't hurt, are ya?" I asked.

"We're fine," Mya answered and turned to the open doorway, staring beyond, into the flames. I followed her line of vision.

"Fuck me! What the hell happened?" I said.

The downstairs window had exploded, and reds, oranges, yellows and blacks were fighting in the living room, squeezing and strangling the life out of each other and smashing up the furniture, clawing up the walls and roaring out a deafening battle cry. As the curtains went up in a sudden whoosh, I stood there hypnotised, feeling the heat on my face.

Then I realised Winston wasn't there.

All four of us had been in that night. We'd watched a movie and chatted about some new project ideas for the Hay Patrollers. Then we'd said our goodnights and gone to bed.

"He's still in there!" Sheila cried, looking up to the bedroom window.

I looked up. It was still dark up there. The fire had obviously started downstairs, but it wouldn't be long until it found its way up to the bedrooms.

"Winston!" I shouted, and Mya and Sheila joined in, cupping our hands and screaming to be heard over the flames and destruction. "Winston! Winston!"

Nothing.

"You call the fire brigade?" I asked.

"They're on their way," Mya answered. But there were no sirens to be heard. I looked up and down the street, which was dead and empty but for some drunk geezer staggering home after a night on the piss.

"Winston! Winston!" we all shouted again. Then I knew I had no choice. I had to go back in.

I ran back to the door. Mya and Sheila were shouting at me, pulling at my bare arms to make me listen, but the only thing on my mind was Winston, The only sounds I could hear were the wild crackles of the fire, laughing at me, threatening to take someone else from my life, but I'd lost too many people already to let that happen. No, I was gonna save Winston, or I was gonna die trying. We'd been friends from birth. We might have lost contact for a while, but we were mates again now, best mates, and nothing was gonna happen to him on my watch.

"Winst—" I tried to shout again as I ran back into the oven, but it was like my mouth was filled with sand, and my skin was sweating and burning again. Then I began coughing again. I pulled the door closed behind me to shut out the oxygen and stop the fire spreading. Now, I have to admit; I was scared. I didn't wanna die, but I couldn't let Winston burn. I rushed at the stairs, but my body was moving slower than I wanted it to as if everything was happening in slow motion, and just lifting my foot high enough to clear each step was harder than I thought possible. The slicing pain of razor blades were back in my lungs, and although the living room door was closed, separating me from the fire, I knew I couldn't take much of this. After what felt like climbing flipping Everest, I reached the landing, passed my door then ran through to Winston's, which was still shut. I'd normally knock before going in, but this was definitely an exception, so

I turned the handle and shouldered it, bursting in and shouting as loud as my lungs let me.

"Winston, man! What the fuck?"

The bedroom looked normal, considering the house was on fire, although I couldn't smell the hair and body products I normally enjoyed taking the piss out of over the smoke and burning plastic, brick and wood. A gap in the curtains lit up the room with a thin line of streetlight, and I could see the geezer was just a lump in the bed. He was in bed! Still asleep! I knew he was a heavy sleeper, but this took the piss.

"Winston! The house's on fire geezer! Get up!" I shouted, and he didn't even stir. "Get up!" I pounded on him now, shaking him hard, then pulled his black duvet off him. "Get out of bed!"

"Hmmmmm! What the—? 'S not funny, mon!"

"I ain't joking, geezer! The fucking house is burning down!"

"Yeah, and I'm Father Christmas! Give it a rest, Degs, you muppet!"

Winston's almost as big as I am, but I managed to reach in and drag him off the bed. He landed with a lump on the floor, and he probably would've killed me if he hadn't started coughing his guts up.

"Believe me now?" I shouted, but my voice was lost to a scary crash, much louder than the ones I heard before. It sounded like a giant boot had stepped down on the house, crushing it like a flipping spider – nar'mean? Shit! It felt like I was that spider, and Winston had balled himself up on the floor and didn't look like he was getting up any time soon.

"What's going on?" he asked, turning to find me in the dark.

"Dunno! But we gotta get out off 'ere!"

I ran back to the door and opened it slowly, scared to see what'd be behind it now. And I was right to be scared. I couldn't even see my bedroom door anymore, or any of the others and the stairs had either collapsed or burned. I had no idea. I think my eyeballs got burnt. It was like looking into the sun's pain-in-the-arse little brother, who'd broken into our gaff and was seriously mugging us off.

I pushed the door shut and fell against it, huffing and puffing and not getting half as much air in my lungs as I needed. Winston was up now and pacing.

"Let me see!" he said, but I wasn't moving from the door. I don't think I could. Then he ran over to the window and pulled it open. It was a two-floor drop, but I could see he was thinking about it.

"You'll break your neck!" I shouted.

"You got a better idea?"

I didn't have a better idea. Ideas were pretty flipping thin on the ground. All I knew was that if we stayed where we were, we'd be toast before the fire brigade could get to us.

"Shift!" Winston told me, rushing back to the door. I wasn't gonna move, but I could see he was serious, so I stepped aside.

"We'll make some rope," I spluttered. "Tie some … tie … get sheets and …" I could barely talk now, but Winston wasn't listening anyway. He'd opened the door again and slammed it shut, just as I'd done.

"We gotta go through," he told me. "There's no other way, mon."

I was coughing too much to answer now, and he was at my side, his arm around my shoulder.

"We'll run for it, Degs. Down the stairs, out the door. It's all we got."

"Window!" I spluttered.

"It's too high. We ain't got time. We gotta go now, Degs!"

I could hear his words, but they were making less and less sense to me. Everything was mashing up in my brain as if it were made of the wrong thing. I could taste the words and see the sounds and feel the sights. It was trippy – nar'mean? And not in a good way. Then I knew my body was moving, and I wasn't in control of it anymore. I'd breathed in so much smoke it was coming out of my ears. My brain to had turned to mush, but I knew Winston had me. My arm was flung over his shoulder, my feet were dragging behind, and he'd taken my weight. I was a sack of spuds, but he was strong, and we were soon at the door. Then it was open, and that's all I remember. I remember that moment clear enough. It was like the world had turned into one of those colour-mirror tubes that kids play with. You know, a kaleidoscope. The door was open, and the purest, most colourful burst of light zapped us full-on in the face. And that's all I remember.

I didn't expect ever to wake up again, but the next thing I remember is doing just that. Waking up. It was confusing at first because there was this black blob in front of my eyes as if I'd spent the day staring at the sun, and now everything was hidden behind a stupid black ball. I could see around it, but when I tried to move my eyes or my head, it followed me. I blinked again and again, but it wouldn't shift.

"He's awake," I heard someone say. I recognised the voice, but it took a sec to put a name to it. I may have been awake, but everything still felt weird, and my brain wasn't doing its job properly yet. "Can you hear me, Degs?"

It was Mya.

I slowly turned my head in the direction of the voice. I could see the outline of her wavy, dark hair. I could see her Hay Patrollers blue hood, zipped up as high as it'd go, one arm reached out to me, but that black sun blob wouldn't move so that I couldn't see her face. I felt her take my hand in hers and I turned, still blinking, trying to work it all out. I was in the hospital. I could make out the whites and greens around that black blob, although all I could smell was burning rather than the antiseptic clean of the ward. There was a curtain to the left of me, and I could feel a soft blanket over my body. Was I alright? I felt alright. Then a more urgent question came knocking on the door.

"Winston!" I said, turning back to Mya. Her face was a

little clearer now. My eyes were coming back into focus, the blob was disappearing, but I wished I couldn't see her expression. She was chewing her bottom lip, looking at me with glassy, serious eyes, but saying nothing. "Is he dead?"

She slowly shook her head, and I let out a deep breath, but there was no relief on her face.

"Well? What? Tell me."

"You just need to relax now, Degsy. You've been through a lot," she said and squeezed my hand, but I pulled away from her.

"I ain't worried about me. Where's Winston?"

She bit her lip again, trying to stop the words coming out. "Tell me!"

She took a deep breath and said, "He's in a bad way, Degsy. The whole place was coming down after you went in. You're lucky to be alive."

I didn't feel lucky.

"The fire brigade got you both out. I don't know; something fell on Winston. I don't know what. You were both out of it when they dragged you out. But Winston ..." She paused, looking as if she might cry. "He doesn't look good. They say he's in a coma. Sheila's with him, and I'm ... well ... I'm with you," she added and then she wouldn't meet my eyes.

"I've gotta get out of 'ere!" I announced to the whole ward, which was made up of old boys in wartime pyjamas looking like they were breathing their last. Everyone turned to look at me, but I didn't care. And then a couple of nurses came running over. One started examining me while the other had a go.

"Mr Hay, I advise you to lie still and wait for the doctor. You've been through—"

"A lot. Yeah, I know!" I snapped back at her. I didn't mean offence, but I couldn't just lie there while Winston was in a coma.

"Mr Hay! If you would just—"

"No, miss, I won't!" I barked. I hadn't lost the habit of calling women in uniform 'miss' from my prison days, and I still wasn't good at taking orders. We eventually came to an understanding, though. I'd be allowed to visit Winston if I let them check me over. Mya could wheel me there in a chair, and I'd come back to the ward after. I'd see the doc after that, and he or she'd let me know what'd happen next. From what that nurse told me, though, I was alright. I sounded like I'd smoked a duty-free box of Marlboro and been thumped in the chest, I was a bit burnt here and there, but there was nothing wrong with me that a bit of rest wouldn't fix, which made me feel even worse when I saw Winston.

He was in a room of his own with nurses coming and going, checking him out and making notes on their clipboards. Mya'd wheeled me to the door, but I wanted to walk in on my own, so I left her in the hallway. She'd been fussing over me all the way there, asking if I was okay, if I needed anything. All I needed was to see my bro, but when I walked in, it wasn't Winston I saw at all. Winston was young and strong, tall and full of energy. The thing on the bed was small and defeated with tubes and wires running in and out of it. His hands were balled up in bandaged boxing gloves, and I just hoped there was some fight left in them because he'd need it. His head was bandaged too and part of his face. My mind started going over it again; should we have stayed put? Tried the window? Was there something else we could've done? I don't know. I was out of it from smoke inhalation. Maybe I'd have burnt to death in that room if he hadn't dragged me out. He was a hero.

Sheila was at his bedside. She was still in her dressing gown. I suppose everything else had burnt. Her hair was gripped tight behind her. It was strange to see her without makeup on. She never let people see her without makeup. It reminded me of the Sheila I'd shared a cell within McAlley-Stokes, but that felt like a hundred years ago now. So much had changed since then, and not just her surgery.

She turned to me, looking tired and upset. "Oh, Degs," she said in that soft voice of hers and started crying.

I went over there and put my arm around her. Her head fell on my shoulder, and I tried to comfort her, but I couldn't take my eyes off Winston.

"What have they said?" I asked as Sheila started to pull herself together.

"Smoke inhalation … first-degree burns …" she told me sadly, and then she hesitated. No one wanted to tell me anything, and I was about to find out why. "It's not good, Degsy. The ceiling came down in him. If he survives, they say he might have brain damage."

"If he survives?" I raged. Then a nurse gave me a look I'd seen a hundred times, and I lowered my voice. "What do you mean *if* he survives?"

"I don't know, Degs. Something about swelling on the brain. All they can do is watch him and hope he comes round. If he does … who knows?"

"That's a lot of hoping and waiting," I said. I could feel my fists balling and took a deep breath. "Ain't there anything they can do?"

She slowly shook her head. "Hope and wait. That's what they told me. We should talk to him, though. They said he might be able to hear us."

I took another deep breath, and it hurt my throat and lungs, but it cleared my brain a little. "Okay, look," I said, "you go grab a coffee, Sheila. Mya's out there. I'll stay here for a bit."

She looked concerned for a minute, looking at my face as if I was the one lying on a bed, crispy and fried. Maybe I looked worse than I felt.

"I'm okay," I said, thinking that was what she needed to hear.

She gave a thin little smile, turned and left. The nurse also left, and I was on my own with him. I didn't know what to do at first. It was so strange. We'd been on our own a hundred times before. We'd chatted through the night and worked together to make the Hay Patrollers happen and draw out the plans for our homeless housing complex, Unit 16-21, but what could I say to him now? How do you chat to a geezer in a coma?

"Alright, mate?" I said, before dropping down into the chair beside him. I hadn't realised how wobbly I was on my pins until I sat down. Maybe Sheila and Mya were right to worry about me too, but Winston was the one who needed worrying about. I leaned in closer and said, "Winston!" Then I said it a few more times, a bit louder, thinking maybe he'd hear me and wake up, but he didn't move an inch. He looked peaceful in a funny sort of way. "I've never seen you this quiet before, geezer," I joked, but I had to wipe a tear away at the same time. Then I heard myself say, "Don't do this to me, Winston. I can't lose you too. I've only just found you again." More tears came, but I swallowed them back and made myself strong again. Then I leaned in close. "I know you can hear me, geezer," I told him. "And I need you to listen to me. You ain't gonna die. Do you hear me? I won't let it happen. You and me against the world, innit. So you just rest, bruv. Take as long as you need. We'll all be here waiting for you, keepin' things going. You just get better. Do ya hear me?"

I hadn't heard anyone come in, but I felt a hand on each of my shoulders. Mya and Sheila were standing behind me, looking just as grave as I felt.

"He's gonna get better!" I told them. "And we've gotta keep it all going for him – the Hay Patrollers, Hay Assist, Unit 16-21. What time is it? We're supposed to be meeting that geezer about the prison visits at nine." I realise now that I sounded a bit bonkers – nar'mean? But I didn't know what else to do or say.

It turned out, I didn't make the meeting or work for the whole of that week. When I got back to my hospital bed, I was asleep before my head hit the pillow. They kept me in for a few days, and then I went to a hotel and slept some more. Sheila and Mya were sorting out a new place for us to live, but, for the moment, a hotel was better than the streets. So I slept. They said it was my injuries, shock and the medication they'd given me. It was almost a week until I was back on my feet again, feeling a hundred per cent. And in that time, Winston had made no progress at all.

2 A SLIPPERY SLOPE

When I got into the office on that first day back, no one knew what to do with me, whether to cheer because I'd survived or hug me because Winston hadn't been so lucky, so they were awkward instead, asking if I needed anything every five minutes without bringing up the fire. I didn't blame them. I don't think I'd know what to do with me either.

Our office was a bit bigger now because we'd grown and things needed to be organised, both for Unit 16-21 and all the things the Hay Patrollers were doing, but at its core were still Winston, me, Sheila and Mya. Everything went through us. It was a bright space, and we'd been lucky to get it. The walls were covered with pictures of the things we'd achieved, media coverage, and charts showing where we'd been and where we were going. When I got in that morning, Sheila and Mya were sitting around the block of desks we shared, and space where Winston should have been sitting was too painful to bear.

"What we doin' then?" I asked as I dropped myself into my seat. I was trying to sound as bright as possible, but I still sounded a little croaky. I knew what we were doing, though – I always knew what we were doing – but it was just something to say – nar'mean? I knew we had contracts in shopping centres all over the place now, with young people patrolling and getting paid for it too. We'd worked so hard to make it happen, and it was amazing to see if taking off. Not just the big picture, but we'd all got to know the kids involved. We'd seen them volunteer with us and then move onto paid work. Some were off the streets; some were in gangs, some had disabilities and had been thrown on the scrapheap. They all thought they were worth nothing, and we'd been able to reach out to them. And then there were the community projects: cleaning graffiti, painting, picking up litter, gardening, raising money. It helped the community and raised our profile, but it did so much more than that. The kids getting involved were the kids who would've been spraying the graffiti and destroying the neighbourhood before. We'd touched so many lives, and I was proud of that. I was starting to believe we could change the world. But then, I hadn't met Slope yet.

"Well," Mya began, filling me in, "if you feel like getting stuck in, Rachel Watson's here to see you. Doesn't wanna speak to any of us." She sniffed as she said the name as if she didn't like the woman, but Rachel had been a great support to us. She was a social worker who'd welcomed what we were doing and often worked with us.

"Any idea what she wants?"

Mya shrugged, and I knew that was all I was gonna get on the subject, then she added, "Phyllis called to see how you are. She wants you to let her know when you wanna see Asha and Ray again."

The thought made me smile. I'd written to Asha and Ray a few times, and they'd sent me some letters and pictures telling me how excited they were to meet their new big brother. As you know, I had no idea my devil mother even had other kids, but now I had a family, I was gonna hold onto it. I'd met them twice now. Once I went over to Phyllis and Trevor's house, their foster parents, and had a bite to eat with them, and another time I took them over to the community centre to see the work we were doing there. They loved it. They're both gonna follow in my footsteps, I think. I was supposed to be seeing them again last week, but the fire took care of that. They were cute kids and we got on well. I couldn't get over how smart they were. They were both doing so well in school and they spoke properly. There was no slang in them. They were getting a good upbringing and would never have to worry about where their next meals were coming from, if they'd get stabbed in the night, or if some junky had stolen all their worldly possessions. They were just normal kids, and I loved being around them.

"We've rescheduled the school visit for tomorrow," Mya was telling me. "And a few more later in the week. Are you gonna be up for doing them?"

"Of course," I smiled. We'd been doing school visits for a few months now, sharing our stories, spreading the word and talking to kids about their lives, so I was looking forward to getting back to it. The juvenile prison visits were a new thing, and I knew they'd work just as well. The surprising thing about the visits though, everybody would hear Mya and Sheila tell their stories. I thought I knew both of them quite well. It turned out I had no idea. Anyway, you'll hear more about that later.

"And Jarra wanted me to tell you he needs a date for your Australia trip. They'll get you the ticket, but they need to know when you're going."

Shit! The Australia trip. They'd been raising money to kick-start the Hay Patrollers over there, and I was supposed to be joining them for a few weeks, helping set things up, but how could I go now? How could I do anything with Winston in a coma?

"I'll give him a ring," I said.

"And, Degsy," Mya added, "I hope you know I ain't your secretary."

I turned suddenly to look at her. She was half smiling and there was some other expression on her face that confused me. "I know that."

"This is special circumstances. Now you're back; you can answer the phone yourself."

"Yes, your majesty," I joked, and this seemed to do the trick, as she left me with a smile and wandered off with an armful of Hay Patroller uniforms. She was a puzzle, that woman, but for now, Rachel Watson was waiting in the snug, and I was curious about what she wanted.

The snug was really just a side room, but we'd thrown in some comfy chairs, tea and coffee, a few candles and pictures, and it was great for having private chats with the parents or social workers who came in to see us. Rachel was sitting down, drinking a cup of tea, but stood up when I went in.

"Desgy, my God! How are you doing? I heard about the fire."

"I'm good, thanks. How are you?" The fire was the last thing I wanted to talk about.

"How's Winston?"

Correction: Winston was the last thing I wanted to talk about.

"He's getting there," I lied. "So, what can we do for you today?"

"Any idea what started it?" She was like a dog with a bone.

I shook my head. "No idea. We're waiting for the police and fire investigators to get back to us. Probably some crappy electrics or something – nar'mean? So, what brings you here, Rachel?"

She was a little bit older than me and always looked and smelled really good, but I'd never go out with someone through work. It wouldn't be right.

"So, there's this lad," she said and flicked open the front of her folder. "Fourteen, Sudanese, came here on his own as a refugee a few years ago, spent some time in detention, on the streets, he's just been moved from a secure unit to a home not too far from here." She took out a few sheets of paper and handed them to me. I read through a list and could see this little geezer had been busy. He'd picked up a couple of suspended sentences, community service, and was going down if he didn't shape up. He was into drugs, violence, thieving; you name it.

"Sadiq Wardi," I read.

"Slope," she told me. "He goes by the name of Slope."

I carried on reading, about his life and all the things he'd been getting up to, as she carried on speaking.

"His parents are presumed dead. They didn't come over anyway. I don't know how much you know about the Civil War in South Sudan, but he'd have been running for his life. To do it on his own … well, he's obviously got something about him, but I don't know, Degs. He's broken. How could he not be? I have no idea what he's seen. I can't imagine what he went through to get all the way here. It's a miracle he made it."

"Why'd he come to the UK?"

"Apparently his brother had made a run for it, lived here, so he had a connection, but no one's been able to track him down. Any record of him ends a few years back. He wasn't reported missing, but he probably didn't have anyone here to miss him. We can only assume he's dead too or legged it somewhere else. Who knows. Anyway, Slope's angry or trying to fit in or … I just don't know. He won't talk to any of us. He's been running around with some lads. Maybe he's never had this kind of freedom before."

"What's his brother's name?"

She leafed through the folder again and said, "Malik Wardi. Big bloke apparently. Also answers to the name Everest. Twenty years old."

"So, when's he coming in?" I asked. "We've got a group meeting up this afternoon at the Unit 16-21 site, putting up more temporary homeless units. I'd need to have a chat with him first, but he can come and get stuck in."

"We're not quite at that stage yet, Degsy."

"I see." I got up and poured myself a cup of tea then joined her again. "You know these kids need to wanna come along and change their lives. I can only meet them halfway, Rach."

She looked me square in the eyes, smiling a little, and said, "I know, but I hoped you could make an exception for him."

I opened my mouth, starting to protest, but she interrupted-
ed.

"I'm scared we're going to lose him, Degsy. It'll be prison if he can't sort himself out. Or worse. I don't know what he's getting mixed up in, and he's vulnerable. He plays the big man, but it's not who he is. I know you'd be good for him."

What could I say to that? I read over the sheet again, and when I looked up, I could see she was holding her breath, waiting for my answer. I could see how desperate she was.

"Okay," I finally said. And I thought she was gonna jump up and hug me, but she restrained herself to a bubbly smile. "Where can I find him, then?"

She tore a page out of her pad, started writing then handed it to me. "This is the name of the home, but it might not be the best way of getting to him. He hangs about under the bridge near the works on the Addie."

I smiled, and my whole life flashed before my eyes. I might have guessed it'd be the bleeding Addie Estate. I'd had enough of that shithole to last me a lifetime, and here I was being sucked back onto it. This wasn't about me, though.

"You can find him there most nights," she added and handed me a picture. He was a scrawny, dark-skinned lad in need of a decent meal, and he obviously didn't wanna have his picture taken because his head was half turned away, and he was sneering, his mouth a little open as if he was about to tell whoever was taking the picture to fuck off.

"Is he carrying?" I asked.

"I don't think so. He's been picked up for fighting, but there's nothing to connect him to knife crime."

"Can I keep this?"

She nodded, and I slipped the picture into my pocket.

"Thanks for this, Degsy," she said, rising to her feet. "I really appreciate it. You'll never know how grateful I am."

I reached out to shake her hand and led her to the door.

"I'll try my best," I told her. "Don't expect miracles, though."

As she walked away, I moved back to our block of desks

and saw Mya was watching her.

"What was that all about?" she said.

"Some kid she wants us to try and work with." "And she couldn't have told us that?" She was really on one today.

"What do you—?"

"Are you blind, Degsy?" she smiled, but there was something strained behind the smile that I couldn't put my finger on. "She's got it bad for you, that one."

I shook my head. "She just wanted to see me because it's a delicate subject and … and,"

"And she fancies the pants off you?" Mya cut in, giggling.

I turned to Sheila for support, but she was miles away. She had been since the fire. In fact, she'd had the hump for a while now. I'd been wondering if telling her story in the schools had been getting her down. I'd have to have a word. But that was for later.

"I've got more important things to think about than some social worker," I told Mya, "and so have you." I realised after that it sounded harsh, but I guess I'd left my sense of humour in the fire.

After a few moments of awkward silence, Mya said, "Good news on the house front," and now Sheila managed a smile too. "Sheila's found us a new place just around the corner."

"Oh yeah?"

"Four bedrooms," said Sheila smiling. "All the mod cons."

"Four bedrooms?" I asked and then smiled. "Good. We'll need them." I reckon all our thoughts turned to Winston then and that fourth bedroom, whether he'd ever be back to fill it, and thankfully the phone rang, giving us a welcome distraction. I snatched up the receiver and said, "Degsy Hay speaking."

A deep-voiced, older woman answered with, "Good morning, Mr Hay. This is Luisa Allsop from London Fire Brigade. I'm leading the investigation into the fire on your rented house last Tuesday. I wanted to let you know that we will be registering a verdict of arson. I'm sure the police will want to speak to you and … erm … your housemates, but—"

"Arson?"

"Yes, sir."

"Arson? How?"

"Did you have a cat?" she asked.

"A cat?"

"Or a dog?"

"A dog?" I realise I sounded more like a muppet, copying everything she was saying.

"It looks like lighter fluid or some other kind of fuel was squirted over the kitchen floor. A cat or dog flap would have given the arsonist or arsonists access."

"Yeah, there was a cat flap from the people who lived in the house before us. We didn't have a cat," I added, although it didn't matter squat.

"Right, well, our findings will be passed onto the police, so expect a call, Mr Hay."

"Right," I answered, dazed, and then hung up.

"What?" Mya asked before I'd even put the phone down.

"It was arson," I told her and turned to Sheila to make sure she heard it too. "Someone set fire to our gaff."

Their mouths dropped open. It was so rare to see either of them speechless, but I couldn't enjoy the moment.

"Who the hell would wanna set fire to our house?" I asked.

"Don't go jumping to conclusions, Desgy," Sheila said. "Just because it was set on purpose, doesn't mean we were targeted. Firebugs are crazies, you know. I met a few inside. They'll set fire to your handbag if you walk away from it for long enough."

"She's right," Mya added. "These idiots go around doing it for kicks. It doesn't mean anything."

I couldn't believe what I was hearing. "Are you two really that green?" I didn't need them to answer that, and I was getting wound up now. "I don't care who started it, and I don't care why. All I know is if Winston doesn't pull through and I get my hands on the bastards, I'll kill 'em."

I had to keep myself busy. A few years ago, I would've gone off the boil, gone looking for a skull to crack, taken care of business, but I had to trust that the police would get to the bottom of things. You know how hard that must have been for me – me and the police got history – but I'd learnt to choose my battles better than before. We went into schools, telling young people to think before they act, take a deep breath, think of the consequences, so I had to do the same. Also, I didn't have the first idea who could have done it. And I couldn't just wander around the streets looking for a kid with a box of matches. So I went off to The Grove that afternoon, checked in with the Hay Patrollers there. They didn't need me to check up on them. They were doing a great job, keeping gangs out of the shopping centre, helping the elderly, disabled and pregnant women with their shopping. They'd been getting great feedback from the management. In fact, they could do no wrong, so I left them to it and decided to pay my new friend, Slope, a visit on the Addie.

I'd bought myself a little run around a few months ago, nothing fancy, which was coming in handy, getting me around town, so I didn't need to blow money on buses or taxis. It was funny not having to think about that sort of thing anymore – where the cash was coming from to live. For the first time in my life I had enough money to pay the rent and bills, run a car, keep enough food in the cupboards, clothes on my back, and then there was enough left over to set aside. I remember a time when the best thing since sliced bread was the shopping trolley I stashed next to the bench I slept on, and food came from the bins behind Patel's. Sometimes it'd hit me all at once, like when I was in the house with the others and we were cooking, watching movies, chilling out. I'd never had that before, and I'd never take it for granted. Whatever was going on in my life, however difficult things got, I'd never stop being grateful for the little things.

I pulled up a few streets outside the Addie and walked the rest. I wasn't daft. My car might have been a banger, but I liked the wheels and stereo where they were. It'd been a scorching day, and there was a buzz as I wandered into the estate. There were no gardens, but people were here, there and everywhere, looking like they thought the concrete was made of sand or grass or something. Lounging around, taking in the last of the day's sun, blasting out sounds from all directions. All sorts of music. No one seemed to care that it all jumbled together into a right head fuck. People looked happy, though. The summer did that. But I knew I'd stumbled into a rare moment, a quiet, peaceful moment. Because the Addie was like a time bomb. Any minute, a fat guy, drunk or Wife Beater, could throw his missus off a balcony, a gang could swarm and leave some poor bastard with a face full of glass, a young person will drop dead with a syringe dangling from their arm or coppers could sweep the place. For now, though, it was a peaceful evening, and I wandered over to the bridge by the works where Rachel had told me I'd clock this Slope fella. I pulled the photo out of my pocket, so I'd recognise the geezer straight off but wouldn't look too obvious. There he was, this Sadiq Wardi, still sneering and trying to hide from the camera, and I didn't know what to expect to be honest with you. He looked like any other teenager, cornered by a camera in the hands of a social worker – scowling and nasty. Didn't mean anything. If I'd cornered Lady Di with a camera, she'd probably have given me the finger and sneered a bit, and look at all the good work she did. Anyway, as I was getting closer to the bridge, the music changed, got a bit darker, the bassline dirtier and heavier. It was a proper drum and bass. I hadn't heard it outside of a club, to be honest, and it was strange to hear it outside on a sunny evening. I could also smell them before I saw them. It was mainly skunked with a few fruity notes of Red Bull clagging at the air. And then I saw them, and I couldn't help smiling. There were about twenty of them, and they looked like they were having a good time, dancing, sitting around, chatting, laughing in the sun under their cloud of smoke. I know people get upset when they see gangs like this, but they were keeping out of trouble for the time being, and I'd met some of them before. They'd either been along to volunteer with the Hay Patrollers and not liked it or they'd been mouthing off about us and stayed away. They weren't exactly the Mafia – nar'mean? Just bored kids who kept themselves busy with a bit of low-level trouble making. They were all older teenagers, some even my age, and then there were a few younger faces, like Slope, who I spotted chatting to a couple of the bigger geezers. Those two were smiling, laughing even, but Slope didn't look like he was enjoying what was being said. As I got closer, I could see he was getting more and more wound up, The more pissed he got, the harder these other two geezers were laughing at him. He was still a skinny, scrappy geezer, just like his picture. No meat on his bones, but he was squaring up to the two bigger boys as if he was eight-foot tall with a shooter in his back pocket. As I got closer, a few people turned to see who I was. One fella, Michael, who I'd met a few times, said, "Alright, Degs." I told him I was and wandered past. I didn't want it to look like I was there for any reason other than just passing through.

I didn't know how I was gonna make contact with Slope, but then it all kicked off. He'd taken as much as he could of being laughed at in his face and had decided to end things. Maybe 'decided' was the wrong word – it was more like he exploded and couldn't control himself anymore; I knew all about that. His face was fierce and changing colour as he let out this growl and ran at the bigger of the two geezers sitting on this pile of tyres. He had some serious spirit this kid, and tackled this massive geezer to the ground. Then he was back up, launching his flipping fists at him, shouting and cursing. Now everyone was shouting and screaming, clapping and stamping their feet.

"Slope! Slope! Slope!" Cheering as if the runt of the litter was taking on an Alsatian and might get a few good hits in before the bigger dog showed him who's boss. The other geezer, who was maybe nineteen or twenty, let Slope run his fists at his mate for a bit, and then he dragged him off. He was still laughing, but the joy was knocked out of him when Slope went for him too. He was twice his size, but Slope was a slippery little geezer. He was all arms and legs. He wiggled free and then was slapping this bigger guy up. Something was missing in his fight, though. I saw it straight away – strength. He could shift fast enough and wriggle, he had fire in his belly, but there wasn't much behind his attack, and I knew he'd be easily overpowered. And that was exactly what happened. For all his kicking and screaming, the second geezer easily got him in a headlock and slammed him down to the floor. And now he was caught, the crowd switched sides. They'd only support the underdog as long as he was winning, and now order had been restored and there was a price to pay.

"What shall I do with him?" the big geezer shouted, easily pinning him down, although Slope was still growling and fighting to get up. "How about …?" this geezer began, then got a handful of Slope's hair and pushed his face into the dirt. The crowd laughed like this was a game they'd watched loads of times before, like a big brother showing a little brother who's boss without doing too much damage or leaving marks that a mum or dad might find, but I didn't like the look of it.

"How about you shift your arse off him and pick on someone your own size?" I said, standing there, looking down on this fella.

He turned his head slowly. I could see the smile still on his face, but it dropped when he saw me. You see, I ain't someone his size; I'm much bigger than him. He knew straight off that if he had to fight me, I wouldn't be the one who ended up in A and E.

"Degsy," he said.

I'd never seen this geezer before, but I guess I had a reputation. I didn't need to say anything after that. He got up and patted Slope in the back, like it'd all been fun and games, but he wasn't the one on the ground with a mouthful of dirt. Slope was up straight away. He was a fiery little shit.

"I'll have you, you fucking wanker!" he shouted, and the whole gang laughed and went, "Ooooo!" and I felt like I was watching something that happened all the time as Slope ran off, red-faced, huffing and puffing about what a shit world it was.

"Pricks!" I shouted back at the gang, and then I ran after Slope. He didn't get far. I found him sitting on the steps of a block of flats near where I used to live. I hated going back there, but this wasn't about me.

"You alright geezer?" I asked him. I tried to sound casual-like. I didn't want him to know I was only there that night to see him. He wouldn't have given me the time of day if he knew his social worker had sent me. As it turned out, it didn't look like he was gonna give me the time of day anyway.

"I can look after myself, you know. Fucking paedo!"

I was more surprised by how well he spoke English than by what he called me. I'd been called all sorts, and this was nothing new.

"I'm Degsy Hay," I told him. "You heard of the Hay Patrollers?"

He laughed at this. "Bunch of fucking do-gooders." His face was flushed and scratched, and he was still out of breath. He was trying to show me how hard he was, but all I could see was a scared lad.

"We look after each other," I told him. "That's all. We help out around the place – nar'mean? Community work and that, but mostly we look out for each other. Never seen any of my gang treat each other the way them geezers treated you."

He looked like he was thinking about what I was saying, then his face hardened again, and he said, "I've got a gang, mate. And I ain't gotta clean no fucking toilets to be in it."

I smiled at him, friendly-like, and said, "Cleaning toilets is a step up from eating shit, mate."

He almost smiled at this, and I could see the decent kid under the armour. I felt as if I was getting somewhere.

"I grew up around here," I told him, looking around at the concrete prison as if it meant something to me. "Right over there," I added.

He looked interested, but then he shrugged.

"It ain't the easiest place to grow up, but then I spent most of my childhood behind bars anyway. I still got friends here though. See that door there?" I pointed and he looked with raised, bored eyebrows. "Nosit and Ivan live there. They're like my folks now, I suppose, and I look out for them." The thought made me smile. Nosit had been so good to me when I got out of prison, and she'd been through so much when she was taken by those dirty bastard attackers, that I tried to get over there as often as I could now. And I didn't need to worry about her being on her own anymore. She'd only gone and hooked up with Ivan. Remember him? He'd gone from sleeping rough on Merson Street, knocking himself out with that crazy-strong hooch that Molly used to make, to leading the work on Unit 16-21, making it all happen there, and falling in love with Nosit. It was a crazy kind of fairy tale.

"Look," I added before he could think too hard and shoot me down. "Some of our lot are putting up some sheds for the elderly folk over at the allotments tomorrow. Why don't you come and check us out?"

"Jokers!" he said. "I'm not putting up sheds. I'm not doing any of that shit."

"Alright. We have some guys painting a mural at the community centre. Do you like art?"

He didn't answer right away, and I could see he was tempted. Maybe art was his thing, but he wasn't gonna show me I'd struck gold. He didn't say anything.

"They're over there every morning. Nine to twelve," I said, and he shrugged and sneered, making the face I'd seen on the photo.

"Why don't you just get fucked?" he barked at me, and I held my hands up to him. I wasn't gonna spend the whole night sitting there trying to win him over. I'd done enough for one night.

"Just think about it," I told him, then I turned and walked away. Now, you might be thinking that was shit. All he'd done was swear and snarl at me, but it felt like I'd made a little crack in that armour, and that wasn't bad for a night's work.

3 A COMMUNITY PROJECT

As I was so close to Nosit's place, I thought I'd pop in. I hadn't seen her since the fire, and I knew she'd been worried about me, but it was more than that. Now Nan was back home in the States, it was like she was a stand-in Nan, and I really needed that. I needed her to make me a cup of tea, hug me and tell me everything was gonna be okay.

"Degsy!" she sang out when she opened the door, and she pulled me in straight away, giving me the hug I was after. "I can't believe what's been happening. How's Winston?" she asked, getting me in and closing the door behind me. I went through to the living room, where Ivan was sitting watching *EastEnders*. I loved seeing him so comfortable.

"Hi Degsy!" he smiled.

"Alright? I don't know what to tell you," I said, turning back to Nosit. "If he makes it, it'll be a bleeding miracle, but we've all just gotta stay positive."

"It's all you can do, son," Ivan said. "Come in, sit down."

I did what he said, and then Nosit brought me in a cup of tea and biscuits then joined us.

"You two ain't heard anything, have you?" I asked. Nosit and Ivan were both well connected. Anything you needed or needed to know, between the two of them, they could get it or find out. They'd both been around the block and if there were anything to know about the fire, they'd know it.

They looked at each other, reading the expressions they found there in the way couples do.

"Sorry, Degs," Ivan finally said. "I'll keep my ear to the ground, but your name's good. People know you're doing good work. I've heard no talk of anyone having a problem with you."

Nosit shook her head and shrugged.

"No prob," I said. "There's something else," I added. "You don't know anything about a geezer called … hang on a sec." I pulled the note I'd written about Slope's brother out of my pocket. "Malik … Malik Wardi. He's a big geezer. Goes by the name Everest." It was a long shot, but I really wanted to find this guy.

Again, the couple looked to each other and drew a blank.

"Who's that then, Degs?" Nosit asked, and I told her about Slope and how his brother had been here before falling off the radar. If ever there was a kid in need of a big brother, it was Slope, so it paid me to put a few feelers out.

"I can ask around," Ivan told me.

"Appreciate it," I answered, and I genuinely did appreciate it, knowing Ivan would do his best for me. He always did. I hadn't had many men to look up to, and I was enjoying having him around. In fact, I loved having the both of them in my life, and I kept taking sneaky glimpses of them as we sat there watching the end of *EastEnders* together, as if we were a proper family, which I suppose we were.

Then Nosit stood up suddenly.

"Hang about. I forgot …" she said and disappeared.

Me and Ivan looked at each other and smiled. It was so good to see her back to her old self. Counselling had worked well for her, and she'd even started volunteering with other women who'd been through the same sort of shit she had.

"This came for you," she said and ran back in with a postcard.

"What's it coming here for?" I said, before even looking at it. I hadn't lived there for ages. I turned the postcard over and saw the loveliest sandy beach I'd ever seen. *Paradise in Perth*, it said. It was from Jarra and Darel.

Get your arse over here! was all the back said. I'd got a few of these lately, at the office, in the house. And the messages. I'd spoken to them, too. Looked like they were getting sick of hanging around waiting for me to organise the trip I'd been promising.

"You going then?" Nosit asked.

"Well, they're all set up over there now. They've got the money together, and I said I'd go over and help them get moving."

"I know, son. You were excited last time we spoke about it."

"I know. We're going global. The Hay Patrollers abroad," I smiled. "But how can I go now? Winston's in a coma and someone's tried to torch the house. I can't just wander off to the other side of the world."

"Maybe it's exactly what you need," Nosit said and pushed the packet of bourbons over to me again. She wouldn't take it back until I'd had one.

I thought for a second. It *was* exactly what I needed. There was no doubt about that. But how could I leave things the way they were? "I'll give them a call, have a word," I told them.

I ain't sure what it was I said, but Nosit reached out and took my hand after that, and she was looking at me like I was a puppy that'd been left out in the rain. "Why don't you stay here with us tonight, Degsy?" she said.

"It's fine. I've got a room, and we move into our new house tomorrow. Don't sweat it, Nosit," I told her, but she wasn't listening.

"I'll get the spare room ready. It's no problem."

I was gonna say no again, but I knew there was no point, so I stayed there that night, and I suppose I was glad I did. I slept better than I had in days. I guess there's nothing better than being close to the people you love.

The next morning, me, Sheila and Mya moved into our new gaff. Luxury, it was, but none of us was smiling. It wasn't the same without Winston. Nothing was the same without Winston, but we tried to get on with it, even managing a few laughs. Well, me and Mya did. Sheila still had a face like a slapped arse.

"Degs," she finally said, looking exhausted as she flopped down onto this second-hand sofa we'd bought, "do you mind if I don't come to the school this afternoon?" I did mind. We were committed to these school visits, going in and talking to the kids about our past, and Sheila was a big part of that. It was a bit bloody late in the day to pull out, and I was about to snap and tell her that, but then I saw the look on her face. I thought she was gonna cry.

"What's up, Sheila?" I asked, but she just smiled, trying to put a brave face on things. I'd heard her story, I knew what she'd been through in her life, but I'd never seen her like this before, so down. "You know I'm here if you need to talk to me."

"Of course, Degsy. It's just all of it getting me down a bit. The fire, Winston."

"The past?" I asked, and she looked as if she was gonna cry again. "You don't have to do it anymore if you don't wanna. It's hard talking about the past, especially if it ain't resolved."

She opened her mouth, as if she was gonna confide in me, and then she just smiled again. "I'm just tired, Degsy," she said, and I had to leave it at that.

When we'd finished unpacking the few things we'd managed to buy since all our stuff burned, I left the girls to it and went to the hospital to see Winston. I wish there was something to report, but there was no change. There he was in bed with the bandages, dressings and wires, a prince who would sleep for a hundred years. And as I took a seat next to him, I tried to tell myself that no news was good news, but Winston's face told a different story.

"Alright, geez," I said and reached out to touch his arm. It made him seem more real and alive if I touched him, less like a body in a bed and more like my mate. I was desperate for anything that would do that or, better still, turn him back into the Winston we all loved, but all we could do was wait and hope, and – as the nurses had told me – keep things as light and normal as possible for him, so I sat there and started chewing the geezer's ear off, filling him in on everything that'd happened since the last time I was there. And it was strange, but I found myself saying things to Winston that I'd never dream of saying to him when he was conscious. We were close, but there would always be a line. So I found myself telling him about the dreams I'd been having about Gabby and Sadface; how I missed them so much sometimes that I thought I'd stop breathing; that I was worried about Sheila and wished there was something I could do to help her. And I told him how scared I was that the fire was just the beginning. I never told anyone I was scared of anything ever, but Winston had become a good listener. Then I started talking about Slope.

"There's just something about him, geez," I said. "I know he's nothing like me. I can't believe I'm saying this, but his life might have been even harder than mine, on the run from God knows what, finding his way to the UK on his own. And there's nothing to him. If the wind changed, it'd take him with it, but there's fire in his eyes. I see me when I look at him, Winston, and I wanna help him more than I've ever wanted to help any of the young people we've met – nar'mean? Maybe it's like sending a hand back in time to help myself. Rewriting history, I don't know. I just know I have to reach him."

Then, as if on cue, my phone rang. It was Katya from the community centre. I'd told her to keep a lookout and see if Slope turned up. I didn't wanna scare him off by breathing down his neck myself, so I'd put Katya on the case. Katya was one of our success stories. She'd been in a car accident when she was a kid and was in a wheelchair. She'd tried to kill herself so many times she'd been on twenty-four-hour watch. Just before her eighteenth birthday, she'd tried slashing her wrists with a torn-up Red Bull can, but painting seemed to bring out the best in her, and she'd led loads of art projects since, including this mural design. I wouldn't say she was happy, but she hadn't been in hospital since she joined us, and we sometimes had quiet chats when she'd open up and tell me what was going on for her. I always think back to what I was like as a kid when these young people talk to me now. I think about little Desgy and what I'd have wanted a youth liaison to say to me. I know little Degsy would've told me to fuck off some of the time, no matter what I said, and sometimes it's what I got from the young people I tried to help, but at least I got it and I didn't ever hold it against them.

"Katya? Good news?" I asked.

"No sign," she said. "Sorry, Degsy."

That was a shame. That project would've been perfect for Slope. I ain't sure if I expected him to turn up or not. I hoped he would, but maybe I was dreaming. I'd give him a week, though. Maybe he was thinking about it and would turn up in a few days.

"Alright, thanks, Katya. Is everything alright there?"

She didn't answer for a while, then I heard, "Fucking stop it!" in the background.

"Ibrahim turned up then?" I said, smiling.

Ibrahim had only been working with us for a few weeks and was a livewire who liked to shake things up a bit. He didn't have the artistic skills of Katya, but if you put a paintbrush in his hand, he'd paint until you told him to stop, like a wind-up toy. Some people don't understand this about young people. They wanna work and feel useful. The trouble comes when there's nothing to do and they're getting a hard time just for being alive. Everything else is from adults fucking them up. That's the way I see it. I ain't never met a kid who was born bad. But, anyway, as hard as he worked, he also liked to have a laugh, wind people up. Maybe he was ADHD. He hadn't been diagnosed, though.

"Does he have to come here?" she asked, and I could

hear the frustration in her voice, but there was something she hadn't realised. Ever since he'd been coming along, she'd changed. He livened her up a bit. She was less stuck in her own head and more out there. She'd stopped locking in on the way she was feeling and was more alive than I'd ever seen her. I don't suppose she liked getting wound up by him, but maybe it was one of the things keeping her alive. I could see her becoming a youth worker or a teacher or social worker in time because she really cared about him. He just drove her round the bend.

Fraid so I told her. "If he ain't painting, God knows what he'll be getting up to." She grumbled a bit, and then I added, "Look, Katya. Let me know if this Slope kid turns up this week, will you?"

She agreed, and that was that. Back to the eerie beeping of Winston's bedside and the background hustle of doctors and nurses hurrying from patient to patient. I stayed a bit longer, chatting a bit, but then just keeping quiet, just being with Winston, hoping that at any moment he'd open his eyes and crack one of his crappy jokes. I'd give anything to hear his voice. *Oi, Degsy, geez, what ya sitting there like a prick for? Who died?* But the only movement was the slow rise and fall of his chest, and I eventually had no choice but to leave him there.

The school we were visiting that afternoon was a dump, plain and simple. The local authorities must have forgotten it existed because it hadn't seen a lick of paint since the seventies, and if they had computers, they kept them well-hidden. Someone still cared about the kids there, though, because they'd got us in to chat to some of the year 10's and 11's.

Someone had spray-painted the word 'fuck' over the sign at the entrance, not even bothering to make a pun or make it funny. Just that simple word, as if anyone entering should abandon all hope, but we were happy enough as we drive through the gates. We'd been to schools like this all over London. We'd been these kids, and they got to see that after we'd spoken for a bit. Some of them could see their lives in our stories, and we always got kids joining the Hay Patrollers after we'd spoken out. We got parents knocking on the doors too, desperate for help with their teens, and we'd helped quite a few young people this way. We'd help the parents too.

That afternoon, there was a madhouse of kids set up in the main hall. We wandered in with a great big, beefy PE teacher. Maybe he was the only one who had any control over them because when he talked, they listened. Other teachers were running around looking like they were about to have a breakdown.

"Thank you!" he shouted when they were almost completely quiet. "This is Degsy Hay and Mya Garcia."

"Wankers!" someone shouted, and the whole hall cracked up again as if it were the funniest thing they'd ever heard.

"Thank you!" he shouted again. "They've come from the Hay Patrollers, working with little shits like you to keep them out of prison, off the streets, and having a decent life, so you need to listen up. Do you understand? I'll be just over there. If I hear any more shouting, I'll be down on you bastards so hard you'll never get up again. Do you hear me?"

This geezer was more like a screw than a teacher, but it was working. All eyes were on us. They may have been bored-looking, angry eyes with raised eyebrows, but at least they were looking in the right direction. And they were quiet. We knew just what to do, though, how to handle a hostile crowd like this, who'd eat us for breakfast if we didn't come in hard, so I let Mya start. She moved to the front of the stage, dropped her hands on her hips and stared them down. She was wearing the Hay Patrollers blue hood and black tracksuit pants, and it was so flattering on her. I could see why the boys in the audience couldn't take their eyes off her, but good looks weren't gonna get her through.

"Bitch!" someone shouted, and I could see this PE teacher getting to his feet, but I held my hand out to stop him. "Mya's got this geezer," I said. A few more shouts went up, some mumbling and laughing. And then she spoke.

"My name is Mya Garcia," she said in that cool, confident voice of hers. "And I'm a murderer."

That shut them up.

4 MYA'S STORY

"Mya! Get down from there!"

"Mya! That's dangerous!"

"Mya! I won't tell you again!"

That's all I heard from my mum when I was a little girl. I wanted to climb trees and jump off things and run fast and, I guess, feel alive. Don't all kids? But my mum, she'd worry about me all the time. I understand a bit more now – course I do. But then, it was like she just wanted to spoil my fun. Anything I wanted to climb was too high; anywhere I wanted to go was too far; anything I wanted to do was too dangerous or cost too much, and, the way I saw it, if it was fun, it was off limits. It ain't like I went around hurting myself and getting into trouble, but the way my Mum saw things, the world was a dangerous place. She'd come to the UK as a kid from the Dominican Republic, and although we didn't speak about it, I know she went through some serious shit to get here. Now I wish I'd chatted to her more, but life doesn't work that way. To me, she was just a boring old cow who wanted to spoil life for me. Of course, I wish I'd listened to her now.

"Mya! Don't talk to any strangers!"

This was the one I got the most. And she wouldn't even let me walk home from school until I went up to high school. My friends used to take the piss, and sometimes I'd do it anyway, run away and leave her standing at the gates, but the trouble I got into wasn't worth it. Funny, now I've been to prison and met kids from all over the place, I know how easy I had it. All I had was an old woman chewing my ear and trying to look after me. I wasn't sexually or physically abused, I had a roof over my head, clothes on my back and a full belly, but there was a spirit in me that was being crushed. I wanted to fly, and every time I tried to spread my wings, she got in the way. I just wanted a bit of freedom, but she wouldn't back off. Every time I tried to be me, she'd step in and tell me I was breaking the rules. So I couldn't believe it when she let me walk to school on my own. I was eleven and felt like I was eighteen. I hated the school, but I was getting my first taste of freedom. The old lady was still coming down hard on me, making me do my chores, my homework, not letting me out over the weekend or at night, but I had that half hour now, from home to school in the morning and then, even better, from school back home at three o'clock. This was when London came to life, and I hadn't seen that when I'd been out shopping with my mum, on a tight leash. I could take my time, look around, have a laugh with my friends and, although I'd live to regret it, I could do all the things my mum told me not to, including talking to strangers, which was how I met Leo.

It was a Tuesday. I have no idea why I remember that. I just do. I was walking home on my own because one of my friends was off sick and the other had started seeing a boy in year 9. I wasn't really interested in boys then, I was too young, but I was covering for her. If her mum asked, she was with me. I'd stopped to buy a can, and when I left the shop, I heard a little voice behind me.

"Excuse me!"

I turned around. A little lad was standing there. Smaller than me, although it turned out we were the same age.

"You dropped this," he said, and held out a £50 note between fingers with grubby, nibbled fingernails, weighed down with a few heavy sovereign rings, bigger than his knuckles. He had the bluest eyes I'd ever seen and such an innocent expression on his face, but it wasn't his face I was focussing on. The biggest note I'd ever handled was a tenner. I didn't even know they went up to fifty, but now I did, the possibilities were running through my head. The shit I could buy with fifty quid! My mum was still giving me the odd fiver here and there, if she could afford it. I was never gonna get this kind of money from her. But, of course, I hadn't dropped it. What the hell did that matter, though?

"Thanks," I told this little kid, then took the note and slid it in my pocket as if it lived here. My heart was pounding, but in my mind, I'd already spent every penny of it, and I couldn't let it go now.

He smiled and skipped off as if nothing had happened, scruffy little fella, and my heart went on thumping as I walked off, carrying this time bomb. And then I broke into a run. I'd never run so fast in my life, and I didn't stop until I got home. I was frantic, looking around when I got to our block, and I didn't stop looking as I walked up the eight flights of stairs (the pissy lift had been buggered as long as we'd lived there), but there was no one around. No one had followed me from town. My breathing started to level out. I couldn't believe it. I had fifty quid in my pocket and endless possibilities in my head. This was the best day ever.

When I got in, Mum was having a go at me about scuff marks on my shoes and how I had to make them last the whole year because she wasn't buying me any more. I felt like telling her I'd buy my own. I had fifty quid now and I ruled the world. She served up yesterday's leftovers, and I thought about all the food I could buy with that note. I wouldn't have to eat that slop ever again. Man, when I think about what was going through my head then, I feel like such a bitch, but I can't change it.

The next day, I couldn't wait for school to be over. I'd spent the day spending that note over and over again in my head, and now I was gonna do it properly. Do you know what I bought? A chunky, gold bracelet. I blew the lot on it. And I'd never been prouder of anything in my life. I was the bollocks in my bracelet. The rest of me was shit. Do you get me? I had my cousin's hand-me-down everything and a haircut my mum had given me one night when she was pissed off with me. Now I had this bracelet; I looked the business. First class, nar'mean. It meant something to me. It turned me into a someone.

So, I was walking home, wearing this bracelet like I was the queen, feeling pretty pleased with myself, and I heard that voice again. My heart sank.

"Nice bracelet," he said.

I didn't turn this time. I wanted to run, but I just kept walking, trying not to look suspicious.

"Hey!" he said. "It's okay. It's a cool bracelet."

Now I dared turned and saw the same little guy with that cheeky look on his face. I hadn't paid him much attention before, but now I could see he was all Nike and gold. Although he was scruffy everything about him reeked of money.

I slipped my fingers under my sleeve and touched the bracelet. I didn't know what to say.

"Relax," he said. "I'm Leo." And when he held out his hand for me to shake, I saw the sovereign rings again and knew they were real gold. This kid either had rich parents or … I don't know what. I guess I was a naïve kid. "Relax," he said again, and I reached out to shake his hand. We were eleven, so it was weird to be shaking hands, but Leo wasn't a normal kid. At least he wasn't like any of the kids I'd met at school. "Your face!" he laughed. "You dropped this!" he added, doing an impression of himself, giggling like a fool. "I didn't know if you was gonna take it at first."

"What do you—?"

"Relax!" he interrupted me again. And I kinda was starting to relax. Whatever this kid was up to, he didn't seem danger-ous. He was friendly, and he'd walked into my boring life like an alien from another planet – one that was gold-plated and decorated with pound signs.

"Mya," I told him, and before I knew it, we were walking together. We didn't talk about the money for the time being. We spoke about school – mine and his – and what a cow my mum was. It turns out his old lady was a lot like mine.

Or that was what he told me at least. She didn't let him do anything, and they didn't have a pot to piss in, so he made his own money.

"You know, there's more where that came from," he said, and pulled up as we were starting to leave the town centre, as if he'd turn to ash if he stepped outside the boundaries.

"What do you mean?"

"You liked it, didn't you?"

I touched the bracelet again and was biting my lip, wondering what to say to him.

"Not just the money," he said, smiling again. Say what you like about Leo, but he was a happy guy, and maybe that did something to my brain. He was like an advert for happiness. He had all the answers to a better life, and it was infectious from the minute I met him. "You know what I mean."

I didn't really know what he meant, but I nodded anyway, and then he reached up to put his arm around me, which felt stupid because he was so much shorter than me, and we were only eleven anyway. But he steered me into an alley, and then I started to understand what was going on.

"Want another one?" he said, holding another crisp, red note out to me.

I wasn't so quick to take it this time. I may have been green, but I knew from my mum that the only thing in life you got for free was the flu.

"What do I have to do for it?" I asked.

"Simples. Take this, run it over to the Chambers Estate." He dragged a padded envelope out of his pocket, and I knew straight away what it was. "Guy there, Mevil, will meet you at the main entrance."

It surprises me now, as I look back, that the only thing going through my head was whether I could get over to Chambers and back home before my mum had guessed I was up to no good. I was just so young.

"Mevil?" I said. "What's he look like?"

"You'll know him when you see him. Big geezer. Built like a brick shithouse." He held the note out to me, and this time I reached out to take it, but he palmed it. "There'll be more where this came from if you don't fuck it up," he told me, and I smiled. Do you know why I was smiling? Because I was eleven years old and I was being given my second £50 note in as many days. I was in Disneyland, and the consequences could fuck off. I'd get some decent trainers and a haircut. I'd get a stash of Mars bars to keep in my room. I'd buy a lock for my door so no fucker could come in. I was riding high, and it just kept getting better.

Leo wasn't wrong when he said Mevil was a big fella. His size twelves were on the steps outside the Chambers, but his great big head was in the clouds. I think he was African or something like that; I wasn't sure, but he had a deep, booming voice and spoke in the same accent like some of the kids at school.

"You Mevil?" I said when I rocked up there. I'd run all the way from town and was hoping I could still make it home in time for dinner.

He barely nodded his head then turned and went into the building. I followed after him, and when we were inside, he scared the shit out of me, running his mouth at me and clipping me around the ear.

"Do you want the police on us?" he said.

I shook my head because I didn't want the police on us, but I didn't really know what he meant.

"You don't know me," he said. "Bring stuff. Leave it. Go!" He was a man of few words, and he made every one of them count. I don't know why I wasn't more scared, but being a kid is a funny thing. I thought I knew it all. I thought I was invincible. I thought drug dealers were something off the TV and in films. But I didn't know shit because drug dealers were on every corner. Not only that, but I was becoming one of them — little old me. At first, it was delivering parcels like this. Then I got to know Mevil a bit. Every time I saw him, he clipped me around the ear and shouted at me, but Leo told me he was happy with me, and he wanted to use me more, which could only mean more money. So I started dealing properly in school and around the estate, and I learnt what this shit was, although I wasn't bothered about taking it. I saw the state of the losers who bought this shit, and I didn't wanna look like that. I was only interested in the money. And it was seriously piling up. In fact, my biggest worry was how I could spend it without making my mum suspicious. So I'm still eating the shit she's serving up while I'm sleeping on my thousands and having McDonald's three times a day. I sound like a bitch, right? If I was gonna do this, why wasn't I helping my mum out? We were poor; why wasn't I giving her money, so she could give up one of her jobs, eat a decent meal and wear something that hadn't come from the charity shop? I don't know. I guess I was a twat. I knew shit about life and even less about what it takes to be a good person. All I knew was my life was shit, I wasn't worth anything, and then it all changed. I was minted, respected, could have or do anything I wanted, so do you know what happened when my mum did get suspicious? I'll tell you. I'm not proud, but I promised to tell my story, and this is part of it.

She'd found a couple of the fifties in my coat pocket. I was pissed at the time she'd been sniffing around my things, and I had nothing to say about it when she cornered me. I just kept telling her I didn't know how they got there, but she was getting all Sherlock Holmes on me. My room was filling up with nice clothes, makeup and jewellery, and she wasn't buying that I was borrowing it off mates. I had an expensive haircut and a ring on every finger.

"You're not leaving this table until I find out where it's all coming from," she shouted, and I sat back in the chair, looking up at her with my eyebrows raised, arms folded. I wasn't saying a word. "I'm waiting."

She tried everything to get me to tell her: shouting, crying, pleading, and finally, she had no choice but to let me go, but she was grounding me. For a normal kid, this wouldn't have been a big deal, but I had a job to do. I couldn't be grounded.

"You've got to be fucking joking!"

Before I'd even finished the sentence, she ran at me and grabbed the back of my neck. She was still a lot bigger than me and easily shoved me out the kitchen, up the stairs and into my room.

"Three months!" she said. "And I'm calling Uncle Frank!"

"Call the fucking Pope! See if I care!"

The door slammed, and I was stuck in my room, but not for long. Before she'd even got downstairs, I was out the window, down onto the balcony below, and I legged it down the stairs and off the estate. There was money to be made.

Later, I told Leo all about it.

"Shall I get Mevil to have a word? Warn her off?" he asked, and I wondered which one of them was really in charge. He was the same age as me, but it looked like everything went through him. And I knew he didn't go to school, and if he had a home, there was no mum or dad in it. The stories he'd told me about himself when we first met were bullshit. Not that I cared.

"Okay. Nice one, thanks," I said, and pictured Mevil having a word in the old lady's ear. I thought it was funny. He'd put the fear of God up her, and she'd leave me alone. It was exactly what I wanted. Only, when I went back home the next day, after staying out all night, the house was quiet. At first, I was relieved. I'd expected my mum to drag me in and ground me even harder, but there was only silence.

"Hello!" I called, but there was no reply, so I made myself some breakfast, chilled for a bit then went out to see my mates. When I went home later that day, she was in the kitchen, piling clothes into the washing machine. I stood in the doorway watching her. Thinking back, she wasn't moving quite right. She was stiff and slow, maybe in pain. If she heard me behind her, she didn't turn around.

"Alright, Mum," I said.

The washing froze in her hands, and then she carried on with her chore, but she didn't turn or say anything.

"Sorry about before," I said, making my voice soft.

Still nothing.

"I know I should have called."

She turned now, slowly twisting her head as if it weighed a ton, and I've relived this moment in my head a thousand times, more and more often as I've got older because these are the things that stay with you. It's the looks, the changes in people and your relationships, when they see into you and show you exactly what they think of the things they're seeing when they lay themselves bare to the truth. To be honest, she didn't even look like my mum anymore; she was a blank as if someone had drained all the emotion from her. It would've been better if she'd shouted and screamed at me, hit out at me. Instead, she gathered up all the love she'd ever had for me and slammed it down on the carpet or dropped it out of the window, and there was none left.

"Ain't you gonna say nothing?"

And now she wasn't even looking at me as she slowly rose to her feet, leaving the washing where it was. "Dinner's in the microwave," she said and walked past me.

From that moment, the only time she spoke to me was to tell me there was some food in the microwave or clean clothes on my bed. I must have been twelve by now, and I know I should've cared more, but it was like I was suddenly free. I was like Leo. I could do whatever the hell I wanted, and that was exactly what I started doing. Only, now the old lady's warnings had stopped, I was hearing them in my head more than ever. Whatever I did, I could hear her words drilling into my brain, saying, "Mya, don't do that." "Mya, that's dangerous." "Mya, what have you become? I used to love you so much."

And I couldn't sleep as well as I did. My mum would pop up in my dreams with Mevil. He was doing terrible things to her, and I couldn't take it. That was when I started drinking, and it was the best decision I ever made. At least I thought so at the time. Life became a party. I'd slipped through the net at school and hardly ever showed my face. I was still making a ton of money, and I was getting smashed most days. I was living the dream. But I was about to learn an important lesson. All good things come to an end.

We had a set patch – Me, Mevil, Leo and a bunch of other kids. I didn't know how many, to tell the truth, but we were pretty big. I guess there's always bigger fish out there, though, and I heard rumblings. A few kids had got their faces smashed in, and there was less money to go around. That was all I cared about. As long as there was a payout, I was still winning, all my decisions had been the right ones, but when the fifties became tenners and fivers, I was spending more and more time hugging bottles of vodka.

So, we arrive at the day.

You wanted to hear my story, and here it is. It was Mevil, Leo, me and a bunch of others on the Chambers estate. To this day, I can't remember why we were all there, but we were. That's just the way it was. We were out in the street. I was shitfaced. I remember that because I still can't see any of it clearly, and believe me, I've tried. We were jumped. There was this other gang eating up our turf, and here they were, bigger kids and grownups, like Mevil. Men and women. And it was just a blur of fists, boots and headbutts until things very suddenly came into focus: Leo's face, frozen like a horror film on pause. A blade. A slash. I can't look, but I can't look away. One of the big geezers has opened up his throat, and I can see inside him. His hand's gripping his neck, and the blood's oozing out between his fingers. I can see it now as I tell you about it. Sometimes it's all I can see. The rest, though, it's a haze of vodka and fear. I know I got knocked down and smashed my head. I didn't even know if I was awake or asleep. I remember picking up the knife. I remember how it felt in my hand as I gripped it. I remember it was already covered in blood and the harder I gripped it, the more it slipped around, so I must have wiped it. I must have been calm enough to give it a wipe before wrapping my fingers around it again. In my mind, I'm thirteen years old, standing there in the eye of a storm with a knife in my hand, surrounded by colour and movement, screaming and shouting. Then it's all blue lights and sirens, and I feel like I'm still standing there, but I ain't. It feels like the knife's still in my hand, but it ain't. I'm face down on the ground with my hands cuffed behind my back. They said I was laughing, like the funniest thing in the world had happened. They said I didn't stop for an hour. I don't remember any of it. I had no idea what'd happened. Still don't, really.

The next thing I know, I'm in a police cell, wearing clothes I don't recognise in a place I'd only ever seen in films. It's like I've just woken up, although I ain't been asleep, Dread creeps up on me like a debt I can never pay as I read the scrawl on the wall. *Fuck the police!* I'm cold, but I know it's hot in there. I jump up and run to the door. I start banging, but no one comes. Then I pace. It's a tiny space, but I must have walked miles. And I'm calling out for my mum. Now I want her. For some reason, I think of school and try to work out what lesson I should be in. I ain't even been there for months. And I know this is a mistake. Whatever's going on, it's a mistake, and I'm just waiting for some copper to let me out, but that was never gonna happen.

Three witnesses saw me murder a twelve-year-old boy in cold blood. They saw him run towards me, unarmed; they saw me draw back my blade and stab him in the gut. Then they saw me standing there in a daze as if nothing had happened. I can't remember any of it, but turns out he was part of that crew trying to take over. He was just like Leo and me, I suppose, and I killed him. I sometimes try and remember that moment, but it's been erased from my brain. It ain't there, so I can't even tell you what was going on. I'd never been violent in my whole life, so I must have been scared. If he was running towards me, I must have done it to defend myself. But I don't know. Bottom line is, I'm a murderer. And I'll have to live with that for the rest of my life.

I was charged with murder and various drug offences. I was thirteen and sentenced to life imprisonment. I was gonna spend my best years locked up like an animal, missing out on all those things kids get to do when they're teenagers: the sweet sixteen, the first car, the first kiss, leaving school, college. And while other kids were doing all that, I was staring out of a tiny window, wondering where it all went wrong, wondering what would have happened if I'd told Leo the truth that day. "Nah, mate. It ain't my fifty," I'd say and go home for dinner. I missed those dinners, the ones my mum cooked. And I tried not to miss my mum, but sometimes it's all I can think about. I ain't seen her since the week before my arrest. I looked out over the crowd every time I was in court, but she wasn't there, she didn't visit, and I don't blame her.

I wish I could say I changed my ways in prison, but I didn't. The mad truth about being banged up with a load of criminals is that you all rub off on each other. If you had a little good on you to start off with, the shit soon started to stick, and you were down in the gutter with everyone else. It's hard to know how to describe what was happening, but it's like, did you ever have the feeling you'd gone too far to turn back? That's what was going on for me. What did I even have to turn back to? This was my life now, and I still thought I was a badass. I kept on drinking so the truth couldn't get through to me, thinking I was the lick, and got more time added onto my sentence for dealing and fighting. And I became the queen of the girl's section at McAlley-Stokes. Everyone was shit-scared of me, and I was riding high. But as time went on, girls were coming and going, serving their sentences, getting out, leaving me behind. Some were cleaning up their act, some were like yoyos and would end up doing as much time as me, and what was I doing? Setting myself up to transfer over to an adult prison when I was twenty-one, to carry on living in a violent limbo while everyone around me was moving on.

I watched films all the time, about normal people living normal lives, falling in love, having jobs, driving cars. Sometimes, I couldn't understand how they could settle for such bullshit, how they could stand to live such boring lives, but sometimes I craved it. I just wanted to stand in a kitchen that belonged to me and make a toasty. I wanted to choose what time I went to bed at night, make plans for the weekend, meet a guy. Only, I was the queen. I had my fingers in so many pies and none of them were apple. So I went round in circles for years, wanting to change and not knowing how. In the end, it was simpler than I'd imagined. I asked for help. Have you ever asked for help? It ain't the easiest thing to do, but it'll always be a turning point. I asked for help, and very slowly, my life began to change. I can't pretend it was easy. I was still going round and round on the crazy carousel, battling myself, fighting the need I had in me for danger, money and power. I still battle it now. But I like this other side of me more. And liking myself at all is an improvement on where I've been my whole life. I started taking classes, help for the alcohol, and I got out after spending eight years of my life behind bars. Eight years of my life I'll never get back. I was even mentoring other inmates by the time I left. And when I got out, I knew I'd never be going back. Now I work with the Hay Patrollers, and we help other young people, steering them away from the kind of shit we've been through because, I tell you this, I wouldn't wish the life I've had on no one.

So, you see. This ain't a story of a good person caught up in some bad shit. I wasn't an angel who killed out of self-defence, behaved, did my time and went on to be a productive member of society. I know people say there's no such thing as a bad person – only bad choices – but I was a bad person. All I wanted were shiny things, freedom and excitement. I didn't care what happened to anyone but myself. I was the lowest of the low, which is what makes my story so important. You might not think it's true, but I'm proof that no one has ever gone too far to change. Whatever point you're at in your life, you can pull up and question it. You can always change direction and you can always ask for help. As for me, I'll always have to live with who I was, what I did and what I lost in the process, but I'm finally proud to be the woman I am.

5 WHERE'S THE CASH?

"Jesus, did that teacher remind you of anyone?" I smiled as I pulled out of the school gates and turned to Mya. Her head was dropped on her hand, elbow on the door, and she was staring off into the distance, as if she was watching her own thoughts. "Any of the screws at McAlley maybe?" I added, but she wasn't biting, so I carried on chatting; thought it might drag her back to reality. "I need to pick up a few bits later: shower curtain, broom, a few shirts," I said, but she was still miles away. "And I was thinking of getting one of them mankini things to wear to work. Probably need to vajazzle me nuts an' all," I laughed, but she was on another planet. She didn't even stir, so I said, "You alright, Mya?"

"Hmmm! What? Sorry, Degs. Did you say something? I was miles away."

"God, you're telling me sis. Penny for 'em."

She didn't answer straight off, but I could feel her eyes on me. Like she had something to say but didn't know if she should.

"It's just, I've been thinking. I'd like to go and see my mum, you know."

She paused to let that sink in. I knew how big this was. I'd heard her story over and over again, and I could only imagine the rollercoaster going on inside of her. I didn't know what to say, though. I couldn't tell her everything was gonna be okay. It probably wasn't. I couldn't tell her it was a bad idea either. It was her life. So I ended up keeping my mouth shut, which was sometimes the best way with Mya.

"And I, well, I ..." she went on, hesitating. "I wondered if you'd come with me."

This was much easier to answer. "Course I will," I said. I didn't even need to think about it.

"You sure? It won't be pretty."

"Mya, you should know by now, I'll always be there for you in a shot. No questions."

She didn't answer, but I could feel her looking at me again. I took my eyes off the road for a second to look at her, and she turned quickly, so our eyes never met.

"Just let me know when," I said, and then she was quiet again, and I left her to her thoughts.

Back in the office, I thought I'd have a go at shuffling my diary, looking at that Australia trip again, but how could I go? I'd promised Mya I'd help her out, and don't even get me started on Winston, then there was Slope and all the work we were doing. Ivan was doing a great job managing the construction at the Unit 16-21 site, but they always needed me to sign off on things. I knew the Australian launch was important, but I didn't see a way out. Then, as fate would have it, the decision was taken out of my hands. I'd only been back in the office a few minutes when I got a phone call. It was Jarra.

"Geez!" I beamed down the blower. It was good to hear his voice, but he didn't sound happy. "What's up?"

"Well, I don't know what's happened, to be honest with ya, mate. It's the cash."

"What about the cash?"

There was silence for a bit then he said, "We're down thirty thousand dollars."

"What do you mean?"

More silence, but I could hear the cogs turning in his head, and when he spoke again, I could hear how upset he was. "We've spent the last year getting that together, Degsy. Fundraising all over the place. Everything's in place to get the Hay Patrollers working over here and now this."

"Wait up, geez. What do you mean you're down thirty thousand dollars? Money don't just disappear?"

"I mean we're down thirty thousand dollars. Simple as. The money's been leaking out and we've no idea how."

"Money don't just leak out, Jarra. If money's missing, it means someone's got sticky fingers. Who had access to it?"

"No one who'd have their hands in the pot, Degs, I swear. Good people."

"In my experience, geez, everyone's good until temptation gets the better of them."

"I just don't know what to do now, geez. Everything we're doing relies on that money."

"Look …" I said confidently, but I had nothing to back it up with. I was thousands of miles away. What did I know about the missing money? Then I knew exactly what I had to do. "Look," I repeated. "I'll look into flights and get over there as soon as, alright?"

"Nice one, Degsy." His voice sounded lighter already. "I'll get some witchetty grubs on the burner for ya, mate."

"You're alright, mate. A sandwich will do fine."

So that was that. I was going to Australia for a week. And after looking at flights, I found one for the day after tomorrow. I was still freaking out about everything I was leaving behind, but Sheila and Mya told me the world wouldn't crumble if I wasn't around for a week.

"Even God took days off," Mya told me, and when I turned to look at her, I could see she was taking the piss. She'd been doing that a lot lately.

"What about your mum?" I asked, quiet enough that no one else would hear.

"I'm sure she took days off too," she smiled.

"I'm being serious."

She smiled half-heartedly and said, "It's fine. I've waited all this time. I can see her when you get back."

The next morning, I got a surprise. Katya called. Slope had turned up to join the work party at the community centre. *What a turnaround*, I thought, and took a wander over there. It was a rundown community centre that'd been left off the government's Christmas list and had to fund itself with coins found down the back of the sofa. The Hay Patrollers had done all sorts of things to help, and our painting group was doing a great job cheering the place up with this multi-coloured mural. There were some real talents among them, including Katya, who wheeled herself over to meet me as I got out of the car.

"How's he doing?" I asked.

"He seems like a good lad. He's getting stuck in."

"Really?" This didn't sound like the Slope I'd met.

"Yep!"

This, I had to see. But she was right. He was outside with a brush in his hand, alongside four other kids, working on the blue-sky background. I didn't wanna single him out, so I shouted an "Alright!" to the lot of them. I got a few smiles, a few of them ignored me, and Slope nodded his head seriously before carrying on with his job.

"You bringing your brother and sister along to see us again?" Katya asked.

I smiled at the thought. "I need to set something up," I told her. "I think Asha's gonna be a little artist. She couldn't stop talking about it. Ray couldn't believe you all turned up and did this. They both loved it – nar'mean?"

Then Ibrahim appeared beside me, as bouncy and excitable as ever, with more paint over himself than on the wall. He wasn't a big geezer, but he looked like he could handle himself. "Hey, Degs! I heard Winston was burnt alive," he laughed.

If this had been anyone else, I would have probably smacked 'em, but the dopey bugger sort of made me laugh.

"Heard his skin was all melty and peeling off his face!"

"You watch too many films," I told him.

"Just saying what I heard. Heard it was the triads, coming after ya for an H-deal gone bad," he said, making his face all dramatic. "Is that what happened, Degs? You got the bleeding mafia on ya?"

"Give it a rest, Ibs," Katya told him, but he wasn't listening.

"Or an insurance job. You torch the place for the cash, Degsy?"

"Alright!" I said, holding my hands up. "Enough of this rubbish. Ain't you got painting to do?"

"But is Winston's face all peely and shit, Degs? Is he all dead and stuff? Is he—"

God only knows what he was gonna ask next, because the next thing we knew, a cannon had broken loose from the work party and taken him down, rugby tackling him, slamming him to the ground. It was Slope, shouting the odds about Ibrahim being a wanker, talking like that. Ibrahim had a few years on Slope, but that didn't seem to matter. He ran at him, and then they were both on the floor and he was throwing punches like he thought this was the flipping UFC. I had to admire his speed and spirit, but – shit, man! – this kid was nuts. And once Ibrahim got himself together, he quickly pulled the switch, so he was sitting on top of Slope, slapping him up.

"Who the hell's this little shit, Degs?" Ibs was asking, almost laughing now, and it didn't look like he was hurt.

A few of the other lads had rushed in to pull him off, and I held onto Slope, who still had the spirit of the lion inside him and was kicking and punching at the air, although I had him up off the floor.

"What the hell you doing?"

"Ahhh! He's a shitbag!" he shouted, his face flushed and sweaty again. I had no idea what I was gonna do with this one, but I knew what it felt like to be where he was. I'd lost it so many times, I'm surprised I ever found it again, and where did it lead me? Prison. I couldn't let that happen to him.

"Just chill, Slope! Chill!" But he was a force that was hard to contain. It didn't help that Ibrahim and some of the others were laughing at him. What were they supposed to do, though? He was a firecracker.

"I didn't even wanna come to your stupid, fucking … I hate this shit! … I didn't even … You're all bastards!" he was shouting, and I was moving towards the car. When we were far enough away from the painting group, and I could feel his body relaxing just a little, I sat him down. Thankfully, he didn't do a runner.

"Get in," I said, opening the car door.

"I'm not getting in the car with you. Fucking paedo!"

"Get in!"

This time he didn't argue, and we were soon on the move. He was even quieter than Mya had been when we left the school, but I could hear his rage pounding inside him, his breathing a hurricane.

"Where you taking me?"

"I'm gonna show you something. I want you to see what can happen when you put your mind to something, when you have a dream and you don't let go of it. I'm gonna show you the difference one little geezer can make. Could be me. Could be you."

He mumbled something, and when I turned for a second, I saw him rolling his eyes and looking off out the window.

"What did you mean?" I asked. "When you were shouting, you said you didn't even wanna come. So why did you?" I caught sight of a shrug, but he didn't answer. Then he said, "My gaff's down there. You can drop me here."

I just laughed and said, "You ain't going nowhere, geez."

A few minutes later, we pulled up at the site of Unit 16-21. I got out and tapped my code into the gate, got back in the car and drove through.

"This is bullshit!" he was mumbling, but he was taking an interest despite himself, watching what I was doing and scoping out the building work, which was still in the early stages. The temporary shelters were up and there were supplies everywhere, people racing around, looking busy, but there was still a long way to go before the place got built. When I parked up,

I told him the full story. I told him how I was born a prison junkie kid, how I'd been in and out of prison, fighting, drugs, alcohol, how I'd lived on the streets when I did get out, no family, no home. It looked like he was listening, but he threw in a sneer every now and then, just to show me that he could. Then I told him how I'd dreamed about building housing and services for homeless people on this site. Now he looked more than a bit impressed.

"You mean you made all this happen?"

I nodded. "I didn't know how I was gonna do it, geez. I just knew I would. That's what life's like sometimes. You don't always have to know how you're gonna do something. You just have to know you're gonna do it. Nar'mean?"

There was a glimmer of understanding, that maybe I'd reached him, then his face went all hard again and he said, "I gotta get going, man."

"Look, Slope. We're doing all sorts of stuff around town. If you can keep it together for five minutes, there's opportunities for you. It ain't just the community centre; we're volunteering all over the place. And it can lead to paid work. We've got teams over at The Grove, doing the patrolling, you know working with other young people that may be causing anti-social behaviour. We also help the pregnant mums and the elderly with their shopping, and more contracts coming up. I know you're still at school—"

"I ain't going no fucking school."

"Well, we can talk about that. Maybe a day release. Get you sorted for when you're in the real world."

"You don't think my world's real?"

"That ain't what I meant, bruv."

"I ain't your bruv."

I could feel this slipping through my fingers.

"It's cool. Get in the car and I'll drop you back at your place. We can talk more when I get back from Oz."

"Australia?"

Now he seemed interested again.

"You going away? When you back?"

"That's a lot of questions. I'm going for the week. Don't worry; you don't get rid of me that easily."

He sneered again, instead of answering with words, and got back in the car. There wasn't much conversation after that, but I felt like I'd chipped away just a little bit more at his armour, knocked down his defences. And, thinking about it, he'd been fighting for my honour in the first place. I don't agree with violence, but he'd flown at Ibrahim because he was getting up in my face, being a pain in the arse. That was something, wasn't it?

After I dropped Slope off, I checked in with the team at The Grove. Everything was going well. The business owners in the shopping centre were telling the boss that takings were up, violence and vandalism were down, and it was all down to our efforts. It was a good feeling, but as I drove away, I couldn't stop thinking about Slope again. It was unusual for one of the Hay Patrollers to get under my skin like this. I'd helped loads of them, but I didn't feel connected to them like I did to Slope. Which reminded me, I needed to let Asha and Ray know I was off to Oz and would see them again when I got back. It was funny; in my life, I'd gone from being completely alone to having family dotted everywhere – not many of them blood, but family nonetheless. The idea of having a brother and sister still made me smile every time I thought about it.

That evening, I was back at Ivan and Nosit's again. She was still set on force-feeding me biscuits, but I wasn't about to turn them down. We chatted about Nan, about old Irish Molly from Merson Road, who was still out there roughing it. Nosit and Ivan had been trying to reach out to her, get her off the streets, but she was a stubborn old boot. And we chatted about my trip to Australia. Despite everything that was going on, I was looking forward to seeing Perth.

"Funny that you'll be so close to Everest," Nosit said, sipping her tea in that noisy way she had.

"What you talking about?" I laughed. "Didn't you go to school? Everest ain't in Australia."

She turned to Ivan, and then the two of them cracked up, laughing as if I'd said the funniest thing they'd ever heard.

"What?" I asked, and this only made them laugh even harder. "Will one of you tell me what the bleedin' hell's goin' on?"

"Not *Everest* Everest. She talking about *Everest*."

I just stared blankly. The two of them had completely lost it.

"The geezer you asked us to keep an ear open for. Everest!" Nosit told me.

"Ohhh!" And now I was laughing, but then I stopped and said, "Are you for real? You trying to tell me Slope's brother's in Oz?"

"Yeah, thought Ivan told you."

"I was just about to. Joe, trady mate of mine, knew him from the railways. He'd picked up a bit of work here and there but couldn't keep it because of his status."

"Because he was an immigrant."

"Sure. He'd even been roughing it on Merson Street same time as us, but I never met him."

I thought about all the immigrants I'd met on Merson Street and all the stories I'd heard. It didn't surprise me that Everest had been there too.

"So how'd he get to Oz?"

"Cut his losses. Met a few guys from Oz, told him there was work there, helped him with a ticket, got a false passport and off he went. Joe told me he said his family were all killed. Doesn't look like he knows your Slope fella's still knocking around. Guess he's a free agent."

I let all that sink in. "So where in Oz is, he?"

"Joe said a place called Bunbury, working in the port."

"He still in contact with him?"

Ivan shook his head. "This is going back a few years. He might not even be there now."

"It's worth a shot, though." I took out my phone and wrote *Bunbury* into Google Maps. There was about 174 km between this city and Perth. A guy like this Everest geezer probably didn't hang around anywhere very long, but I might find someone there with a few answers. I had nothing to lose anyway.

After I said my goodbyes to Nosit and Ivan, I turned up back at our new gaff. If I was going to Oz the next day, I needed to pack, but I didn't have much to my name after the fire, so I thought I'd take myself shopping the next morning. I didn't need much – a few tops, jeans, underwear. Thankfully, we had enough Hay Patroller uniforms for me to take one of them. I was thinking all this as I turned my key in the door, but it all fell out of my head when I was stepping inside. I knew straight off that something wasn't right. There was something hanging in the air, a kind of dread, and when I got into the living room, I saw Mya and Sheila sitting there together, looking like the Child Snatcher come knocking and taken all their sweeties.

"What's going on?"

They looked up, and I could see them both take a deep breath at the same time, but they didn't say anything. It was the hospital all over again, when Mya wouldn't tell me about Winston.

"What is it? Is it Winston? Tell me!"

"It's not Winston," Mya told me then looked to Sheila again.

"Will one of you just bloody tell me what's going on?"

"This came through the door," Sheila said and held out her hand to me. I took what she was holding and could see why they'd lost it. It was a box of matches. A bloody great big one: the kind you keep in the kitchen. My heart sank.

"And this just came through the door?"

They nodded, and then Mya said, "That ain't all. Look inside."

I gave it a shake first. It sounded empty. Then I slid the box open. There was nothing inside, but as I pulled it, I saw something written on the bottom:

Degsy
~~Winston~~
Mya
Sheila
X

"Are you fuckin' kiddin' me?" I shouted and started pacing back and forth, trying to keep a hold of myself, but I didn't know what to do. Someone was coming for us, all of us. They'd already taken Winston out, and now they had their eyes on us.

"We called the police," Mya said.

"What good's that?"

"Don't fucking shout at me!" she snapped back, and I held my hands up to her. The last thing I wanted to do was upset her.

"What did they say?"

"They're sending someone over to get it."

"When?"

"Dunno. This was about an hour ago."

I dropped it on the table. "And now our prints are all over it."

"You know as well as I do, there'll be no prints on it," Sheila said, sighing. "Look, I'm going to bed."

"You're going to bed?"

"Yes, I'm going to bed."

"Just like that. We get this, and you're just gonna curl up and go to sleep?" I looked closely and could see she'd been crying. This wasn't the Sheila I knew. This was all hitting her hard.

"Sometimes all you can do is curl up and sleep," she said,

looking so grave and not like herself, and left Mya and me to it. I needed to have a good, long chat with her, see what was really going on, but for now, my hands were full.

"Well, I can't go and see Jarra and Darel now!" I snapped, still pacing.

"Will you please sit down, Degsy! You're making me dizzy."

I picked up the box again. "A fucking kiss? The joker's put a kiss at the end, Mya. Whoever it is, they're laughing at us."

"Just calm down. This ain't helping."

"Ain't ya pissed off?"

"Of course I am, but what can we do? We have to try and trust the police and keep each other safe. Safest place for you at the moment is on the other side of the world."

"That ain't how I work, and you know it. I need you lot to be safe."

"We will be, Degs. We'll stay in a hotel again for a couple of nights. Jarra and Darel need you, and it's booked now anyway."

I thought for a minute about Mya and her story, how she'd been as a teenager, and couldn't make the connection between that and the big-hearted woman standing in front of me with the big, brown eyes. She always made me feel like she had my back, even if it was just handling a nightmare parent or making sure there was loo roll in the house. Yeah, she busted my balls, but it was done with love. I didn't wanna go, but would be staying change anything? I was completely powerless. At least I could make myself useful in Australia. And It'd stop me doing something I'd regret, which would happen if I came face to face with whoever put Winston in hospital. So it was settled. I was going.

"I'll miss you," Mya said, and looked down at her hands gripped in front of her. The sight of her made me miss Gabby, but I realised as I stood in front of Mya that I hadn't dreamt about her for a few nights.

"I'll miss you, too," I said.

6 HAY PATROLLERS DOWN UNDER

I ended up having the same conversation over and over again, fuming about the matches and telling Mya and Sheila that I couldn't leave, but they did a good job keeping me together, and as I boarded the plane to Australia, I was almost excited to be getting away. I still felt like I was letting them down and should have been staying, but Mya had said something that stuck with me: If I was going, I couldn't spend my time moping about what was going on in London. It wouldn't change anything. If I made the decision to go, then I had to give the trip my all, so that was what I'd planned to do. I owed Jarra and Darel that much.

Until a year ago, I hadn't travelled further than Romford in my whole life. We travelled a lot after we brought down MR-K and his cronies, getting awards and that, but I didn't get to spend any real time anywhere, so once I'd had a word with myself and got into the idea, I was almost looking forward to this trip. I know there was shit going down in London, but we'd given that bloody matchbox to the police, the girls were in a hotel, the office was shut for the week, and everyone connected to the Hay Patrollers had been put on alert. I wasn't totally satisfied, but that was life. And there'd been no change with Winston; the geezer was still sleeping for England, and the hospital had told me I should go. Getting a break and coming back strong would be good for me and good for Winston. People in comas can't just hear, they can pick up on vibes; that's what Jane, this hippy-dippy nurse told me anyway. I didn't know white people could have dreads, but she saw nothing weird about walking around the hospital with them. She was lovely, though. Anyway, I didn't know about no vibes, but in the end, I knew Jarra and Darel needed me, and there was a chance of finding Slope's brother. It was only a week anyway – seven days. What could possibly go wrong?

Because I'd booked the flight last minute, the plane stopped first at Abu Dhabi, and then we flew into Brisbane. I thought it'd be a bonus to see more of the world, but thirty-one hours later, I was at the end of my rope and starting to think I lived on the flipping plane – Nar'mean? All that was forgotten, though, when we touched down at Perth Airport, into the hustle and bustle of luggage and noise, and out through the arrivals gate. Now I could take a breather, and I couldn't help smiling when I clocked the Aboriginal brothers I'd come to see. How could I miss them? Both big lads, massive smiles, and did I mention the sign? Where other families and drivers were waving signs with names on them, they'd painted this bloody great banner with just one word on it – *Trouble!* They were waiting for trouble. That sounded about right! They always did have a wicked sense of humour, and I couldn't stop laughing and yawning as I slung my bag over my shoulder and had to stop myself running over to them. They dragged me in for the biggest hug I'd ever had, then held me out at arm's length to look at me, as if they were a couple of nans looking at how big their boy had gotten.

"You've changed, mate and you stink like a kangaroo's backside as well."

"Oh yeah, so would you if you had flown all that way?"

"It's like you were a kid when we last saw you. You're all grown up now."

"Do me a favour!" I joked, then said, "Where's a fella to get a bite to eat around here and a bloody good wash?"

They were right, though. It was only a few years since we'd been banged up together in McAlley-Stokes, but so much had happened. I felt like I'd been an adult since I was a boy – I'd had to be – but this was a different kind of adulthood.

I hadn't lost the fire of my teens, but I'd found the dial, so I could turn it up and down when I chose. I controlled it now rather than the other way round. Maybe this was what they were seeing.

They hadn't changed a bit, though. They were always big lads, always smiling, and nothing seemed to have changed.

We picked up a burger to keep me going then spent an hour trying to find their car, joking with each other all the time. It was so good to see them. When we pulled out of the airport at last – no lie – I felt just as happy as I had when I'd been released from the nick. The sun was shining, although I'd picked the right time to come, and it wasn't too hot, and as Jarra drove and Darel pointed out areas of interest, my nose was glued to the window. It was all so much cleaner and more spacious than London, and was I imagining that everyone looked happier than back home? I probably was, but then I'd just spent the best part of two days banged up on a plane.

We passed over the Swan River, and Darel told me how it'd been at the heart of his culture for more than 40,000 years, before the Europeans arrived. The Derbal Yerrigan they called it, created by giant serpents who carved waterways and valleys as they made their way to the mouth of the river at Fremantle. "We have a responsibility to protect and care for the land and its waters as a part of their spirit and culture," he added proudly.

I'd never seen this side of the boys before, and I knew I was gonna enjoy being in their manor.

We drove on, over the bridge, and as the skyrise of the city appeared before us, I felt as if I was in one of the postcards Jarra and Darel had sent. We drove through, with Darel still doing the tour, now pointing out places where he or Jarra had gotten lucky with girls, then out into the suburbs, which were more interesting to me than the city. I had all day every day to look at cities, and although Perth City looked slightly different, I was pretty sure it was related to London in some way.

But the suburbs were like nothing I'd seen before. Not in real life anyway. I'd seen the odd episode of *Neighbours*, but it was hard to believe life could be this comfortable, with miles and miles of detached houses and space, so much space. I thought about the Addie and how many hundreds of people had to live in a few square miles of towering flats, how many family members had to share a room. I could see why Jarra and Darel hadn't hung around. But then, like anywhere else in the world, Perth began to reveal its secrets: there were the rich, and there were the poor. There were people owning global restaurant empires in one part of the city, and the people who couldn't even afford to eat in another. I guess that was why the Hay Patrollers would be so valuable here, which got me thinking.

"So tell me about the money, geez," I said to Darel.

"Well, mate, we didn't leave things to chance. Kaleigh's mum's been looking after the funds."

"Kaleigh?"

"My missus," Jarra chipped in.

"Anyway," Darel went on, "she's an MP. She's been putting the word out, supporting us and looking after the loot."

"And you trust her?"

"Course. She's an MP."

This made me crack up, but the brothers weren't laughing.

"What?" Jarra snapped. "She's my girlfriend's mum. She's not on the rob. It's peanuts to her, anyway. She's got a great big house, cars."

"Doesn't mean anything, geez. These MPs, man …"

"Well, you're gonna meet her back at my house, mate, so …" he hesitated, so I helped him out.

"Keep my mouth shut so I don't ruin things for you and Kayleigh?"

He laughed and said, "You got it."

"Punching above your weight a bit with this Kayleigh anyway, ain't ya?" I said, smiling. "An MP's daughter?"

This made them laugh, and that was all we said about MPs and the money for a bit, because whatever else we had going on, this was a day of celebration. I'd travelled all the way around the world to see them, and we were gonna have a good time, which started the moment we pulled up outside their family home. They tooted the horn as they turned into the road, and a bunch of people came running out of a house that wasn't as big as some we'd seen, but was still comfortable.

"We're a traditional people," Darel said seriously, and it sounded a bit like he was warning me, but then he smiled and said, "We know how to eat, drink and make our guests feel welcome."

He wasn't lying. As I stepped out the car, I was hit by the smell of food cooking on a barbeque and could see the smoke rising behind the house.

"Welcome! Welcome!" a tall, smiling man was saying with arms wide, before pulling me in for a hug, as if we were old friends. Turns out this was Jarra and Darel's old man. Their old dear was just as welcoming and pushed a drink into my hand before I'd even reached the house. There were children running around everywhere, aunties, uncles, music; it was a hero's welcome. Jarra led me to the bathroom so I could have a quick shower and change my smelly clothes. I was also dying to brush my teeth. God my mouth smelt shitty.

When I'd cleaned up and caught my breath and been led out into their massive yard, I finally met this Kayleigh that Jarra had been talking about. She was about eighteen, red hair, pretty, but she also looked a bit cheeky, a bit of a handful. I liked her straight away. As soon as she walked over, I saw Jarra's eyes light up. I hadn't seen him in love before. It was nice.

"Degsy, this is Kayleigh," he said, and we shook hands.

"So you're the Degsy I've been hearing so much about. Good to know you," she said and wasted no time pushing a mysterious paper plate of food into my hands, covered over with another plate so I couldn't see what was on it.

"What's this?"

"Little welcoming gift," she said, and I saw the boys look at each other and smile. I lifted the cover and wished I hadn't. There on the plate was – well, I don't even know how to describe what was there – bugs and grubs and insects and all sorts of things that should be in the ground, not on the plate. Something on there wasn't even dead yet and was still wriggling. I thought I was gonna puke and jumped up to my feet, nearly toppling the lot.

Jarra, Darel and Kayleigh looked serious now.

"You have to eat it, Degsy," Darel said. "You can't disrespect our culture." And then they eyeballed me as I watched the creatures and critters on the plate. I thought he'd been joking on the phone when he was talking about witchetty grubs. I looked at them again, watching me. I was in their home. I couldn't disrespect them, so I reached my hand to the plate – shaking, it was – and I picked up the smallest, deadest-looking critter there. It was still too big and had too many legs for my liking. I had it in my hand, though, and even managed a smile. Then I slowly brought it up to my lips, looking for the exit already, so I could run and chuck my guts up. I was really gonna eat the bloody thing. Then I realised that everyone had started laughing.

"Your face!" Jarra roared, and grabbed the plate from me. "This is more you, isn't it, mate?" he said and switched it for a burger.

"You shits!" I shouted, and now everyone was laughing and cheering. Then I noticed I still had the little bug in my hand and threw it in the bush. That was where bush tucker belonged after all – nar'mean?

A little later, Jarra came over with a serious-looking woman beside him in a beige suit and sensible shoes. She didn't look like the partying kind, but she smiled as she got closer, and I knew this must have been Kayleigh's mum, the MP. My body tensed up a little, but I'd agreed not to show Jarra up by shouting the odds, not today anyway. Thirty thousand dollars may have gone missing on this woman's watch – thirty thousand dollars of Hay Patrollers' money – but a promise is a promise.

"Degsy Hay, this is Mrs Malone, Kayleigh's mother."

I held out my hand to shake hers, and although the sun was shining, her skin was cold. Close up, she was a pale, drawn woman, not at all full of life and playful like her daughter, and I couldn't help being suspicious, but I said, "Pleased to meet you, Mrs Malone. Jarra here says you've been helping us out, getting things started over here and that."

"It's an enterprising scheme, Mr Hay," she said, managing a distracted smile.

"Call me Degsy."

"Degsy. Right. So how long will you be in Perth, Degsy?"

"Just the week. Perth's a sight for sore eyes, but I got things need doing back in London."

She smiled again, almost laughed, and I could now see something of her daughter in her features.

"What did I say?"

"Nothing, it's your accent, Degsy. You've quite a turn of phrase."

"Is that a good thing?"

"It's a very good thing," she mouthed and took a long sip of her drink, keeping her eyes on me the whole time. I couldn't bloody believe it. She was flirting with me. I was sure of it. She wasn't bad looking, but bloody hell.

"Well, lovely to meet you, Mrs Malone. I'm sure we'll speak again before I'm off."

"I'll look forward to it," she said and wandered back into the party, but not before giving me a cheeky grin.

Me and Jarra just looked at each other then burst out laughing.

"Was I imagining—?"

"Nah, mate! You got a fan there!"

"So she was flirting, yeah?"

"Looked that way."

Then I twigged. "I trust her even less now," I said.

"What do you mean?"

"It ain't a new trick, geez: flirting your way out of trouble. I seen girls in court flirting with solicitors and judges, hoping to bring down their sentences."

"Does it work?"

I shrugged. "I know it ain't gonna work with me. I don't trust that woman as far as I can throw her."

"She's alright, Degs. Believe me. She's been a great help setting things up."

I watched her across the garden, scrutinising her. It's a big word isn't it and i didn't need that DWB (dodgy word book,) anymore. Then I snapped out of it, for Jarra's sake. This was his future mother-in-law after all. "Course she is, geez. Course she is," I said, slapping his back. "Let's grab a few more drinks."

The cans of beer were going down well. Infact it was keeping me awake from the jet-lag.

"Darel, can I ask you a question mate," I said laughing.

"Yeah, what is it geezer."

"Is it why you Australians can't spell, cos you have to write XXXX on this can of beer."

"Cheeky bastard. Come on have another one."

We were all smiles after that, and the celebrations went on long into the night, with dancing, eating, drinking and games, which surprised me a bit, but I think they were showing me who they were – their culture and that. Darel explained that a lot of the games were traditionally used to train warriors and hunters in the wild. He was right when he said they were proud people, and I'd never been made so welcome in my life. I'd also never been so exhausted and I thought I'd sleep for England (or Australia maybe) when I hit the sack, but as nice as the day had been, there were still a hundred things going through my head, and I gave Mya a quick call just to put my mind at ease. London was eight hours behind, so it was still afternoon there. She told me, as I hoped she would, that the whole world hadn't collapsed while I'd been away, that there was no change with Winston, and we hadn't had any more nasty little messages from our arsonist.

"And are you okay?" I asked when she'd finished giving me the lowdown.

"Of course. Why wouldn't I be?"

"Just checking. And Sheila?"

She paused for a second. "She's a bit more complicated. I don't know, Degs. She's kinda shut down, if you know what I mean. She ain't really there at the moment. I've tried speaking to her."

"Maybe she just needs some space."

"Maybe."

We both paused for a moment, thinking about Sheila, or maybe leaving a respectful gap before moving onto the next subject, and then I told her all about the trip so far, Darel and Jarra's family and the plate of bush tucker.

"I tell ya, Gabs, I nearly puked – Nar'mean?"

She was laughing and then stopped. "Gabs?"

"Huh?"

"You called me Gabs, Degsy."

"No, I didn't!"

"You did. You called me, Gabs."

My heart started pounding. "Slip of the tongue, Mya. Look, I should go. It's late here and we've got shit to do in the morning. I'll call again tomorrow." And I didn't give her a chance to say anything else before I hung up. I was so tired, but now I'd wound myself up over calling Mya Gabby. When I tried to sleep after that, I had even more to think about, but the jetlag thankfully got the better of me, and I was soon out for the count.

I wondered where I was when I woke up the next morning in a cool, simple room with white curtains and small paintings on the walls of beautiful, Aboriginal designs.

"Breakfast, Degs! You can't sleep all day!" I heard shouted from the other room and headed out to the colourful, homely kitchen to see what was on offer. "There he is! Sleepy head!" Jarra greeted me. He and his brother were dressed in their Hay Patrollers uniforms and already looked as if they'd been out and done a day's work. They still worked in the mines, but they split their time now so they could get the Hay Patrollers up and running.

"What time is it?"

"One."

"In the afternoon?"

"We thought you could do with it, mate, but now there's work to be done."

"One in the afternoon?" I yawned, rubbing my head.

"Get a grip, Degsy. Here, eat this." He flung a pancake in my direction and it nearly landed on my head. I caught it and began to munch, making them both laugh. There were more on the table and loads of fruit and sauces. It wasn't what I'd normally eat for breakfast, but I got stuck in, and so did the brothers.

"So we need your advice on a few things today, Degs, mostly about publicity, getting businesses onboard, recruiting young people, that kind of thing. You in?"

"That's what I came for," I said, and when we'd finished eating, we spent the next few hours going through their plans and swapping ideas. I shared everything I knew about making the Hay Patrollers work in London, and it was great to see how that could be applied in Perth. There were just as many young people in need here, and gang- and knife-related crime was on the rise. Where there're cities, there're always gonna be gangs, even one as pretty as Perth, so we had lots of work to do.

Over the next few days, we were out visiting sites and chatting to the young people who were already part of the program. We stopped in on a small mall where the boys had landed a youth liaison contract, and they told me about their plans for the train stations, to have Hay Patrollers keeping people safe there, giving the young people that hang around there, up to no good, a purpose. That was the idea behind the Hay Patrollers after all, to have young people look out for each other and the community, and it looked to be working, although they were in the early stages and had lots of work to do. For a start, very few Hay Patrollers even had uniforms, and they had so many ideas for training and courses, which was why the missing money was so important.

But it was the individual stories that told me how important all this was, just as it had been back home, and I met so many young people whose lives had been changed by this. The one that will always stay with me is Mohammed, a twenty-year-old immigrant who lost an arm and a leg to a landmine. He'd spent most of his life banged up by the regime in his country, lost all his family and did a runner to Oz. Here was a young man who was severely physically disabled, and God only knows how his head had been mashed up by it all, but when I caught up with him, he was leading a group of volunteers to clean graffiti in a graveyard. There were no complaints; the boy was full of smiles. He was happy to be a part of this and help his community. I knew geezers who hadn't been through half as much who were holding hands with heroin as they staggered through life, stealing and fighting. He was an inspiration.

It was when we were visiting this volunteer party that Jarra got a call. I didn't pay too much attention until I heard him shout, "Are you taking the fucking piss?"

Everyone turned around, but the Hay Patrollers quickly got back to work, although they were laughing and mumbling to themselves.

"What's up, mate?" Darel asked.

"It's Kayleigh," he said, shaking his head. "Looks like you were right, Degs. She thinks her mum *has* been nicking the money. I don't understand it."

"What do you mean?"

"I don't even know, Degs, but she told us to meet her in the city now," he said and was already on his way to the car. Me and Darel ran behind him, and we were soon cruising the streets, heading off to God knows where, back over the river before skidding into a carpark. When we got out of the car, it all made a bit more sense. We were running towards a massive casino that wouldn't look out of place in Vegas.

"Hang about!" I was shouting. "What's going on?"

But Jarra wasn't listening. He burst through the entrance and found his girlfriend in the foyer. She looked as if she'd been crying.

"What the fuck?"

"Just try not to freak out," she was saying when we'd caught up. "It was what you were saying yesterday," she said, "you know, about how Degsy laughed at you for trusting an MP and something about temptation turning people."

"So?"

"So, Mum's the only person with access to the money other than us."

"So?"

"So, wake up, Jarra. I followed her, and here we are. Look."

She opened the door behind her and the pinging ker-ching of the slots had hit us.

Jarra poked his head in, scanned the room, and I saw his face change as he locked on his target. Then he stepped back. He'd obviously seen enough. "The fucking pokies?" he spat. "She's blowing our money on the pokies?"

I poked my head in the door. It was a strange sight. It was light and sunny outside, and this was a porthole to another world and another time, where it was always midnight and the game was always on. It hurt my head just peeking in, but by the look of some of the people in there, they'd lost days on the pokies, as Jarra called them. And there she was, flirty Mrs Malone MP, in the same beige suit and sensible shoes. Maybe she had a whole wardrobe of the things, so she never had to slow herself down in the morning by deciding what to wear. She had a look of determination on her face as she pumped the buttons on the machine in front of her, but she was a robot, like everyone else in there, hypnotised by the flashing lights and spinning reels.

Before we could stop him, Jarra had marched over there, so me and Kaleigh followed behind, and we were soon surrounding Mrs Malone's machine. She didn't notice us to begin with, over the din and intense pokey focus.

Then Kayleigh said, "Mum?"

She didn't move at first, but she stopped playing, and then her head fell slowly forward and she gripped the sides of the fruit machine, propping herself up. She'd been sprung good and proper.

"What the hell's going on here?" Kayleigh asked, and we watched as Mrs Malone took a few deep breaths before braving it and turning to face her accusers. When she turned, she didn't look surprised to see the three of us standing there, and she even managed a smile, but it was the most pitiful smile I'd ever seen.

"I can explain," she said.

7 A BAG OF FISH GUTS

"I really hope you can, or I'm calling the police," Jarra said. I hadn't seen him raging like this since we were banged up together, but he had a right to be angry. We all did. He'd worked hard to raise the money, to get sponsors and donations, and there she was pissing it all up against a wall that flashed and made crazy beeping noises.

"There's no need for that!" Kayleigh protested.

"Are you for real? She's blowing the lot on the pokies."

"We don't need to get the police involved."

"What do you suggest?"

Mrs Malone stood there, not saying a word, as Jarra and Kayleigh argued over what to do. And I could see her fidgeting and giving the fruity side-eyes. I almost laughed. She still had credits in there, and she was twitching to press the button.

"I think we need to talk about this somewhere else," I said, and began walking back to the foyer. The sunlight was a shock after the seedy, fake night of the arcade, and we all squinted and shielded our eyes as we walked through and into the car park. Jarra didn't wanna let Mrs Malone out of his sight, but he finally agreed to let her drive back to her house, and he and Kayleigh would meet her there. The condition was that I'd stay in the car with her. Keep her on the straight and narrow. It was probably too late for that, though. It wasn't the way I would have chosen to do things, but I didn't complain as I climbed in the car beside the shamed MP and waited while she started the engine. I was surprised I wasn't angrier. Maybe I was just relieved that we now knew what had happened, and we could work on getting the money back. It was why I'd come to Australia in the first place.

We drove in silence for a few minutes, and although she

hadn't said anything, I could now feel the sadness dripping off her. She seemed so different to the woman I'd met the day before, but I couldn't gather up much sympathy, especially since we were driving a car that cost more than all the money I'd see in a lifetime. What kind of woman takes money from a project like ours? Then, as if reading my mind, she said, "I suppose you think I'm a monster?"

I didn't answer. What could I say?

"It's not what you think."

"So tell me."

There was no flirting now. She looked like a broken woman, but I still didn't trust her. Growing up in the UK, we learn that MPs are full of shit pretty early on. I'd met a few good ones recently, but Mrs Malone's mug didn't fit in with that lot.

"Peter, my husband, Kayleigh's dad …" she began, and stopped. She was getting choked on her own words already. I thought it was best if I stayed quiet and listened. "He passed away eleven months ago. Eleven months, two weeks, three days, four hours and" – she looked at her watch – "seven minutes ago, to be precise."

"I'm sorry."

"Have you ever been in love, Degsy?"

I sighed, my head getting chocka with Gabby, our whole relationship flashing in front of my eyes, from the moment I met her on the streets, bundled up in the snow, to the moment I'd scattered her ashes in the Thames. I nodded slowly and was already starting to feel more sympathy with her. I knew what it felt like to lose someone.

"We met when we were fourteen, fell in love and hadn't spent a moment apart since. We were so different. I wanted to run the world, but he was a gentleman, and he wanted to save it. Over the years he showed me that that was a far more noble ambition, and we set about doing it together. That's the kind of MP I am, Degsy: one that is trying to help people, make the world a better place, strive for change from the inside. We learnt when we were young, on endless demos and protests, that you can't change the whole world, but you can strive to be a good person and change the world around you, and that's what we did. He was an MP too, a better one than me, if I'm honest, but he was my light, Degsy. He made my world a better place. He made me a better person."

"He sounds like quite a man."

We were driving on streets I hadn't seen with Jarra and Darel, and as she rounded a corner and drove past a row of shops, she said, "None of us saw it coming. He had been so healthy. He ran a few times a week, took a yoga class, swam, ate well. And then …"

"You don't have to tell me, Mrs Malone."

"I want to. I want you to understand. It was a heart attack. He was fifty-five. Fifty-five, Degsy. That's no age. He was visiting a homeless shelter, serving soup and bread, and he dropped down dead. Just like that." She turned the steering wheel again, and we were heading out into the suburbs, where the roads were wide and the houses lush. I just knew this would be the kind of house she lived in.

"When he died, a part of me died to. Do you know what I mean? I was empty. For weeks, I couldn't even get out of bed. And when I did, everything hurt. Everything. I couldn't breathe most of the time. I really thought I'd died too. Then … I don't know. Life goes on doesn't it. It'll get easier, they say. Time is a great healer, I was told. But I was just as hollow and empty as I had been in my bed. Now I was a zombie walking through life, doing my job, talking to people, but I wasn't there. Nothing mattered anymore. Nothing *matters* anymore, Degsy. I wish I could make you feel how I feel, so you understand."

"I know how you feel," I slowly began to say.

"How could you?"

"Because my fiancée was killed in an accident."

Suddenly the car swerved, scaring the life out of me, and we pulled up at the side of the road. She turned the engine off and swivelled round to look at me. I didn't know what was happening at first, and was worried she was getting flirty ideas again, but she was almost in tears and said, "I'm so sorry, Degsy." Then she lost it completely. "Here you are, grieving, and you're coping somehow. You're not spending all your days on the pokies just to feel something. You're not trashing your life because it hurts too much to wake up every morning." She was sobbing now. "You're not—"

"It's alright, Mrs M," I said and took her hand. It was still cold.

"Sarah. Call me Sarah."

We sat like that for a bit. She was sobbing, and I was holding her hand, trying to comfort her, but what could I say? Nothing made me feel better when I lost Gabs, and I wanted to punch the people who dragged out the crappy phrases that might have made them feel better, but did nothing for me.

When she'd calmed down a little, she said, "How did you cope, Degsy? How did you get over it?"

I thought for a minute and wondered how to answer her. Was I over it? The thought made me sad. "I don't think you ever get over it," I said.

"But I've seen you laughing with the boys. You've set up the Hay Patrollers. You're a smiler, and I know it isn't a fake."

Then I took myself by surprise by laughing.

"What?"

"No, it's nothing. Just that I hated it too – all the people who said all that crap about time healing and it would get easier and things would get better. It's just, sitting here with you, I think it's flippin' true – nar'mean? I hadn't even noticed, but you're right. I am happy, I guess. I still think about her. I still talk to her sometimes, but I'm living my life too. I know how you feel, Mrs M. I remember that feeling, and I know it's still there sometimes, like some kind of animal's died and crawled up inside where your heart used to be, like someone's taken a great big ice cream scoop and hollowed you out. But you're right; it ain't like that all the time anymore. I can't believe I hadn't even noticed. I still love her, though."

Mrs M's tears were drying as I spoke, and although she wasn't smiling or anything like that, maybe she looked a little more hopeful. Maybe there was a little less loss in her face.

"Thank you, Degsy," she said, letting out a deep sigh, and reached for the ignition.

"I think we need to talk about the money, though, don't you?" I asked, and her hand fell to her lap again. "How bad is it?"

I thought she was gonna cry again, but she sniffed back her tears and stared straight out of the windscreen. We both watched as a black cat ran across the street, and then she said, "It's pretty bad. I'm not a thief. I'm really not. I'm … It's …" she tried to say, and then she was crying again. "I need help, Degsy. I know I do. I've lost all of it: our savings, Kayleigh's college fund, the Hay Patrollers' money. It's all gone. I'm going to have to sell the car and re-mortgage the house. My God, Peter would be turning in his grave."

"Nah," I said. "He sounds like he was a cool dude. What do you think he'd say to you if he was still around?"

She thought for a moment then said, "He would put his arms around me and tell me it was all going to be okay. We'll get some help for me, and money isn't everything anyway."

"Well then?"

She turned to me and said, "I will get help, Degsy. I know I need it. Maybe I needed to get caught to make a change finally."

"You can do it, Mrs M. I've got faith in you."

"Thank you, Degsy."

Again, we sat there as silence passed between us, and maybe a little healing: for her, and maybe for me too. Then she said, "Look, Degsy. I have an idea about the Hay fund. I have a few contacts and can call in some favours. I think I can arrange a government grant for you guys."

"Nothing illegal, right?"

She laughed. "Of course not. It's just knowing the right people to ask, and the right palms to grease. I'm going to try for fifty grand. I really want to make it up to you guys."

"Fifty?" I beamed. An extra twenty grand would change the project completely.

"It will take a few weeks, but I know I can do it."

"And what about the rest? The savings? Kayleigh's college?"

"Well," she began, and I couldn't believe how much lighter she looked, and younger. "I don't need a car like this really, do I. Peter always wanted us to get rid of the cars and start cycling, look after the planet, so maybe I'll do that. And I can re-mortgage the house if I need to."

"And the pokies?"

"I'll get help. I can see it all so clearly now. And thank you, Degsy. You don't know what you've done for me today."

When we drove on, the tension between us had clearer and she was even pointing out landmarks, just as Darel had done, and when we got back to the house and had to face Jarra and Kayleigh, I got out first and did the talking for her. Then me and Jarra stood there watching as Kayleigh slowly walked over to the car and got in the passenger side. They sat there for some time, talking and crying, and then they were hugging, so we thought we'd leave them to it. It was so sad they'd lost their husband and father, but perhaps things would be better now they'd laid their cards on the table. And we were happy. We had another twenty grand to play with. The Hay Patrollers Down Under was gonna be a success.

As the days passed, we managed to check out a few more of the projects set up by the lads, but it wasn't all business, and we managed to fit in a bit of sightseeing here and there. We shopped, checked out the cafés and bars, and Jarra and Darel made sure I didn't leave without seeing some of Perth's hottest landmarks. We saw the Bell Tower and the Quay, and we even drove out to Splash City waterpark for the afternoon. I felt like a kid again and hadn't smiled so much in as long as I could remember.

With only a day left of my trip, I decided it was time to have a go at solving the other little problem I'd brought to Australia with me, and Jarra agreed to help. We were gonna drive along the coast to Bunbury and see if there was still any trace of Slope's brother, Everest: Malik Wardi. To be honest, the odds were stacked against us. For a start, we knew he'd travelled on a false passport, so he could've been going by any name now. I'd managed to score a photo from Rachel at social services, but it'd been a few years since he'd gone there, and he didn't seem like the kind of geezer that hung around. Add to that the fact that Bunbury wasn't exactly a big, exciting place. Jarra said he'd be more likely to move as soon as he got there, to Perth or somewhere exciting like Sydney or Melbourne. Or he could've gone even further north, out of Australia all together, where the living's cheap. The fact that he worked at the port made us even less confident. He would've been meeting people from all over the world. Bottom line is: he could've been anywhere. But I soon forgot my troubles as we headed off south along the west coast of Australia. We'd been to the beach during the week, sunbathed, swum and hung out, but that was nothing compared to driving alongside it with tunes blasting, following it's glorious, shimmering bends, winding our way through a freedom I'd never felt before. And I really did feel the wind in my hair and breathe in the sea air like I was in a flipping movie or something. I thought about what Mrs M had said again. I *was* happy. Life wasn't perfect, but I was cruising along sandy beaches on the other side of the world with a good friend beside me. What was there to be sad about?

I was glad it was just me and Jarra. He was the more world-ly of the two brothers – Nar'mean? Darel was great for pointing out landmarks and messing about, but Jarra had been around the block a few more times, so when that phone call with Mya came back into my head again when we were about halfway there, it felt easy to talk to him about it.

"You called her by your dead girlfriend's name?" he roared after I told him what I said. "Man, you know how to make an impression!"

"It just came out, natural-like."

"And do you like her?"

"What do you mean?"

"Wow! Degsy, for a smart guy, you can be a dummy sometimes."

"Nah, it ain't like that, geez. She's my friend."

"A friend you called Gabby – the love of your life."

I didn't know what to say to that. Was that what it meant?

"I don't think about her like that."

"Maybe you should start, mate. It's about time you got back on the horse isn't it."

"She ain't a flipping horse. She … well … she's special, I suppose."

"Special? But it's 'nothing like that'," he joked, and I was starting to regret bringing it up.

"A friend. She's a special friend, you mug."

"Well, you want my advice? Shit or get off the pan, brother."

I lost it then, laughing my arse off at the joker. "Thanks, dude. I'll bear that in mind."

When we arrived in Bunbury hours later, Jarra started pointing out landmarks, although he'd never been there before.

"That's a lighthouse," he said, pointing at a crazy-looking, black and white checked lighthouse overlooking the beach.

"No shit!"

"That's the Dolphin Discovery Centre," he said, pointing out a building with 'Dolphin Discovery Centre' written on it.

"You don't say."

"And that is the port," he told me, and I had to stop myself from clouting him, but the sight of the port, which was bigger than I'd imagined for a small city, made me smile and take pity on the dopey sod.

We parked up and made off on foot, gazing off into seas to die for. I'd never been to the coast in the UK. If it was anything like this, I'd move there, but I didn't think it would be. We have bleeding pebbles for a start. What I was looking at was pure gold, and we couldn't resist dropping down to feel the warm sand on our feet then paddle a bit. But there was work to do. And as soon as we hit the port, I started asking questions, but people were cagey. I know I didn't look like a copper, but they really didn't wanna talk to me. I thought Jarra would get on a bit better, but they didn't wanna talk to him either. Talking to people around there was like banging your head against a wall – a wall that knew more than it was letting on.

Meanwhile, Jarra was having the time of his life, catching rays, daydreaming about owning a boat, buying up souvenirs to take home to his old lady. It was like he was the one who'd never been to Australia before. Then he bought this stinking bag of fish heads and guts that made me wanna heave.

"Look in there," he said before I knew what it was, and I wished I hadn't because the sight and smell of those gory bits of fish and guts put me in a right bad mood. He told me his old lady would make a stew out of it, as if it was a good thing. I didn't care what she made out of it. I wasn't going near it.

Anyway, after walking around the boats for nearly an hour, with the reek of dead fish up my nostrils, asking just about everyone we ran into if they knew this Everest geezer, we were fit to give up. Then we heard this shouting behind us and turned quickly. This great big geezer had this small fella against the wall by the neck and was shouting the odds, screaming in his face. The little guy was no match for him, but this didn't stop the other guy. Then he slammed him down on the deck and was punching him, laughing as he did it. It was just the two of them, no other geezers around, so me and Jarra didn't even pause. We weren't having that. We ran in there, shouting, and pulled this big geezer off him. We could smell the booze before we even got there. As the little bloke scurried off to the side, nursing his punched-up face, this big dude was straight up on his feet. He was all muscle, hair and fists, but I'd seen bigger and scarier, and me and Jarra ain't exactly small lads, so we squared up to him, and we could see the cogs turning in his head, working out whether the fight was worth it. In the end, he thought better of messing with us. It was a good decision for all of us.

"Watch your back!" he snarled in a thick Aussie accent before turning and marching off, leaving us with the little guy, who was still on his arse with blood dripping from his nose and eyelids bulging like plums.

"You alright, geez?" I said, giving him a hand up. He was even smaller than he looked, and giggled nervously as he found his feet, as if he thought we might batter him and all.

"It's alright, mate. We ain't here to hurt ya. You okay?"

He nodded sadly and wiped his nose on the back of his hand. "You guys not from around here," he said. His voice was just as tiny as his muscles.

"Perth," Jarra told him.

"London," I added. "What was that all about?"

"Nothing, mate. Debts, that's all. That fella there, Bones, he runs things around here, and I can't say I'm in his good books. If I were you blokes," he added, moving closer while looking around in all directions, "I'd get the hell out of here."

"Why's that?" I asked. I wasn't about to let some meathead scare me.

"Well, mate, you've got about three minutes until he's rounded up his boys and coming after you."

Me and Jarra looked at each other then back at the scrawny

Aussie. I was trying to keep my head up, show I didn't run from no bastard, but the idea of a whole bunch of raging, big blokes chasing us off the dock didn't sound like the ideal way to spend an afternoon, and whatever happened, my fist weren't about to come out of retirement in a hurry. I knew Jarra felt the same because he nudged me and nodded his head away, trying to move things forward. All I saw when I looked at him was that carrier bag of stinking fish, though. The bugger had lost his say in anything we did when he bought that and made me look in it.

"Just a minute, geez," I said. "I've come all the way around the world, and I ain't leaving this port until I get some answers. I know these mugs we've spoken to know more than they're letting on, and I want some info." I'd met little fellas like this geezer inside, and I knew that shouting my mouth off, making a scene, was enough to get him onside. The last thing he wanted was trouble.

"What you after?" he said, and he was twitching now, like a junkie after a fix. He just wanted to see the back of us before the big blokes came back.

"This guy," I said, turning the photo towards him. "Goes by the name of Everest or Malik."

His face dropped, like I'd just shown the geezer a council tax bill that he had to pay this week or he was going to jail, but his mouth stayed shut. He looked over his shoulder, more cagey than ever now, and chewed on his lip. Then he finally spoke. "I'm only telling you this because you guys helped me, but you didn't hear it from me, right? His name's mud around here, and if Bones finds out I've blabbed then …" He dragged his thumb across his neck and I knew he was serious. He took my arm and led me a few steps closer to the wall, trying and failing to take us out of view, and said. "We run all sorts from here, you know?" his eyes widened, asking if I understood what he meant, and I nodded. 'All sorts' could've meant anything, though. They were in a position to run a million different scams. This geezer was so cagey, though, I'd bet my arse it was drugs – nar'mean?

"I don't know about no Malik or Everest. That fella there's Kinsy. Kinyeti, I think his name was, but who's got time for a mouthful like that?"

I made a mental note. He was definitely a slippery fella. He couldn't keep the same name for more than five minutes.

"I felt for the fella. He had no one in the world. No family. All dead. But he wasn't one to mope. Maybe being all alone in the world gave him freedom or something, because he was a cool guy, charming, lots of stories and lots to say for himself. He knew how to schmooze."

It worried me a little that he was talking about him in the past tense, but that could just mean he wasn't around anymore. I tried not to think the worst.

"Then it was like he just didn't want to do it anymore. Do you know what I mean, mate? He'd made his money and he always talked about opening a little café on the coast, serving up African grub or something. I tell ya, mate. We laughed our arses off when he told us about that. Well, most of us did. Bones's face didn't crack a smile. Kinsy had brought in a load of new punters. He was a fucking cash cow, and he wasn't about to let him go."

"So?"

"So … I haven't got a clue. One day he was here, the next he wasn't. Ask me, he's down there." His eyes drifted over to the ocean and my heart sank. "Once you're in, you're in deep. I should know," he frowned. "Now, you blokes need to get moving or that's where you'll end up."

I didn't move, but Jarra had taken a few steps out into the open and said, "Er, Degs."

I had a hundred questions to ask, but when I turned to Jarra, all the colour had drained out of him, and his mouth was wide open. I followed his line of vision and turned to see about twelve beefy geezers strolling towards us, all tooled up and ready to have a go, led by that massive fella, Bones. They were all in sweaty vests and overalls or dungarees, hanging loose at the waist. The sight of them made me laugh for a second – like the Chippendales if they'd got really fat, ugly and oily.

"Run, Degs!" Jarra grunted.

But you know me. Am I the kind of geezer who just turns and runs? Nah! I folded my arms and stood my ground while Jarra and our little informant shit themselves. Then I put my hands in the air and said, "We don't want no trouble." And I was starting to regret not doing a runner. I could hear the tension in them: grinding their teeth, slamming their tools on their palms, salivating over the taste of my blood. "We're looking for Kinyeti! We don't want no trouble. We just wanna know where he is."

Groans went up, and I knew I was on a hiding to nothing, but I had to know, for Slope. He had a right to know if his brother was dead or alive.

"You're a brave man, I'll give you that, you Pommy bastard!" this Bonehead roared. The geezer was easily forty, but he was all muscle and anger. Me and Jarra might have stood a chance against him on his own, but the only chance we had of taking out the whole army was bugger all. "Kinsy was a brave man, too, and look where it got him. Remember Kinyeti?" he shouted behind him, and his boys cheered and laughed as if they'd eaten him for breakfast and were hungry for more.

"Get ready to run," I mumbled to Jarra, and I felt his body tense next to mine. Then I shouted, "So you killed him, then? Good! Saved us the job! Fucker owes us big time," but Bones wasn't listening, and he wasn't about to be fooled by a mouthy chancer like me.

"You wanna know what happened to Kinsy? We'll show you. Get 'em boys!" he roared, and his crew were on their toes, taking us by surprise, flying towards us before we could even think. But I was quick with a plan and grabbed that stinking bag of fish heads and guts and tossed it into the air. For a bunch of sea heads, they made a right fuss when fishy gore and bloody bits started to rain down on them, and it stalled them long enough for us to jam, sprinting away and buying ourselves a head start. Turned out we needed it, because these fuckers might have been older than us, but they were fit old sea dogs, and they weren't gonna let us go in a hurry.

"Where's the car? Where's the car?" Jarra was shouting.

"Fuck should I know? You were driving?" I shouted back, my heart pumping on overtime as we made it back out onto the long drive, whizzing past shrubbery and houses, and almost getting ourselves knocked down. Then I saw something I recognised and said, "Down here." We turned suddenly then I dared sweep a glance over my shoulder. Those bastards were still coming, roaring a death cry that showed they meant business, and if we didn't soon make it back to the car, we'd end up looking a lot like the fish guts I'd thrown at them. "Round here!" I shouted, and the car was in sight. Jarra dragged the keys out of his pocket and pressed the button to unlock it before we even got there, then – I swear – I've never thrown myself in a car as quick. "Go! Go! Go!" I was shouting, but when Jarra put the key in the ignition, the bastard thing made this stupid chugging noise, and I knew we weren't going anywhere.

"Start, you bastard!" Jarra was screaming, and I was looking out the back window. We had about two seconds before a dozen guys landed on us, and we were sitting ducks in his old banger. "Start! Just start!"

Then, the next thing I know, my ears are ringing with a smash, and the window's exploding beside me. A fist has come through and clobbered the side of my head and then two fishy hands, closing in around my throat, dragging my face through the broken glass, pulling me up out of my seat. I can hear myself screaming out as my arms windmill punches that don't quite manage to hit anything. "Fuuuucccckkk!" Then I hear a sound I've never been so happy to hear in my life. The engine's purring and we're skidding off so fast that Bones can't keep hold of my throat. I dropped back into my seat, breathing like I've just been dragged out of the Thames, but I can't help laughing.

"You see Kinsy, you tell him we still got business!" I heard that massive fucker shouting as we skidded off, and now Jarra was laughing his arse off too. We might have left our criminal days behind us, but a little adrenaline still went a long way, and it was like being a kid again, getting away from the old bill or a gang by a whisker. I watched those shitheads getting smaller and smaller out the back window as Jarra sped off down the road until they disappeared altogether and we could finally relax. But Jarra kept on driving like a maniac for a few more miles, until he was certain we were out of danger. It must have been the adrenaline.

"We were right about you at the airport, mate," he said as he finally started to slow down.

"What do you mean?"

"We knew we were waiting for trouble."

And now we were laughing even harder. There was nothing like nearly being killed by an angry mob to bring a couple of geezers together.

"Sorry about the window, geez," I told him.

"Don't sweat it. I just wish there was better news about your little mate's brother."

"Well, at least we know he ain't dead. Or at least he didn't die here, or they wouldn't have sent us off with a message for him. And …" I said, and let my voice trail off as I got my phone out. "This geezer's clocking up the names too. What did they call him? Kinsy? Kinseti or something?" I searched the name in my phone, but there were too many results and none of them shed any light on the geezer we were looking for.

"Do you think he ever got his little café on the coast?" Jarra asked.

"You're a genius!" I told him and typed *Kinseti Café* then *Wardi Café, Kinsy Café, Everest Cafe* then finally *Malik Café*. Now we were cooking. I saved the searches and decided to start calling and sending emails when we got in. For now, Jarra had the loudest speakers I'd ever heard in his car, and I had that feeling of bliss again. For the next few hours, my life was cruising along the western coast of Australia with a mate, some banging tunes and the sun shining down on us. I even wondered if this could be my life now. I could just leave it all behind, take to the road and follow the sun, but I knew where my home was, and in a funny kind of way, I was looking forward to getting back.

As soon as we got in, I started making phone calls, all over the world as it turned out, getting a jump on those different café names. I knew it was a long shot, but I promised myself I'd do everything I could to find him. I sent out a bunch of emails too, but after a long evening chasing my tail, I came back with nothing, pretty certain I'd hit a dead end again. If Slope's brother had managed to get out and open a café on the coast, he hadn't used any of the names I had for him. But we already knew how slippery he was. He could've called the bloody place anything, or instead of a café on the coast, he could've opened a shoe shop on the shore or a hairdresser's in the hills, or he was six feet under somewhere. I had so little to go on, and I knew I had to give up for now anyway. The trip was at its end. The break had been good, and I really did feel refreshed; we'd sorted out the money, made a little headway with Slope's brother, but now matters in London needed my full attention, and it was time to go.

I spent my last few hours in Australia breaking bread with Jarra, Darel and their family. Jarra made me apologise for throwing the fish guts away, but I probably saved our lives, and I think I'll still be laughing about the state of those fishy blokes when I go to my grave. When the time came to leave, the farewell was as warm as the welcome had been. I wasn't looking forward to another marathon in the air, banged up in a 747, but it felt quicker this time, and I couldn't help smiling thirty hours later when the lights of London came into view out the plane window. Australia was great, but I knew where home was. I also knew I was whacked. I'd spent so much time in the air and flown through so many time zones that all I wanted to do was hop in a cab and find my bed. Maybe I'd find some fish and chips on the way, but after that I'd sleep for a week. Then my phone rang and I knew straight away that I wasn't gonna be getting any sleep.

"Degs!"

"Mya? What is it? What's going on?"

"It's Sheila."

My heart started rolling again, pumping the blood around me too fast.

"The matches?" I asked.

"She's been beaten up," she said. "I'm at the hospital."

"I'll be there in five," I told her then hung up and hailed a cab, trying to stop myself crying. I'd come to think of Sheila as my sister. She was funny and smart, and she was a driving force in the Hay Patrollers. I couldn't bear thinking of what it'd be like if something bad happened to her. And she'd been through so much to get to where she was now. I'd heard her tell her story in schools all over London, and it never got easier to listen to. I don't know what I'd do if I lost her.

8 SHEILA'S STORY

I'm often asked when I first knew, and I always answer the same way: by asking the same question back to them. "When did *you* first know?" I say, and they look at me strangely and ask what I mean. "When did you first know you were female?" I ask if I'm speaking to a woman. "That's different," they always answer – some of them smiling, some of them getting agitated – and they add, "I *am* female. It's not something I ever had to know." And then I smile, and once or twice out of ten times, there will be a dawning realisation. I'll see it growing on their faces. They understand what I'm saying. They understand that I didn't suddenly realise that I wanted to be a girl. I *was* a girl. The fact that I had been born in the body of a boy made no difference to that whatsoever. The other eight in ten are less positive. I got spat at once. Well, I've been spat at lots of times, but I was spat at then by a woman who felt so strongly about my words that she had to resort to violence. I've been hit, shouted down and laughed at, but I won't change my answer because I never know when it's going to change someone's mind and make them view the world just a little bit differently. Perhaps they'll go home and tell their family what they've learnt – *I met this trans woman and she was just like me.* This is how the world gets changed.

I suppose the question they really want to know is when I realised that I was in the wrong body. When did I realise that there had been a mistake somewhere and I had been born Malcolm when I should have been Sheila? The simple answer is that I don't know. I have spoken to so many other trans people who can pinpoint the moment: it was usually when they started school and had to conform to a male or female role that was as uncomfortable as a jumper made of bees and hair. My parents didn't let it get that far. There must have been a time when I played with dolls and dressed up in my mother's heels, but my mum and dad must have stomped down on it, because in my first memories of myself I have a shaved head and I'm wearing a soldier's uniform, holding a gun that lights up red and makes machine gun sounds. I'm playing with my dad in the garden, and I already know not to complain. I know what happens if I do. I'll lose something. It could be something I own (although I hated most of the things I owned), a meal, time in front of the TV, pocket money. More often, I would get a thump. My parents were early champions of aversion therapy.

"You're running like a girl."

Thump!

"No, you can't grow your hair out."

Thump!

"No, you can't watch *The Clothes Show*!"

Thump!

Not surprisingly, I learned to keep my mouth shut, but I wasn't without secrets. Every kid has secrets, and I kept mine in an old Quality Street tin, well hidden under my bed. I saved clippings from newspapers, anything I could find about people having sex changes, and pictures of beautiful women that I wanted to be, beauty tips, and I bought makeup and stored it in the tin. I knew I would never be able to wear it, but just having it comforted me. I bought a few outfits too. I didn't get much money, so they were nothing fancy, and I kept them hidden under my mattress. I hadn't even dared try them on. If you'd met my parents, you'd understand why. Not only did they have me running around the garden, declaring war on the neighbours' kids, but they were deeply religious, and I often heard them praying over me. We went to church every Sunday and helped run different groups throughout the week. Whenever I was too feminine for them, I wasn't only disappointing them, but I was condemning myself in the eyes of the Lord. They showed me pictures of the hell I would face in the next life. I was an abomination. I was just a little kid who was a bit girly, but they saw me as a child of the Antichrist himself. And I got my first taste of how powerful they were when I was nine.

If I could go back and change it, I would. I would whisper in little Malcolm's ear, "Stop! They're on their way home," but I don't think he would have listened. He had had those outfits and that makeup in his bedroom for so long, and if he didn't try them on soon, he would explode. Mum and Dad had gone to the church for a meeting that didn't concern him, and they would be away for hours yet. So little Malcolm pulls one of the dresses out from under the mattress. It's too old for him and too big. It's crinkled up, but he doesn't care. It's perfect. He takes off his boy clothes and steps into it, one foot and then the next, and pulls it up over his body then stands in front of his mother's full-length mirror. He looks funny, wrong, but he stuffs it with a couple of balled-up socks and it's a start. His mother has a couple of hair pieces, which he arranges into a wig. Then he fools around with the makeup. He doesn't know what he's doing, but he takes it seriously, exploring the lines of his face and experimenting with different colours. He doesn't even hear the front door open and close; he's too lost in the moment. And then he sees him in the mirror: the towering figure of his red-faced father, with his toecapped boots and shaved head. And then fists fly and everything goes black. When he wakes up, he is in a room with a group of big men. He recognises a few of them from church. The pastor is there, looking on, rubbing his hands together, his eyes boggling out of his head. It's a small room with a low ceiling, lit by candles, which smells the way the church hall does in the winter: damp and earthy. He is flopped over the back of a busted-up, damp sofa, arms thrown in front of him, massive hands hold him down. He's naked. There is pain as he is thrusted into. There's laughing as he tries to move. The pastor grabs his hands, squeezes them and digs his nails in, distracting him from what's going on behind him for a few seconds. Then he screams out and something is forced into his mouth. Something dirty, like a sock. And then he passes out again.

Actually, if I could go back in time, I would go back to the moment when little Malcolm wakes up again in his own bed. I would hold him and stroke his hair and tell him that everything is going to be okay. I would show him the woman I am now, and tell him to hang in there because life is difficult, but it will all work out in the end. Stay strong.

My dad burnt the dress, the makeup, the cuttings, and I welcomed it. I had got the message. I played the war games as hard as I could, and I prayed for myself, although the men I had seen that night were in the church whenever I went. I tried to make friends with boys, although none of them really liked me, and I finally found my salvation in books. There was nothing girly about reading, and it became acceptable. So, I could lose myself in adventures and romances, always casting myself as the leading lady, and I could learn about the world, about science, nature, culture, the law, the stars; I sucked up books with a straw. And as time passed, I was happy. I was living my life in my head, I suppose. Then I hit puberty, and I still don't know what the hell went wrong. I was still living my life in my head, trying to hide what I was from my parents, so I don't know what upset them so much. My soft voice? My walk? I don't know, but I did everything they told me to, and I never dared try on women's clothes or makeup again. But when I was twelve, I was snatched from my bed one night, kicking and screaming, and found myself back in that basement, thrown over the back of the sofa. I was bigger now, but they still overpowered me easily. I had almost managed to convince myself that it hadn't happened to me before, that I had dreamed it, but here was the proof. To this day, I don't know if my father knew what they were doing to me. He called it The Cure. He thanked the Lord for The Cure as he prayed over our Sunday roast. He boasted to his friends that The Cure had purged the demons from his son. But all it was doing was breaking me. I receded further into my books and was terrified to walk or talk in front of my dad in case Sheila leaked out of me. But as well-behaved and boyish as I tried to be, it made no difference. In just a few months, I had gone from being dragged out of bed for a one-off 'cure' to being handed over to the church for weekly intervention. Every Friday night after school, my father would wait for me at the gates then drive me to the church and wait outside. He would tell me how successful he thought this was and how proud he was to call me his son. And every Friday night I died just a little bit more. I never tried to tell anyone; I was too scared. I tried to run away a few times, but it was only worse when I got back, so I was trapped.

This went on for nearly two years, until a few days before my fourteenth birthday. I was never a big girl, and still looked young for my age, and the church was still enjoying me in the name of aversion therapy. I was a shadow, just the way they wanted me to be, but I was always listening out. It was my superpower, and it was what would finally save me.

"Just get the blue ones," my dad was saying. They were talking about cushions or curtains, something like that. I can't remember now. "And make sure you keep a receipt."

"And what's the pin?"

My ears pricked up.

"It's nine four three eight. You should know it by now."

My mum grabbed a pad and pen.

"Don't write it down," he snapped. "Use that thing on your shoulders. It has to be good for something." He always spoke to her like this, but I found it hard to feel sorry for her.

Nine four three eight. Nine four three eight. I kept saying it to myself, over and over in my head. *Nine four three eight.* I didn't do anything straight away. I knew better than that. If I was going to do this, I needed to give myself a head start. So, a few days later, I left for school as I always did, strutted down the garden path with the butchest walk I could imagine, but when I got the school gates, I just kept on walking. When I got to town, I changed into jeans and a shirt in the public toilets and dumped my school uniform. It was the only outfit I took with me. I couldn't risk arousing suspicion by walking out with a fully packed bag. I looked at my face in the mirror: my shaved head and sadness, but there was hope there now, and I couldn't help smiling as I pulled my dad's credit card out of my pocket. *Nine four three eight.* At the first cashpoint I came to, I managed to take out £350. It was the daily limit. I would do this for the next two days before the card was stopped. I bought a train ticket to London and waved goodbye not only to my parents, my school, my town, but to Malcolm. I was going to be Sheila from now on. I didn't know how I was going to do it, how I was going to live, but I had what felt like a fortune in my pocket, and I couldn't wait to arrive in my new life.

I was naïve, though. If I had my time again, I'd stash the money and go to a hostel, but I felt like a queen. I booked into the nicest hotel I could find and paid £100 per night for a room. Then I bought some sequin tops that hung off my shoulder, and enough makeup to open my own counter at Debenhams. I'm not sure where I got my courage from, but I was nearly fourteen, pretty and ready to hit the town. All I remember from those first few days is the colour, the music, the lights, the alcohol and lines of coke, the sex: a blissful blur of blooming into a magnificent colourful butterfly. I was having the time of my life.

The bubble burst a few days later. The hotel wanted me out. I had taken a crowd back there and we had partied through the night. Things had got smashed. I got a big bill and a boot out of the door. I suddenly found myself standing on the cold streets of London with nothing but a bag of makeup, a few pairs of killer heels and a bag of outfits to die for. I didn't even have the money for a sandwich.

"What now?" I asked the boy beside me.

I couldn't remember meeting him, but he had been there almost from the moment I arrived in London. We had partied together, danced, snorted, drank, laughed and become sisters. Michael. This was my Michael. He was the first gay boy I had met, and he was outrageous in a T-shirt that was so torn I wondered why he bothered wearing it and purple hot pants. His hair was shaved like mine, but it looked fabulous on him and brought out his cheekbones. He wasn't trans, but he was the first boy I ever saw wear mascara on wide, defiant eyes that challenged anyone to pull him up on it. I thought that gay people were gentle or weak before I met Michael, but he was anything but. His body wasn't quite masculine, but he knew how to look after himself. We were never lovers. More like sister and brother.

I turned to see him smiling.

"Well that was fun," he told me. "What now, sweet cheeks, is I take you back to the palace for a royal fry-up." He grabbed my hand and we skipped through the streets, hangovers and all. I was still in a daze, a face full of makeup, and I loved the fact that everyone was staring at us.

"Have a good look!" Michael sang out to them. "Superstars coming through!"

I couldn't wait to see the palace. In my mind, I was being whisked away to be a Disney princess in Buckingham Palace. What a shock to the system it was when he took me back to a squat that I smelt before I could see. At any one time, about twenty people lived in it, and we shared a room with four other people who'd just got to London and looked as shocked and scared as I felt. After they moved on, we had it to ourselves for a while.

"What do you think?" Michael announced, sweeping wide arms over the place, holding his head up high. Maybe he really did see a palace as he showed me around.

"It's fabulous!" I told him, buying into his vision, as I would whenever we were together. If it was raining, it wasn't water falling from the sky but glitter. If we were hungry, it wasn't uncomfortable; we were fasting for Miss Universe. If we were hit by punters, we became damsels in a fairy tale of our own making, the latest in a long line of leading ladies to fall victim to affairs of the heart. Yes, he showed me the life and how to live it without going insane, getting depressed, or getting too hurt or killed. More than that, he showed me how to grab life by the balls and dance with it. We were living in a horrible, noisy, damp squat, turning tricks for a tenner a time, eating whatever shit we could find, but I will always remember this as the time of my life. I was happier than I had ever been, which might sound weird, but compared to the life I had at home, with my family and The Cure, I really was living the life of a Disney princess. It was me and Michael against the world. We worked hard and we played hard. We became known as the Sparkle Sisters on a scene that embraced us as a couple of lost boys, and we partied for days at a time, hardly bothering to come up for air.

We went out on the streets together, and the punters were easy to come by. Most days we'd get our first offer before we'd even had breakfast. Working in this way kept us safe. One of us would take the guy around the corner or down an alley, and the other would keep lookout. And we saw all sorts of guys. It wasn't just the pervy old guys that you've probably got in your head. There were young guys too. Cute guys. Students from the college, squaddies, coppers; we saw it all.

One day we ran into a musician guy we'd seen out busking around the Bracker Road. He was seriously cute, and we both fell in love with him. We couldn't believe our luck when he flashed us a tenner.

"He's mine!" I shrieked at Michael. We were never very discreet.

"Mine! Mine! Mine!" Michael screamed back at me.

"Paper hats, rock star, pinking shears?" I said. It was our variation of paper, rock, scissors.

Michael looked the guy up and down before turning back to me and agreeing to play for him. We pounded our fists in front of each other then both made scissors of our fingers. This happened again, and then Michael switched to stone. I had stayed with scissors, hoping to bluff him. The gorgeous, blonde busker with the cute stubble was his. Just my luck. I'd probably end up with some old, sweaty fart having a nervous breakdown.

"Lip gloss," he said, rubbing it in, and I reached into my bag to give it to him. It wasn't often that one of us got a job that we might actually enjoy. He then slinked over to him, working his hips, forcing the guy to watch him, and took him by the hand. I followed behind, jealous as hell, as he led him down an alley that we had both used a hundred times. It was out of the way, but light enough to feel safe. I stood in the open and watched as he turned back to wink at me. Sod!

I stood there for five minutes, folding my arms. It was summer, but it wasn't a warm day. It wasn't unusual for Michael to spend a bit longer with punters, especially if they looked like this guy, so I left them to it. I thought about going down there and joining them, but Michael wouldn't have liked that. So I waited, and I waited. Then I had no choice but to go down there and get him. A tenner would only get you so far, and I couldn't have this guy stopping us from getting the money we needed to party at the weekend.

"Pull your pants up! Prossie police coming to get you!" I called as I walked, laughing to myself. Then I got there and just stopped. I didn't say anything, and it wasn't like you read in books or see in films. I didn't scream or hyperventilate. I didn't drop to my knees or pull him into my arms. I just stood there, feeling nothing, my body still and calm, looking down at Michael the way I looked at him in the squat when he was asleep – the only time he was ever quiet. He was bare-chested, but his red, velvet trousers were still on him. They matched the blood. I would never find out how many times he had been stabbed, but if I had to guess, I would say it was eight or nine, and then his throat had been cut, but he was sitting upright with his legs thrown out in front of him as if he were at home relaxing, drinking a cocktail before we hit a club. And he didn't look in pain or scared. His face, drained of all colour, was locked in an expression that seemed to ask what was about to happen but had frozen before it got an answer.

I stood there for about an hour, not moving or making a sound, then I simply turned and walked away. I stopped at a phone box and managed to tell the police that I had found a body, but I didn't hang around. He wouldn't have wanted me to get taken into care or back to my parents. And then I just walked. I was still numb, and all I could do was walk. I just kept putting one foot in front of the other, propelling my-self forward, because it hurt too much to do anything else. I walked and walked for days, and I'm still not really sure what happened, but I woke up in a hospital. They kept me in, on a drip, too exhausted to move, but as soon as I was able, I was off again, walking the street of London like a ghost. I stole food and drink and slept for just a few hours in the day when my body absolutely demanded it. I must have gone on like this for months. I couldn't bear to think or be anywhere or talk to anyone. As I saw it, I had also died with Michael that day. My life was over.

I'm not sure if it was the grief lifting or the days getting colder that made me snap out of it, but I was starting to need and want things again – warmth, new clothes, shelter, good food, just the basics – and I went back to the squat. I couldn't go back into our room; it was too overcrowded now, and I didn't want to anyway. So I lived out of the kitchen, slept on the floor, and got myself together enough to start looking for punters again. I didn't care about the danger; it was the only life I knew, and although I didn't have a partner, I knew the local faces, and we looked out for each other the best we could, but it wasn't the same. I hated it, and I hated every man that flashed me a tenner. I hated the other toms, too, and we would get into fights all the time. I started getting arrested, drinking and taking too many drugs, making scenes in public. My life was in the toilet. But, in all the chaos, I started reading again, escaping into books. I read about the lives of people who had it harder than I did, stories from around the world, and it gave me strength somehow. And then I started volunteering. I know that sounds weird, and I guess it was. I was a seventeen-year-old rent boy, squatting in a kitchen, getting into trouble with the law every five minutes and fighting with my 'co-workers', but I took it seriously, and turned up every morning to help refugees who had newly arrived in the country. I dished up food and drink and chatted, sat with kids, even helped in the English language classes. Looking back, I was just as in need of help as the people I was supporting, but this was a kind of support for me. It was giving me a purpose and taking me out of myself. It was showing me that I didn't have the monopoly on suffering; it was all around me. And often those who were most hurt were the strongest people I met. They had learnt so much by walking the deep canyons of their own wounds. I suppose that was what I was starting to do. I was healing and getting stronger, seeing the world and my role in it differently. I cut back on the drink and drugs, although I wasn't ready to completely leave them behind, and started looking for a way out. I finally confided in a woman at the centre, and she was helping me to view my options. I didn't want to go into care – I wasn't far away from being eighteen anyway – but I was thinking about getting an education, working, having my own home. Then, at the worst possible time, my luck ran out and I was arrested for fighting. It was the typical after-hours kind of drug-fuelled slapping session with a couple of other prossies. I can't even remember what it was about now, but one of them – Cheryl

– was so wasted that she could barely stand up, and when I pushed her, she went down so hard that she cracked her skull. Before I knew it, the street was full of sirens and I was arrested again. The difference this time was that the police had seen my face once too often. So I was given three and a half years for prostitution and GBH. I think I would have been less terrified of prison a few years earlier, when I didn't give a shit about anything, but I was a different person, I had learnt so much from the shit I had been through, and it seemed unfair to be cut down like this, especially as I had started to help other people, and this was really what I wanted to do with my life. But sometimes things are meant to be, and I met Degsy before I even made it to McAlley- Stokes. I should make it clear that prison is not somewhere I recommend. I could tell you stories that would make your hair curl, but, for me, it was the right place at the right time. Degsy was as hard as nails and became the prison boss, but underneath that, he wanted to make the place better, reach out to people and keep them safe. His life had been hard too, and he had taken the same things from it as me – he didn't want other people to go through what he'd been through. He just wanted to help people. And that was how the Hay Patrollers was born.

It was also while I was in prison that I reconnected with my mother. My dad had died a few years earlier, and she reached out to me. She wanted to be a mother to me, and I even went to stay with her when I got out. She was going to pay for my surgery, but things didn't work out. She said she didn't have the money after all, but it was more than that. She still didn't completely accept who I was. Not that that's easy to do – I know. So, we're still in touch, and I'm patient with her. I want her to get to know me as a person and not a freak. I don't know how much she knows about The Cure, and I don't really care. That's all in the past.

The message I leave you with today is one of hope. When I was a child being abused, when I was on the train to London, when I was standing over Michael's dead body, when I was walking the streets, when I was taking drugs and fighting, when I was facing three years inside, I thought it was the end for me. I thought I was in a pit that I would never be able to crawl out of. But every single time, without fail, a light has appeared and showed me a way through, and every single one of my experiences has made me the woman I am today. Would I change my past? Of course I would, but I'm not going to spend my life wishing things were different. Wherever you are, however bad life is, take a look around and see what other people are going through. If you can, reach out to them. You may think you have nothing to give, but you are wrong. Everyone has something to give. And giving might be the thing that changes your life.

9 THE NOTORIOUS

I thought about the speeches Sheila had made as I rushed to the hospital. She always ended them so positively, trying to get school kids to put others first and find a way out of suffering by helping others, and it worked; we had more young people getting involved in the Hay Patrollers after her speeches than when me, Mya or Winston told our stories. That was just her personality, I suppose; her warmth and positivity were catching, but I hadn't seen any of that in her for a while. She'd been keeping herself to herself, drifting off to another planet in meetings, taking herself off to bed early, and now this. Who the hell would wanna beat her up?

The taxi driver took me and my £50 note seriously when he skidded into the ambulance docking area at forty miles per hour. I had the door open before he'd even stopped and legged it into A and E. The thought of seeing Sheila hurt was still making me sick, but I relaxed a little when I saw her in the packed waiting room with Mya beside her. She hadn't been admitted, but that didn't mean anything with the NHS. She could've come in with her head hanging off, and she'd probably still have to sit and wait ten hours to see a doctor – nar'mean?

"What the fuck?" I was saying as I marched over there. All sorts of walking wounded turned around, but I didn't care.

Mya stood up, walked towards me and led me to the side, leaving poor old Sheila alone on the red plastic chair. Her nose was busted open, and she was gripping her elbow and wincing when she moved as if her arm or her ribs were broken.

"What the fuck?" I repeated.

"Just chill out, Degs," Mya whispered. She looked tired and pissed off. "The last thing Sheila needs is you jumping in with your size tens."

"Just tell me what happened. Who did this to her? Is it some prossy from her past? That Cheryl she put in hospital?"

"It's much worse than that, Degs. She said it was a gang. They dragged her off the street and took her into this house. She was terrified."

I looked over Mya's shoulder at Sheila. She was staring blankly into space, a blur of tears, blood and mascara. Rage burned inside me.

"What mugs would do this?"

"She said they were called The Notorious. Their leader, X, sent her back with a message."

"Hang on. X? Like the X on that box of matches? So it wasn't a kiss."

"Looks that way."

"I ain't heard of no Notorious gang."

"I think that's the way they roll, Degs. They're low key, high impact. Striking when it's least expected. That's what that X prick told Sheila to tell us anyway. Some of them are from the TWC."

This didn't sound good. Most of the TWC were banged up because of us. Winston was a part of them when we met up again after all these years. Maybe we should've expected something like this to happen. Gangs don't just let their members walk away.

"This X geezer's a bit of a firebug. Looks like he torched our house, and he ain't stopping any time soon. Said we need to clear out, and if we don't … well, all this is only the beginning." She let that sink in then said, "What we gonna do, Degs? These guys mean business."

"We'll sort it," I said, but really I didn't have the first idea how to sort this. If this Notorious gang wanted us out, what could we do about it? It's not like we were a fighting gang. We didn't walk around tooled up, looking for trouble. We were the opposite of that, which, I guess, was what this geezer had a problem with. As long as we were around, cleaning up the streets, getting kids out of gangs and into work, geezers like this X wouldn't be able to spread their wings and stomp their feet. I sighed and said, "Do we know anything about them? Where to find them and that?"

Mya shook her head. "Maybe Sheila'll be able to tell you more."

I looked over at Sheila again, lost and broken. She wouldn't be telling anyone anything for a while. "Look, you stay with her," I said. "I'm gonna sort this shit out!"

"Wait! … Degs!" she called after me, but I was already on the move. Two of us were already in the hospital. I couldn't just sit around and wait for something to happen.

I spent the rest of the night driving around London, talking to anyone I thought might be able to shed some light on this shit. I marched right up to faces I knew, and those I didn't, and demanded info. And my reputation hit before I did; most people on the street knew who I was. Some knew I was doing a good thing and were happy to talk to me. Others probably hated me as much as this Notorious gang. Either way, I fronted right up to any mug I met, and I didn't walk away until I knew they'd told me everything. I even got Ivan on the blower to see if he'd heard anything about a new crew, but it was news to him too. In the end, the break came when I marched over to a couple of lads outside the Flag and Thistle pub. They hid what they were doing when I walked over – some shady drug deal – but they carried on with business when they saw that I was alright.

"Alright, boys," I said. "You ain't heard of a new crew around here called The Notorious, have ya?"

They looked at each other then back at me, and then the taller, uglier one bolted into the night as if I was a copper and he had a meth lab set up under his coat. The other geezer tried to run, but I caught him, crunched his arm behind his back and shoved his face into the wall.

"Got something to say?" I said, pulling his arm so hard I was almost breaking it. But not quite. I knew how that felt, and that sickly feeling just before the crack of a bone always loosens the lips.

"I don't know nuffin'" he said, and I slammed his face into the wall again. Blood exploded from his nose.

"You need to start talking."

"Alright! Alright! Just don't break my fuckin' arm. I heard whispers, but I ain't seen 'em. Some guy called X puttin' the shits up everyone."

Jackpot!

"And where do I find this X?"

"I don't know."

Slam! More blood, and his arm might have been broken now.

"Alright! Alright!"

"Where?"

"St. Francis!"

"What?"

"The church! They're holed up in the church."

I let him go and he crumbled to the ground, holding that battered arm. I know violence was a thing of the past for me, but that didn't mean I wouldn't use it if I had to.

"You piece of shit! They're gonna have you!" he shouted as I walked away, and I was one step away from turning back and filling that mouth of his with my boot, but I was on one now. There were a load of St Francis Churches across London, but I knew straight off the one he was talking about. The one that'd been a shell for as long as I'd been alive. It wasn't a big place, and if someone thought to break in, it'd probably make a great hideout for a crew.

As I got back in the car, I tried to make it all make sense. How had I never heard of this outfit, and why were they bothering with us? But the whys and hows didn't mean squat. As I started the car, all that mattered to me was looking after my own. Then, with the sunshine of Australia a distant memory, I was driving through the night way too fast, heart pounding, thoughts flying. Twenty minutes later, I was outside St Francis's.

I sat in my car, looking out and up at it for a few minutes. There were no lights on, and it still had those heavy steel doors that keep the homeless out of empty buildings. Perhaps if society tried harder to get the homeless into empty buildings, we'd all be a lot happier, but that was a problem for another day. It wasn't a big church, but it would've once been magnificent, with stained-glass windows that'd since been smashed though and a statue of Jesus outside who'd lost his head and been decorated with bog-roll by kids. I didn't move. This couldn't be it. But the other St Francis Churches I knew were still being used as churches. This was the only lead I had after two hours of asking, so I got out and started to case the joint. It was cold outside, and maybe all the gravestones dotted around the overgrown grass made me feel even colder. And it was dark and silent. If this was a major gang hangout, either there was no one in or they were all dropped down to their knees in silent prayer. Neither seemed likely.

So I circled the old place, looking for a way in, listening out, but it was bloody Fort Knox. That geezer with the broken arm and smashed face had said what he needed to get me off his back, and I can't believe I bought it.

I circled around one more time. I even started looking for secret openings and passageways, like I was flipping Lara Croft or something. But then, when I got back to the tall, arched doorway at the front, I couldn't believe my eyes. The bloody thing was wide open, and this massive geezer was standing there with his hands on his hip and so much gold hanging from his neck I was surprised he could hold his head up.

"You Degsy?"

"What's it to you?" I asked, and when he folded his arms and I could hear his muscles grind, I said. "I'm Degsy."

"Inside! Now!"

I marched towards him and then past him, showing that I didn't care how big he was; I was in charge here, and I'd take him out if I needed to. That was the mood I was in. I was a kid again and angry as hell. I'd take out anyone who got in my way, or I'd die trying.

This guy stepped aside as I walked in, and the door slammed shut behind me. When I turned, he'd gone, and I was left standing there on my own, in an entranceway that'd seen better days, with yellowing notices on the boards about choir practices and church fayres that were supposed to take place decades ago. The plaster was hanging off the walls and the door was splintered with flaking paint, but it didn't smell old and abandoned. It smelt of weed.

I reached out to open the door, but it didn't budge. I turned back to the main entrance and tried that. It didn't move either. I was stuck. Then I looked around again and saw the video camera in the corner. I was being watched.

"You armed?" A voice from nowhere asked.

I tried to find the speaker, but it was well hidden.

"Nah!"

"Show us!"

I lifted my shirt and turned around to show there was nothing in my waistband. Then I lifted the legs of my jeans and patted myself down. When I'd finished, there was a clank and a beep, and I moved towards the door again. This time, when I tried it, it was open. I stepped inside and regretted it when I was pounced on. I didn't even get a glimpse of the inside or who was there before they had a sack over my head and my hands tied behind my back. Then I was slammed down on my knees, and every time I tried to move, some mug booted me in the stomach. Maybe coming here on my own hadn't been the smartest idea.

After forever in silence and darkness, a voice broke the silence.

"Degsy, mate! How the fuck are you?" Then he said, to whoever was in the room with me, "Take that off him. Show him some respect."

The sack was pulled off, and I was blinded by the light. As my eyes got used to it, a young guy came into focus. He'd called me mate, but I didn't recognise him. He was dark-skinned, maybe Indian or Pakistani, about my age, sitting back on a leather sofa as if owned the place, in fat trainers and a tracksuit that cost a fortune; chains, rings; this guy was minted, and I knew straight away that this was X.

Now I could see, I took the chance to look around the place. It was old and abandoned with graffiti on the walls, but warm, and they'd done it up a bit; there were sofas with PlayStations, Xboxes and top-of-the-range speaker and kit everywhere. A few people were dotted about, chilling, drinking, smoking weed, doing lines. There was even a bit of a kitchen where the choir would've sat, with a couple of two-door fridges, microwaves, coffee machine, beer taps. It obviously served as a getting ready area too as there were tubs of wax, mirrors and cans of Lynx around the place. Over on the other side was a bleeding dancefloor, decks and light rigs, although none of it was being used. Whoever these geezers were, they were well set up and they had cash, which worried me, but I didn't let it show. I was impressed to tell ya the truth; it was the coolest man cave a guy could hope for. This X geezer looked happy enough anyway. He hadn't stopped smiling since he took my hood off.

"Sorry about that," he said. "Can I get you a drink? Spliff? Line of coke? Oh no, you don't do that shit anymore, do you. Maybe a cup of tea and a cucumber sandwich? That's more your level, innit?"

Everyone around him was laughing. I was not.

"To be honest, Degsy, I would've got some herbal tea and muesli in if I knew you were coming, but you've taken me by surprise, bruv. I knew you'd get here. Full marks for speed, though."

More laughter.

"Let's just cut to the chase, shall we?" I said. "You want us out, and we ain't going nowhere. I can't forget what you've done to Winston and Sheila, but I'm prepared to let it go if you back off."

Again, there was laughter from all around.

"I have some names for you, Degsy. Mya – you know her, right?"

I didn't answer. I knew from the box of matches that they had her in the frame with me.

"What about Nosit and Ivan?"

My heart sank, but I wasn't about to show them that. I made my face as hard as I could. Nothing could touch me – or so I thought.

"What about little Asha and Ray?" He said their names in a childish voice then fell about laughing. The dude was a complete nutcase.

I tried to jump up off my knees, but another boot in the stomach reminded me of my situation and knocked the wind out of me. I fell hard on my face, coughing and spluttering as this merry band of jokers killed themselves laughing. Then they pulled me back up onto my knees, and I tried to get myself together. "You leave them out of this!"

"Why would I do that when I wanna see them burn? I wanna see your face when they all burn. I ... well ... I just want to have fun, Degsy. Ain't nothing as fun as a box of matches and a bottle of lighter fuel, innit."

"You're nuts."

"You've got a week, Degsy. Then it's open season on every-thing and everyone you love. D'ya feel me? We can't have a crew like the Hay Patroller running around, spoiling every-one's fun," he laughed. "You have to go. Simple as," he added, but then his face changed and he said, "Or I suppose there is another option ..." and left it hanging there. He was enjoying this.

This guy was starting to well and truly piss me off. "What?" I asked, but he didn't answer. "Stop dicking around, geezer, and tell me what I have to do."

"Well, I'm not an unreasonable man, Degsy."

"That ain't the impression I got."

Another kick in the stomach. This one doubled me over and I landed, cheek-first, on the stone ground. When I was dragged up to my knees, he'd made himself comfortable, sitting back with his legs crossed as if he was a fucking prince or something. I would've loved to get up and lump the geezer.

"There is a compromise, Degsy."

I thought for a minute. What was the midground between torching me, my friends and family and all of us getting out of town?

"I'll give you a clue, bruv. It's got the queen's mug on it, and it ain't a stamp."

I couldn't help smiling as I looked around their luxury church again. "I should've known. Cash? You want cash."

"Yes, Degsy," he said and sprang forward again, talking in my face. It took everything I had not to nut him. "I want cash. I want lots of cash, Degsy."

I thought for a moment then said, "Alright. I got a few thousand. Take it and fuck off out of our lives."

The place erupted again.

"Have I said something funny?"

"Oh, Degsy! Degsy, Degsy, Degsy!" he said, smiling like a loon. "I got a few thousand in the bathroom. I wipe my arse on a few thousand. Try a few million. Then try a few more million and you're close."

I felt hands on my shoulders again. Maybe I looked like I was gonna dive on the geezer. Maybe that's exactly what I wanted to do.

"Are you having a fucking laugh? A million? I can't get my hands on that kind of money."

"Five million."

"Five million?" Now I was laughing. "You're in a dream-world, geez. You think I got five mil knocking about? You're having a laugh."

He dropped his elbows on his knees and his chin on his fists, eyeing me as if he was so much better than I was. "I'm gonna do you a favour, Degsy. You see, we've been doing a bit of research."

"You said."

"Not on you. On the Cliff Vault."

I didn't like where this was going.

"There's a window, bruv. There's a security van, a pick-up and a drop-off, and we know exactly the best time to strike. One job and we walk away with five million cash."

"You want me to rob a bank?"

"No, we want you to rob a security van. Not the same thing."

"And you think I can just walk away with five million?"

"We know you can. Tony over there's got a brother, works with SecuriFirst. Knows the codes and has got you the key. All you gotta do is knock the bloke out, unlock the box, take the cash and we're quits."

"You know there'll be dye in there, and they'll know the serial numbers."

"Why don't you let me worry about that?" He was getting up now, sticking an envelope in my pocket, leaning down to me so I could smell his champagne breath. He wasn't like any gang gaffer I'd ever seen before. Little shit.

"Few details for you," he smiled, and then he stood up, and before I could say a word, another boot landed me in the face and threw me halfway across the room. I didn't hear the laughter that time because I was out cold.

When I woke up, I was outside on the wet grass among the gravestone. The church, towering beside me, was so dark and lifeless that I wondered if I'd imagined it all. My busted face and bruised stomach told a different story, though. We were all in serious shit, and I had no idea how I was gonna get out of it.

10 HEART-STOPPING

When I got back to the hospital, Sheila was still in the waiting room, curled up on two chairs with Mya's jacket thrown over her, sound asleep, but she looked anything but peaceful.

"She still ain't been seen?" I asked Mya, taking her by surprise. I must have looked a right state because her face dropped when she saw me.

"Looks like you're the one who needs a doctor, Degsy. What the hell happened?"

It was pushing four o'clock in the morning now, and the waiting room had thinned out, with just a few drunks and a geezer who'd been in a fight waiting to be seen. It was peaceful and cool, which was exactly what I needed, so I took a seat beside Mya, wincing as I took the weight off my feet. She was right; I was pretty hurt, but it was the last thing on my mind.

"What happened?" she repeated, lowering her voice.

"Don't worry," I said. "It's sorted."

Sheila stirred and Mya pulled the jacket up higher, making sure she was warm enough. "How can it be sorted?"

"It just is."

"You mean you ain't gonna tell me."

"I mean, Mya, it's sorted. End of." I folded my arms and turned away.

"Okay," she said. "If you ain't gonna tell me, why don't you go home. You've only been back in the country five minutes. Get some sleep and we'll chat tomorrow."

"What about Sheila?"

"I'll take care of her. Just go."

I didn't know how to take that. She didn't sound angry, but sometimes girls don't sound angry but they're bubbling under inside. I know she didn't believe I'd sorted a thing, but I had no more to say on the subject, so I said my goodbyes and left her to it. I wasn't going home, though. I needed help, so I went to the geezer I always turn to in times of trouble: Winston. It was late, but the nurses had let me sneak in before. Jane, that hippy-dippy nurse with dreads and peace badges, was on tonight and she let me in, no problem. She looked quite worried about me, though, but I played it down.

I don't know what I expected when I walked in. Maybe I thought he'd be sitting up with his head in his phone. He'd give me an "Alright, mon," and we'd chat and laugh. But my week away had had no effect on him whatsoever. He was still in the land of nod, but he looked even smaller in the bed now, as if he was slowly shrinking, and I'd go there one day to find he'd disappeared completely.

"Bit of a head scratcher, geez," I told him. I was feeling my face and my head as I chatted to him. Although it all hurt like hell, I didn't think there was any real damage. "I know you'd know what to do."

I took the envelope out of my pocket and opened it. It was all there: codes, dates and a loose key I'd use on the guard's handcuffs.

"Next Thursday," I said. "Seven days. What d'ya think?"

He didn't answer, so I lumped down in a chair beside the bed. The jetlag, pain and the weight of what I'd got myself into hit me all at once, and my eyes felt heavy. I couldn't stay awake another second and fell asleep on my arms, leaning onto the bed. It was heaven, and I'd have slept forever too, but I was dragged from my sleep later that night by a long screech. I thought I was dreaming at first, but it was so piercing, it made my teeth hurt and my eyes flick open.

Everything had changed.

The room was full of doctors and nurses, and I was being led away. The door closed on me, but I could see through the window, and I could still hear that long beep. They'd slammed his bed down, so he was lying flat, and were pushing electric paddles onto his chest. I watched as his body heaved, possessed, every time they thumbed the button.

"Don't do this, Winston!" I begged with both hands on my head. I couldn't look. I turned away, but then I turned back again. I couldn't *not* look. They were still shocking him and breathing oxygen into him with a squeezy bag. The room was a blur of wires, injections, white coats, black skin and hope. Then, all at once, they stepped away from the bed. I closed my eyes. I really couldn't look now. I'd lost him. Everything we'd been through together, and I'd lost him. This was it. It was over. It didn't matter about X or Mya or any of it now. Nothing mattered anymore. It was over. When I opened my eyes, though, there were smiles and high fives. Then the doctors started piling out of the room, and only a few nurses stayed behind.

I didn't waste a minute before I was back in there.

"He's going to be okay, Degsy," that nurse, Jane, told me. "For now, anyway."

I thought I was gonna cry or explode or float off into space. It was relief on a scale I'd never felt before. But I didn't know how much more of this I could take.

"Why don't you get off home?" she added, taking my arm. She was about my age, and had been great from the moment Winston was admitted.

"I should stay," I said.

Then, more forcefully, she said, "No, Degsy. Get some sleep. Nothing's gonna change tonight. Get some sleep. You look like you need it."

I couldn't argue with that, but I had to go back to A and E first to tell Mya what had happened. Maybe I shouldn't have told her; she had enough on her plate with Sheila. Maybe I was telling her for me, because I really needed someone to put their arms around me and tell me everything was gonna be okay, and Mya did just that. Everything that could have gone wrong had, but I felt comforted in her arms and waited with her a little longer, and then she sent me home too. This had been one of the longest days of my life, and when I finally got into my bed, it was twelve hours before I was out of it again. I missed the whole next day at work, and I probably would've kept going if Mya hadn't come in with a coffee. With my eyes half-open and the light glowing behind her dark, curly hair, it looked like she had a halo. I didn't tell her that, though.

"Thanks," I said, sitting up. My head felt like I'd spent the night partying. I brought my fingers to my hair and felt a bump the size of a plum.

"Well, you look like shit," Mya smiled.

"Thanks." I couldn't help smiling. I was pleased to see her. I'd missed her while I was in Oz, and we were both calmer than the night before in A and E. "How's Sheila?"

"Not great. Physically, it's a broken nose, few broken ribs, she'll live. Mentally, I don't know."

"I'll speak to her."

"Give her some time. It's like she's trying to organise things in her mind, I think."

"You think she'll be okay?"

Mya shrugged then said, "Will any of us?" I knew what she meant by the look on her face.

"I told you, it's sorted."

She didn't answer, but her silence was more of an interrogation than any words she could come up with. She was like good cop and bad cop all rolled into one, and I cracked straight away.

"Alright, I found this X geezer. We had a scrap and we've sorted it out. He ain't gonna get in my way, and I ain't gonna get in his."

"Just like that?"

I could tell she didn't believe me, but I couldn't tell her the truth. "All you need to know is nothing else is gonna happen to any of us. I've sorted it."

She tilted her head, getting the measure of me, then said,

"Drink your coffee, Degs. I've gotta get going."

"Where you going?"

"To see my mum." And then she left the room.

I bolted out of bed in my pants and ran after her. "Wait up, Mya! Wait up! I was supposed to be coming with you."

She turned but didn't stop. "Well, if you can't be honest with me, why should I trust you with my life?"

She had me there. "Alright," I said. She'd won. "Look, come back in."

She didn't look like she was going anywhere for a minute, and then she finally came back into my room and sat on the bed. As I threw on a pair of jeans and a shirt, I told her everything. I'd promised myself I wouldn't, but how could I not?

"So we're screwed!" she said. "Why'd you tell me everything was okay?"

"Because it is."

"What planet are you on?"

"I can sort it."

"What kind of relationship are we gonna have if you don't trust me with things like this?" she said, dropping her face in her hands.

I opened my mouth to answer then tripped up on the words she'd spoken. "Relationship?"

She brought her head up and rolled her eyes. "You know what I mean, Degsy. Friendship. We're all in this together."

"I know, but I thought it'd be easier to deal with it myself."

"Easier for who?"

"I'm sorry, alright!" I was starting to miss Australia. The idea of being thousands of miles away was heaven. "Look, what time are you seeing your mum?"

She pulled her phone out of her pocket and said, "I'm going now."

"Just give me five minutes and I'll take you. I wanna do this with you, Mya. We can talk more later."

She blew out her cheeks, making me suffer, before she nodded and said, "You've got two." Then she marched out of the room and I couldn't help smiling.

Almost half an hour later, we were sitting outside a block of flats on the other side of town. The engine was off and the car was silent, but Mya hadn't moved. I was staying quiet. I knew this was her moment. Either she'd go in or she wouldn't; either way, I was gonna support her, but it was her decision to make.

"I ain't seen this place since I was thirteen years old," she said. "It ain't changed a bit."

"Reminds me of the Addie," I said.

She smiled weakly, but I don't even know if she heard me. Her eyes were fixed as if she wasn't just looking at the building, but into the past itself, watching herself as a kid going up and down those stairs, going to and from school, and then going out on deals, getting richer and more powerful.

"I can't do it," she said. "I thought I wanted to know, but I don't. All these years …"

"You don't have to go in, Mya."

"But I owe it to her, don't I? Whatever Mevil did to her to warn her off was my fault, wasn't it? I didn't want him to hurt her, but I didn't tell him that. I let him go ahead and intimidate her so I could go on dealing, living in luxury without her bending my ear. What kind of person does that make me?"

"It was years ago, Mya."

"That's not an excuse. What if he raped her?"

This silenced us both. I'd wondered this before but never said the words. Mya's old lady had hardly spoken a word to her since that day. Whatever had gone down must have been pretty nasty. I didn't know what to say, but then she unclipped her seatbelt and opened the door, so I did the same. We were on the move.

"Okay?" I asked as she pulled open the main door, and she nodded. She looked great; she'd made a real effort for her old lady, to show her she'd changed and life was different now, but we both knew there was every chance she wouldn't wanna speak to Mya. She hadn't turned up to Mya's trial or visited her in prison when she was doing life for murder; it wasn't likely she'd welcome her daughter with open arms, so I admired Mya for trying.

We walked up a few flights of stairs then through a door and along a corridor with *Tories 1, You 0* spray-painted across the wall. It smelt of booze and fags, which was better than the smell of most of the blocks on the Addie – nar'mean?

"Here," she said, rounding another corner, and we were standing outside number fourteen. "This is it."

"You okay?" I asked again, and she didn't answer this time. She raised her fist to knock on the door, and I could see she was shaking. The door had a frosted window, and we could see a light inside, so when there was no answer, she knocked again. This time, we saw something stir inside. A tiny figure was moving around and then opened the door a few inches before it caught on the chain.

"Yes?" The voice was like Mya's but smaller. Mya was a powerful woman; this was what she'd sound like if she'd been shrunken down and hollowed out. It must have been her mum.

"It's me."

No one said anything, and then two dark, little, emo- tionless eyes appeared in the gap. After a few seconds, they were gone again and the door closed. Me and Mya looked at each other. Her face was flushed and teary. I reached out and took her hand, gave it a squeeze. Then there was more movement. The door opened again, this time with the chain off. The woman who opened the door was much older than I'd imagined she'd be. Life had definitely booted her around a bit, as her wrinkles, white hair and sad eyes testified to. Her face was difficult to read, though. She didn't look happy to see Mya. She didn't look sad either. She was blank, and it was unsettling to watch. And she didn't say anything. Mya said nothing too. It was weird. Then the old lady went back into the flat, leaving the door open. I squeezed Mya's hand, hoping it helped in some way, and we followed in behind her, into a flat that smelt of greasy fried chips.

Mya led me through to a simple living room, with the TV left on and blaring, but her mother wasn't in there. We heard noises from what must have been the kitchen, but we stayed put. I looked around and noticed some nice paintings and ornaments, but there wasn't a single photograph anywhere nor trace that Mya had ever existed. We didn't sit down. It seemed rude, so we just stood and waited for Mya's mum to come back in.

Minutes later, she was there with three beakers of squash. It was a strange choice, especially as she hadn't asked us what we wanted. She set the colourful beakers on the coffee table and sat in the armchair facing the noisy antiques program on the TV. Me and Mya sat down on the sofa and grabbed a drink. She didn't look at us at all.

"Are you okay, Mum?" Mya finally asked.

I waited for an answer, but none came.

"Mum?"

A little smile rose on her cheeks, but it was because of the antiques program rather than anything Mya had said. And we just carried on like this; the three of us sitting together, watching some old geezer telling an old lady her prize vase was worthless, as if we were a family or something and this was just a normal evening. It was weird, but comfortable in a funny kind of way. We were doing this for some time before Mrs Garcia spoke. And all she said was, "Victorian," and turned to smile at us. I wondered what the bloody hell she meant until the old geezer on TV made a comment about this little figurine being from the Victorian era. She was in her own little world. Me and Mya looked at each other once again. Then, before either of us could say a thing, there was a buzz. We stayed seated as Mya's mum got up and went into the hallway. She moved as if she was on her own in the flat, oblivious to us, as if she was being operated by remote control even, stooped over and shuffling. When she got back in the living room, she was joined by a full-figured, joyful-looking, Nigerian nurse. Her smile dropped for a bit when she saw us.

"I didn't know you had company, Maria," she said loudly, smiling once again. "Who's this then?" But Mya's mum was back in her armchair again, playing Name That Antique.

"Can I help you?" the nurse asked us, looking more concerned now. I suppose it didn't help that my face was a bit smashed up from my meeting with X.

"I'm Mya. I'm her daughter, and this is my friend, Degsy."

The nurse's face relaxed, and her voice raised again. "I didn't know you had a daughter, Maria," she said, as if talking to a deaf person. "And a pretty one too. Let's just get you comfortable, shall we?" she added, moving over to Mya's mum. Then a routine of pill-taking and other medical checks began before talk of a bath and bed, as Me and Mya looked from her mother to each other, shrugging at this latest development. When the nurse came walking back across the living room, taking some old plates and cups through to the kitchen, Mya caught her arm and said, "Can I talk to you outside for a minute?"

"Of course, dear," she answered, and I was left alone, wondering what the bloody hell was going on. I liked Mya's mum, though. She obviously wasn't well, but she'd made us drinks and given us a welcome. She was a good person.

When Mya came back in, I could see she'd been crying, but she wouldn't meet my eye. "I'm off, Mum," she said, and now she raised her voice, too, as if the old woman was on another planet and they had to shout to reach her. "I'll come back and see you soon," she added, and that was that. We left. Or rather, Mya left and I was running to catch her, which seemed to be happening a lot lately. I caught up with her outside and opened the car for her. When we were safely back inside, she started to sob.

"It's dementia," she said, wiping her eyes.

"Shit, I'm so sorry."

"She doesn't even know what day of the week it is."

I didn't know what to say, so I pulled her in for a hug. What else could I do? As her body fell towards mine, I could feel the weight of her sadness and the trembling as she sobbed. "I wish I could take this away from you," I told her. "And we'll do everything we can to help her, Mya. We can get some of the Hay Assist volunteers over there to keep her company, take her out, make sure she's got shopping and that, and I'll come and visit her with you."

She pulled away from me, half smiling. "You'll do that?"

"Of course," I smiled. "I really liked her. She seemed kind."

Her half smile broke into a full smile and then a laugh, and the last of her tears broke. "I love you, Degsy," she said and then her hand came to her mouth. "Sorry, I didn't mean … I mean …"

I didn't give her a chance to take it back or explain it. I moved towards her and found her lips. It was only now I was kissing her that I realised how much I'd been longing to kiss those soft, full lips and feel her fingers running through my hair. I closed my eyes, and the world inside me lit up. I can only remember that happening once before: when I kissed Gabby. The kiss could've lasted seconds or hours; I had no idea. Time had fallen away into this single moment, and I didn't want it to end. When we finally pulled away, her face was flush and her gaze had softened. She reached out to wipe her tears from my face and I closed my eyes at her touch.

"It's all gonna be okay," I told her.

Then her face turned cheeky as she said, "Let's go home."

11 HAY ASSIST

I had no idea what time it was, but the sun was shining through the curtains, the birds were singing and Mya was sleeping close to me, her face against my chest, her hair flowing down her bare back. I reached out and ran my fingers through it, and memories from the night before hit me, lighting me up again all over again, sending goose bumps up and down my body. As I touched her face, Mya began to stir, and then those dreamy brown eyes were looking up at me.

"Morning," I said, and a smile crept up on her face. She ran her hand through her hair, propped herself up on her elbow, and then we were kissing again.

It was mad that I could feel happy with everything that was going on, but Mya had this effect on me. It was mad that I could even think about finding love again after Gabby, but here we were, in bed together, waking up together, and nothing had felt more right in my whole life. We were a fit. It had taken me a long time to see it, but sometimes you have no idea that what you're looking for's right under your nose until it slaps you in the face. I could've stayed in that bed with her all day, but she had other ideas.

"Where you going?" I asked as she sat up and started to pull her clothes back on. "Don't put that on. No, not the bra," I joked. "Don't put the bra back on. Not the T-shirt."

She smiled back at me, but my complaining didn't stop her.

"Where you going?"

She was on her feet now. "To see my mum."

There wasn't much I could say to that. I knew she'd have her hands full with her mum from now on. But then she was coming back to the bed and we were kissing again. When she pulled away this time, she said, "I meant what I said last night, you know."

"About Beyoncé kicking Rihanna's arse in a fight," I joked, remembering all the daft stuff we'd chatted about long into the night.

"About loving you, you muppet," she told me, "but I need to go, and so do you. Holiday's over, Degsy. You've got some serious shit to sort out," she added, and now she looked serious as she kissed me on the head then left me to it. She was right, but there was nothing I could do today. It was six days until this robbery was going down, so I had time to think of a plan or make a decision; I just hoped something came to me because the options were looking pretty shitty: either I rob this van and probably land myself back inside or get shot, or we pack up everything we've worked for and get out of dodge. But how could we do that? It wasn't just me, Mya, Winston and Sheila; we had people and projects all over the place, and it was growing all the time. Maybe there was another option. Maybe I could take this X geezer and his boys down, but I had the feeling they were no small operation. And I wasn't that geezer anymore anyway. Giving a few black eyes to get info ain't the same as wiping out a gang boss and his crew. It wasn't me anymore. That only left the police. We'd already been to the police about the arson; they had the matchbox. But now I knew what we were dealing with, I knew the police would be as useful as a Cadbury's kettle. The day I would see coppers turn up at St Francis Church would be the day everything I loved was torched. I had to face it: X had me by the balls. The only thing I had on my side was time. There was still time to think of a plan and, in the meantime, it was business as usual.

I pulled myself out of bed, which was so hard because Mya was still all around me – her scent on the pillow, memories of her in every crease of the sheets. I took a shower, got dressed and popped into Sheila's room to see her, but she wasn't there. I'd expected her to be in bed, resting and healing her injuries, so I was surprised when I saw her sitting at her desk, working on her computer, when I got into the office.

"Hey! You're looking better!" I said as I dropped myself into a chair near her.

"And your pants are on fire," she said, managing a smile, but the sadness was there to see, along with a bandaged nose and two black eyes.

"How you feeling?"

"I just want to put it behind me," she said, and carried on with her typing.

"I found them, Sheila. It's all gonna be okay."

Her fingers stopped for a split second before she was speed-typing again, paying me no attention at all. Then she said,

"So how was Oz?"

"Didn't you hear me? I found them."

Now she stopped. "Look, Degs, I don't mean to be funny, but I don't care. Someone like me will always be beat up, and it doesn't really matter. I'm glad you've found them. Maybe you'll sort things out, maybe you won't. I don't really care one way or another."

"This doesn't sound like you, Sheila," I said, but she just shrugged and was back to business. I was gonna leave her to it, but she looked so sad, so I said, "No one deserves to get beat up, Sheila. No one like you anyway. And by that, I mean good people, good friends. I don't know what's going on for you, but I need you to know I'm here for you. Anything you need, I'm here."

Once again, she stopped typing for only a second before carrying on and giving me the weakest smile I'd ever seen. "Thanks, Degsy," she said, but I wasn't sure if she'd even heard me. I didn't wanna push her too hard, though, so I got on with business. Then she came to life and said, "There's someone waiting for you in the snug."

"Thanks," I said, and left her to it. But I couldn't believe what I was seeing when I made my way over there. Slope was sitting on the comfy chair, head in hands, and stood up, almost respectfully when I walked in. Whatever he wanted, I decided I wouldn't tell him I'd been looking for his brother. I didn't have anything to tell him anyway – all my leads had turned to dust – so it made sense to keep shtum.

"Degsy," he said, sounding a little surprised.

"You expecting someone else?"

"Nah, it's just …" He sat down again, and I joined him.

"You alright, Slope?" I asked. "Good to see you." I didn't wanna make him feel awkward. He might have hit out at Ibrahim last time I saw him, but all these kids deserve a second, third and fourth chance in my eyes, especially Slope. He was too young to be doing all this on his own.

"I'm sorry, alright," he huffed and folded his arms. "I just lost it."

"It's alright. Don't sweat it."

He looked surprised. Perhaps he expected me to shout or make him feel like shit, but it wasn't my style.

"So you back on board?" I asked.

He rolled his eyes, and in that moment, I didn't really know why he was there. He still looked like he hated me and everything we were trying to do with the Hay Patrollers. He'd turned up, though, so I had to give him credit for that.

"Suppose," he said.

"So you wanna get back in with the painting group, get a bit of training? Have you had a look at the other stuff we've been doing?"

He shrugged and said, "Don't care really," then looked out the window.

"Am I missing something? Is someone paying you to be here?"

I was joking, but he looked like he was taking me seriously, shrugging and looking shifty. He was a tough nut to crack.

"Let's just start at the beginning, shall we?" I said, trying to be patient with him. "I've got a bunch of forms for you to fill out, and you can have a look at our programs, see what takes your fancy."

"I wanna work with you," he said, surprising me, all his indecision gone. Then he added, "I ain't bent."

I couldn't help laughing. I didn't know what to make of this little geezer, but he was begging to be taken seriously. That much I knew. I'd seen him take on the big lads, trying to be a big man, doing anything it took to be the gaffer, and laughing at him wasn't gonna help. Maybe having some responsibility and working with me was exactly what he needed, so I surprised us both when I said, "Alright. Let's start now. See how you get on. I'm checking in on a new project this morning. You in?"

He sat up straight and said, "What do I gotta do?"

"Keep your mouth shut and your eyes open. That's a start," I said, and I might have been mistaken, but he almost cracked a smile.

I left him filling out forms and reading, and called to check in with the Hay Patroller at The Grove, and all was well. Then I turned my attention to the Hay Assist project. First, I wanted to make sure Mya's mum was added to the schedule. Then, as it was still quite new, and we only had a handful of old dears on our books, I thought me and Slope could spend the morning dropping in on a few of them and getting an idea of how things were going. The project was a great idea, with volunteers going into the homes of the elderly and disabled to help out with things around the house, shopping and keeping them company. The idea of these old dears being lonely or even scared in their own homes broke my heart. So with the project only just up and running, I'd heard good things, but there was no replacement for getting in there and checking it out with my own two eyes, and if Slope really did wanna get involved and climb the ladder, this was a good place to start.

We stopped in first to Mrs Henry's place, and she was full of praise for seventeen-year-old Joa and nineteen-year-old

Ahab, who'd been stopping by to help with chores and take her shopping. Slope didn't say a word, but he looked to be taking it all in. Just down the road was Mr Sehmi, who also couldn't speak highly enough about Han and Three Pies who were looking after him.

"What the hell is Three Pies?" Slope asked when we got back in the car.

"It's this nineteen-year-old geezer who used to be on crack, but he turned his life around."

"Why's he called Three Pies?"

"I ain't got a clue," I told him, and we were quiet again, but as he'd started the conversation, I thought I might risk asking him a few questions. "Do you like the UK?"

He shrugged and looked out the window.

"Do you miss Sudan?"

The look he shot me made me feel stupid for asking. Why'd he miss a place where he lost his family and had to leg it out for his life? But that didn't shut me up. "That bad, huh? There must be something you miss about it, though. I spent years in prison, hating every minute of it, but I still miss their rice pudding sometimes. I've tried making it, but I can't make it taste like theirs. Probably had mould and all sorts in it, but I couldn't get enough of it."

He didn't answer.

"No? Nothing?"

"You need to go left," he finally said, taking his role as navigator seriously, and I left it at that.

"Listen, I've had an idea, and you might be just the man to help me," I said, feeling energised. "I think we should put on an event, raise awareness for the Hay Assist program, invite all these old dears. We could do it at the community centre and unveil the mural at the same time. You wanna get stuck in, you can help me organise it."

My brain was a runaway train, but Slope just shrugged and said, "Sounds like a lot of work."

"It will be," I told him. "But you wanna get involved, yeah?"

He shrugged again and looked out the window. Then my phone rang, and I was glad of it because I was one step away from asking what the bloody hell was wrong with him.

I didn't like answering the phone while I was driving, but it was Phyllis, Ray and Asha's foster mother, so I had to take it, and I put it on speakerphone.

"How was your trip?" she asked, and I filled her in. I didn't wanna talk about anything private with Slope in the car, so I got around to asking what I could do for her.

"Asha and Ray have been missing you. I wondered if you wanted to pick them up from school one day this week, take them out for a few hours."

"I'd love it," I said. "How about tonight?"

"Great. If you're sure. They'll be thrilled. They get out at three twenty."

"St. Mark's, isn't it?"

"That's it. I'll let their teacher know you'll be getting them."

We said our goodbyes and once again I found myself feeling content. I'd been missing my brother and sister too. Now I was back in the UK, I wanted to see them regularly and be a proper brother to them. It'd be nice to see their school too. Then maybe I could take them to see the work being done on Unit 16-21. I really needed to check on the building progress there. It was good for them to learn more about what life's really like too and how they can make a difference.

Mine and Slope's last stop was a council flat where a Mrs Bukhari lived. A couple of the patrollers had been popping in just to keep her company. She liked board games, and had already told us what a difference it made having someone to play them with her, but it couldn't hurt to pop in just to make sure all was well. She was only a few floors up, so we went up, knocked on the door, and a tiny Pakistani woman answered. She looked worried when she saw us, but she welcomed us in when we both showed our photo ID's and told her who we were.

"Wonderful! Wonderful!" she said, and was straight in the kitchen to bring us tea and biscuits. Slope couldn't believe his luck and ate as if he'd never had a biscuit before. Mrs Bukhari laughed at him and said, "You remind me of my grandson." Still smiling, she reached out to a photo on the mantlepiece and handed it to me. I nearly spat my tea out when I saw who was on it, posing for a school picture as if butter wouldn't melt in his mouth. It was only that nutcase X.

"You see that shop we passed on the way here," I said to slope, turning the picture away.

He shrugged, sneered and nodded all at the same time.

"I need you to run down there and pick up some milk for the office."

"But—"

"Semi-skimmed. None of that full-fat nonsense." I must have looked like I meant business because, although he didn't look happy, he took the couple of quid I was holding out to him and left us alone, dragging his feet and slamming the door behind him. I looked at the photo again. He was much younger, but it was definitely him, in his school uniform with his head held high, arrogant-like. He may have been smiling, but even then there was something crazy-looking about him, something not quite right.

"He looks like a good boy," I said, and stood him up on the coffee table.

"Aziz? Nah, he's a little shit," she said, and I burst out laughing. I didn't expect that.

"Say it like it is, Mrs B."

"Don't get me wrong," she added, slurping at her tea, "boy's had a hard life, but he's not one to be a good boy."

My ears pricked up, and I knew all I had to do was keep quiet and she'd fill me in. If there was one thing I knew about old dears like this: they loved to talk.

"It was tragic, Degsy. I don't know how any of us got over it. They were killed, both of them, in a house fire. He was only five."

"What? His parents?"

"My daughter and her husband. Aziz's parents. Yes. He lived with me after that, but I couldn't control him. He was a wild one. Loved setting fires. Sometimes I even wondered if …" the thought trailed off, but I knew what she was wondering. Just how much of a psycho was this X geezer? "I don't suppose you could reach out to him, could you, Degsy? I ain't seen him for more than a year. He'd be your age by now. Maybe you could get him to join your lovely programs and be a good boy like you? Maybe you can change him?"

She looked so hopeful that I couldn't disappoint her, so before I left, I told her I'd see what I could do. I hated lying, but what else could I say? I didn't think rocking up to St Francis's Church and asking X to join the Hay Patrollers was gonna get me anywhere.

I spent about half an hour with her, and promised I'd pop in again. Even gave her my personal mobile number in case she ever needed anything. I really liked her, and it was sad that she was all alone. X didn't deserve to have a nan like her, but we were gonna look after her now. As she spoke to me, I listened out for anything I could use on X to get me out of my fix, but there was nothing. The fact that his life had been savaged by trauma when he was a kid explained a lot, but it was hard to feel sorry for him.

When I got outside, Slope was waiting by the car with a four-pinter milk in his hand.

"Alright?" I said, and all I got was another shrug for my trouble. Then we got in and set off, and the drive back was mostly silent, with me trying to make conversation and then giving up. I wasn't gonna break my back trying to reach out to this kid. I'd held my hand out; it was now up to him whether he took it or not. But then, finally, it felt like I was getting somewhere, like all my effort had been worth it, like I was getting through. It wasn't a big moment, but it was moment nonetheless, just as we were getting out of the car. I pulled up and turned as he moved to get out, but then he stopped. I thought he was gonna say some shit about today being a waste of time, or he didn't wanna come anymore, but he turned to look at me and said, "The mountains." His face was still made of stone, but I could see something had shifted. I didn't know what the bloody hell he was going on about, though.

"Eh?"

"You asked what I miss about Sudan. I miss the mountains," he said, and then he got out of the car, and I watched him walk away. Maybe there was hope for him after all.

I drove off, smiling, thinking about him and wondering if there was any hope of finding his brother. Then I started thinking about that idea of putting on an event at the community centre, celebrating the Hay Assist program and unveiling the mural and all the other work we'd done there. It was a great idea, and my mind was on overdrive, but then my heart sank. X wanted me to walk away from all of this, leave behind all this good work, and there I was planning a new public event. If that wasn't rubbing his face in it, I didn't know what was. But I knew deep down we weren't going anywhere, that this event would happen. I just had to work out how to dig us out of this hole with my life and freedom intact.

I spoke to Mya on the blower for a bit before going to pick up Asha and Ray. It felt the same as ever, talking to her on the phone, but completely different at the same time. It was like we now had secret access to parts that we didn't know about before, and she spoke with a voice that was new and fresh, and it drove me wild. I think it meant we were together now. It wasn't just a one-off thing; we were talking like a couple.

"How'd it go with your mum?" I asked.

"Well. Surprisingly well. I mean, she ain't got a clue who I am, but … I don't know. I can be there for her at least. I can make sure she has everything she needs, even just sit and watch programs with her. She smiles at me, you know."

"Of course she smiles at you. Who wouldn't?"

She laughed at that, and we chatted for a bit longer. She told me more about her Mum and that she wanted to meet Asha and Ray soon. I told her how it'd gone with Slope and how worried I was about Sheila. It was a comfort to talk to her. I didn't think I could do the love thing again, but here I was whispering sweet nothings and loving every minute of it.

After that, I swung by St Mark's and picked up the kids. It was such a posh school, and I felt out of place, but they ran up to me and hugged me. In the car, I couldn't stop smiling. I swear, them two could talk for England, and it was exactly what I needed to take my mind off things.

"Can we go to McDonald's after?" Ray asked. I looked in the rear-view mirror and saw his hopeful face. He was ten years old now and a right little chatterbox.

"Can we go to the park?" This was Asha. She may have been a year younger than her brother, but she was the one who had the control.

"Where are we going, Degs?"

"Will there be tigers there?"

"Why's your name Degsy?"

"Why's the sky blue?"

They had so much energy and I loved it. I hadn't spent much time around little kids before, and they always put a smile on my face. I looked in the mirror at them both again. They were play fighting now, squabbling over something or other. As I watched, I wondered if they got stick at school, since he was black and she was part Chinese, or because they were fostered and had a dead junky for a mother. But then I put the thoughts out of my head. They looked like a couple of happy kids. And now they had a big brother to look after them if they got any trouble anyway.

"Yeah, we can go to McDonald's," I told them, and they

stopped their squabbling to say, "Yay!"

"We can go to the park too if you like. And to answer your other questions: we're gonna visit some amazing people who do great work for homeless people. No, there won't be tigers there. My name's Degsy because no one wants to be called Derek. And the sky's blue because when the world was being built, they run out of green paint."

They giggled at this.

I thought answering all their questions in one go would settle them, but it only set them off again.

"Why didn't they use a different colour paint then?"

"Why are you called Derek?""What's a homeless person?"

I decided it was time for them to get the answer to that last question, and I'd put them to work at the same time, get a paintbrush in their hands, build their characters, their sense of community and have some fun at the same time. Then we turned into the site of Unit 16-21, and all that went out the window. I couldn't believe what I was seeing. People had scattered all over the place – running, waving their arms, screaming. I recognised most of them, wearing their Hay Patrollers uniforms, or the older workmen and women in their high viz, scattering all over the place. It was chaos.

I drove through the open gates, pulled the car over and just sat there.

"What's happening?" Asha asked, but I couldn't answer. I was just staring ahead of me. I couldn't get my head around it. How was this happening? Everything we'd worked for and achieved? I couldn't believe it. The whole bloody site was on fire.

I told the kids to stay put, and I ran out of the car. A group gathered around me, all trying to tell me what was happening at the same time.

"Just stop!" I said, and then I pointed to Carl. He was an eighteen-year-old geezer I trusted to give me the lowdown. He'd come such a long way in the time I'd known him, knocking the drugs on the head and mentoring some of the younger members.

"It's a fire, geez," he told me.

"I can see that. Is anyone hurt?"

"I don't know. We're all meeting at the gates. We had a fire drill a few days ago, so we know what we're doing, innit."

Looking around, I could see there was more order than I first thought. Everyone was at least running in the same direction, even if they were screaming and shouting.

"Okay, do a count and let me know," I told him, and as they walked away from the fire, I walked towards it. I thought I'd had enough fire to last me a lifetime, but I couldn't take my eyes off it. I felt like crying, to tell you the truth, but what good would that do? Months of work was going up in flames. Months. And all that money we'd got to get it going. Would we even be able to do it after this? It'd been a dream: knock down the old school and hospital, build the units and sort out housing and employment for so many people who needed it, and now it was all going up in flames and I was raging. And I didn't need to think too hard to know who was behind this. I wished he was standing in front of me right now. I'd kill him. I'd do him once and for all. Bollocks to living a peaceful life. I'd rip his throat out. Then my phone rang, stalling my rage, but it was back as soon as I answered it and heard the voice on the line. It was him. I was so shocked, I couldn't even say anything. The boy had a serious set of balls on him.

"Pretty ain't it?" he said, and then I had to move the phone away from my ear because he was laughing so hard.

"We had a deal! The job's a week off. What's this all about?" I was screaming at him.

"Oh, Degsy. I just wanted to make sure I had your attention. I need to know we're on the same page. Do you get me? I need to know I can rely on you. I need to know—"

I'd heard enough. "Go fuck yourself!" I shouted and hung up before he could say another word. I didn't care about the consequences. Fuck him! All I cared about was getting those flames out and making sure everyone was okay. I could hear sirens in the background now, and I finally turned away from the fire and moved back towards the car.

"Shit!" I shouted and started running. Ray was there, but the door was open, and Asha was nowhere to be seen. "Shit!" I leaned in and grabbed Ray by the shoulders. "Where's Asha?"

"I-I-I" Ray mumbled.

"Where?"

"She went to find you," he said and started to cry. I wanted to hug him and tell him it was alright, but I had to find Asha. I turned and scanned the whole site. Thankfully, I saw her straight away. She'd wandered close to the fire and was staring up at it, just as I'd done. I ran over to her and snatched her up into my arms.

"It ain't safe!" I was shouting, trying to make myself heard over the flames and sirens. And now I'd scared her, and she was crying too. I ran back to the car and bundled her inside. "You two need to stay put," I told them. I could see they were scared, but I had to make sure everyone else was okay. "Carl!" I barked when I got to the gates.

"Everyone accounted for, Degsy," he told me. That was something at least. I don't think I could have coped with another hospital visit.

"What about these gates? When did they get opened?"

"Just now, Degs. They've been closed all day, just like always."

"How did they get in, then?" I mumbled to myself, but then my eyes were drawn back to the site when some electricals exploded, and all I could do was watch as the fire raged, torching everything in its path. Then the fire brigade arrived and soaked all trace of my dream, putting out the flames, leaving a black mess that was less use than the abandoned school and hospital we'd torn down in the first place. All I could think about as I watched was what a mug I was. How could I have spent the night with Mya, having the time of my life, and cruised around London with Slope, chatting to old dears as if I didn't have a care in the world? How could I have dragged my brother and sister out at a time like this? How could I have thought carrying on like nothing was happening was a good idea? I knew, though, that I wouldn't make the same mistake again. If X wanted my full attention, he had it.

I told all the Hay Patrollers and other workers to go home, and then I knew I had to get Asha and Ray back to their place. They were still upset and had been in the car on their own for a while, but I promised to take them to McDonald's next time, and anywhere else they wanted, and they gave me a hug before I took them back into their house. Then there was only one place for me – back to the site. I'd called Mya to meet me there, and we just stood there, not talking, surrounded by a fizzing, black nothing. Mya took my hands and stroked my palm with her thumb. I thought I might cry, but I held back my tears. This wasn't the time for crying; it was the time for thinking, coming up with something that might save us all. I wished Winston was with us too, and Sheila. We were stronger together, but thoughts of them just made me more determined to steer our ship to safety.

"What we gonna do?" Mya asked.

"We?"

"Yes, we. We're in this together, Degs. I told you."

I turned and pulled her towards me. We started kissing, and then we just hugged, and it gave me strength. I wished it'd give me wisdom too because I was still clueless.

"You wanna go after them?" she asked.

"How can we? They're a serious outfit, Mya. And do you really wanna end up back inside again?"

"You'll end up back inside if you do that job."

"And we'll all end up dead if I don't."

"So you're gonna do it?"

I took a deep breath and regretted it. The smoke on the site stung my throat and took me back to the night of the first fire. "I don't know. I don't know how the hell they got in here to start the fire either. The security's tight – nar'mean? If you ain't got the code, you ain't coming in."

"What? You think it was one of our own?"

"Nah. Course not. I just don't know what to think or what to do."

We stood there holding hands, saying nothing. Then my phone rang and Phyllis's name flashed up on the screen again.

"Shit! It's Asha and Ray's foster mum," I told Mya. "They weren't in great shape when I took them home."

"Answer it."

I took another deep, smoky breath and pressed the green button. "Hi Phyllis," I said. "Before you say anything, I know—"

"That they're both in tears, Degsy? Is that what you know?"

"Phyllis, I—"

"No, Degsy, this is not alright. These kids need stability. They don't need to be traumatised by you; they got enough of that from their mother."

"Wait a minute! I didn't start the fire."

"No, but you left them alone and shouted at them. You scared Asha out of her mind. She hasn't stopped crying since she got in."

I didn't know what to say. I thought I was looking out for them. "I … I'm so sorry. I didn't have a clue."

"You only get one chance with these kids, Degsy. One chance. We told you that when we started to let you see them."

"No, please, Phyllis. I love them. They're my blood. They're all the blood I've got."

"I'm sorry, Degsy," she said, and then the line went dead.

As I slowly lowered the phone, staring down at the floor, I must have looked like shit because Mya said, "What was that? What happened? What did they say?"

"I can't see them no more," I told her. "I thought I was

looking out for them, but I was making it worse." I couldn't stop the tears now. I didn't think they'd ever stop, and Mya pulled me into her arms and held me. "It's probably the safest thing anyway. I'm no good to be around at the moment," I said.

"Don't say that."

"I mean it. As long as X's out there after us all, they're safer away from me."

She didn't answer that. She knew it was the truth. "You'll see them again, Degs, when this as all blown over."

"And when will that be?" I asked. I didn't mean to snap, but I could feel my anger building. "Tomorrow? Next week? Next year? D'ya think we'll make it that far, Mya? Do you really think X is ever gonna stop this?" I was pumped now. The adrenaline was Red Bull in my system, and I couldn't stand there with her any longer. I had to do something, and I had to do it now.

"Where you going?" she called after me as I ran back out through the gates, but I didn't answer. I didn't even look back. I was gonna sort this once and for all. I was going to St Francis's Church and heaven help X if he was in.

12 WITH THE CURTAINS DRAWN

I was lucky I didn't crash my little banger as I skidded away from Unit 16-21 and tore off down the street with all sorts flying through my mind. My knuckles turned white as I gripped the steering wheel, imagining my fingers closing around X's throat and squeezing until the life was drained out of the bastard. Every time I slammed a foot on the pedal, it was pounding down onto his face, stamping the smile off it. I'd show him he couldn't just march into our lives and take it over. We wouldn't go down without a fight. We were the Hay Patrollers and we weren't gonna let a snake like X stand in the way of the work we were doing. "He'll have to kill me first!" I heard myself shouting. I was shouting other things too, getting seriously pumped, and by the time I skidded onto the grass outside St Francis's Church, I hardly knew what I was doing. I jumped out of the car, slammed the door behind me and stomped up to the steel door. It was still early evening, but this wasn't a busy road, and there was no one else around. I wouldn't have cared if there had been; I wouldn't have even noticed.

"X! Get out here!" I was shouting, pounding my fists on the door. I didn't care that it was reinforced steel. "X! You bastard!"

There was no sound or movement from inside, but that didn't mean anything. I gave the door a last kick and ran around the side. I already knew there was no other way in, but I wasn't leaving until I'd grabbed a handful of X's hair and pulled the scalp off his skull. I hadn't felt like this for years, and I know it wasn't my finest moment, but something takes over when the people you love are in danger. I'd spent so many years of my life with nothing and no one; I couldn't lay down and let him take away everything I'd built up without a fight.

"X!" I was shouting, but there was still no answer, so I started kicking at the broken-down stone wall just outside the church door, driving my boot into it until it was boulders on the grass. The one I picked up was so heavy I couldn't stand up straight with it. I powered it into the main door and it thudded down to the ground. I'd dented it a bit, but I knew I couldn't get in like that. I picked it up again and managed to get it on my shoulder. Then I hurled it at the camera embedded in the wall. Then I picked up smaller stones and threw them up at the bits of window that hadn't been boarded up. The smash didn't get me anywhere, but it was satisfying to hear. I thought about getting back in my car and driving it into the bleeding wall, but I was sane enough to know I'd come off worse in that one. My phone had been ringing in my pocket since I left Unit 16-21, but I was in no mood to answer it. I just wanted to smash and shout and break X's face, but as my energy faded out and I slumped down onto what was left of the stone wall, I took it out and looked at it. Nineteen missed calls from Mya and a bunch of messages telling me not to do anything stupid. Then it rang again. It was Mya, and I answered it this time.

"Look, I'm sorry," I said. "I ain't done nothing daft. No one's in. Just don't give me a hard time, alright."

I'd expected her to go on at me, but there was a pause before she said, "Have you seen the news, Degs?"

I almost laughed. I'd left her half an hour ago and gone straight to the church with adrenalin burning a hole in me. Course I hadn't seen the bloody news.

"St Mark's. That's your brother and sister's school, yeah?"

I stood up. "Yeah."

"It's on fire, Degsy. It's all over the news. Started a few minutes ago."

"I'll get over there," I said.

"No. Stay away, Degsy. Your face doesn't need to be caught

up in this. The kids are safe. You've seen them. School finished hours ago."

"Damn!" I shouted. "Look, I've got another call coming through," I said and switched caller. I wasn't surprised to hear X's smug voice on the line again.

"We could play this game all night," he said, and I could hear he was smiling, enjoying himself. "I set fire to your stupid project, you huff and puff and kick my church. I set fire to your brother and sister's school, you cry about it. I go over and see what Ivan and Nosit look like when they're thrown on a bonfire, you wish you'd just agreed to do the job in the first place and saved everyone a lot of pain. Do you see where this is going, bruv?"

"Alright!" I said. "I'll do it." I slumped down onto the broken wall again, all my energy gone.

"What was that, Degsy?"

"You heard me. I said I'll do it. I'll do the job and then we're quits. You stay the fuck out of our lives. We're done."

"And you won't forget? I don't need to send you any more reminders closer the time, just to let you know you're in my thoughts."

"Do me a favour! I'm in, alright. Then we're done."

This was Friday. The job was the following Thursday. Six days, and then, one way or another, this would all be done. When I told Mya about it, she agreed; there was nothing else to be done. We were out of choices; this was the lesser evil, and if I managed to pull it off, we might all walk away from it. I ain't sure if we believed that, but now the decision had been made, the pressure was off a bit. I was still as mad as hell, but I had to accept there wasn't a thing I could do to change things. Me and Mya even spent most of the weekend going through a few tactics, about how I could do the job as safely as possible, without hurting the guard and make off without being seen. Then, to take my mind off things, I started planning this event I'd thought of when I was out with Slope. It'd grown in my mind and was gonna be a fundraiser too. I'd spoken to the gaffer on the site of Unit 16-21 and we were lucky that work was at such an early stage. We'd lost everything we'd done so far and some supplies and equipment, but it was gonna be possible to restart if we raised a bit of extra cash. I started phoning around too, getting some backers, and by Tuesday the pot was starting to look respectable again. I even spoke to Mrs M in Oz; she was doing a lot better, staying off the pokies, and she agreed to send some of the grant money she'd squeezed from the government our way. The fundraising was an important thought; it'd build awareness, bring the community together, celebrate our work and show that we can overcome anything. We were holding it on the Sunday after the robbery, and I was determined it'd go ahead with us all safe and present. The only person who wouldn't be there was X. After Thursday, we'd never have to see his mug again. Maybe even Winston would've stopped messing about and come out of his coma by then to put in an appearance. Or maybe I was living in a dream world. But life's taught me to plan like that, as if anything's possible, and I'm always gonna be the one coming up smelling like daisies. What's the point otherwise? So, we were moving forward, the days were passing. The robbery and fundraiser were marked on the calendar with two massive Xs, and we were hoping for a nice, quiet week, but, as it turned out, there ain't no such thing.

Tuesday had been a long day. There'd been a few issues with our Hay Patrollers at the Grove. The shopping centre manager was accusing one of them of spraying graffiti, so I had to go down there and smooth things over. Of course, it wasn't one of our guys, and we found the culprit. I was gutted, though. I thought the manager thought more of us and the work we were doing. Just goes to show that some people will always be suspicious of young people, even when they're working hard and doing a good job. I was ranting and raving on the way home, and Mya was letting me get on with it. She knew me well enough to know I sometimes just needed to blow off steam and then everything would settle down. When I was happy I'd said my piece, I really did feel a bit better. Then Mya started talking.

"I think we should talk to Sheila tonight."

I didn't answer straight away. I'd been putting it off, to be honest. Not because I didn't care or because I didn't wanna help, but because I was hoping she'd snap out of it on her own. I'd known her a long time, and I knew how strong she could be. I knew this wasn't her. And we'd all heard her story. She went through so much for so long when she was a kid, and she found the strength to run away. She was working the streets and her best friend was murdered, but she didn't give up. She kept going and found her way out of it by helping others. She was bloody inspirational. I was just waiting for her to turn up at the office in a new outfit with a smile, excited about a new idea she'd come up with, ready to get going, like she always was, but it wasn't happening. She hadn't shown for work since the day after her attack, and I wasn't sure if she'd even left the house.

"I'll do it," I told Mya. And that was all we said on the subject. I suppose we both knew it was serious, and we couldn't leave it any longer. She was our friend, and she needed help.

When we got in, Mya took our bags of Chinese through to the kitchen, and I popped my head in the living room. It was empty and the curtains were still drawn from the night before. If Sheila was here, it meant she hadn't been out of her room all day. My tummy flipped a bit when I set foot on the stairs, and I was in no hurry to get to the top. The house was still so unfamiliar. We all liked it, but we were only there because our home had been torched, and we could never forget we were there without Winston. And nothing good had happened since we moved in. There'd been more fires, Sheila had been beaten up, and it was starting to look like she was disappearing down the plughole. As I slowly walked up the stairs, I only hoped I could pull her out of it.

I was still in no hurry as I crossed the landing. In fact, I was walking slowly. I wasn't sure why I didn't just march over there, but my legs wouldn't move any faster, and my stomach was still turning somersaults. It was a full circus in my gut by the time I reached her door, and then I just stopped and stood there. I didn't knock straight away. I leaned in close to hear if she had the TV on or some music. I could hear Jeremy Kyle's voice, which was a good sign. If she was watching TV (even crappy Jeremy Kyle), it meant she wasn't just sitting there staring at a wall. I slowly raised my arm to knock and it stopped in mid-air. I suppose I didn't really know what I was gonna say to her or what she was gonna say to me. I'd lost so many people in my life; I didn't want her to tell me she was leaving London or anything silly like that. I just wanted things to go back the way they were. Then, I have no idea why I did this, but instead of knocking on the door, I just opened it and burst in. It was like I was possessed, like all the stomach-flipping and dragging my feet had built me up to this moment, as if there was something going on in the back of my mind that I didn't have a clue about. But as soon as I did it, I knew why I had. I wasn't scared of anything Sheila might say or if she wanted to leave London; I was scared of what I'd find behind the door, and I'd been right to be.

"It's okay, Sheila," I whispered as I crept into the room. Her room usually smelt of makeup and perfume, but now it smelt as if the window had never been opened before. The curtains were drawn, but the TV blaring away in the corner lit the room just enough for me to see her. I turned the sound down and edged towards her. "It's just me, Degsy. You're okay. Just stay where you are. Everything's gonna be okay." I made my voice as soft and gentle as possible, but my brain was screaming. "Ahhhhh! What the fuck!" She was sitting on the floor, cross-legged, leaning up against the bed, wearing a dressing gown, open, showing her nighty and bare legs. One hand was resting on a thigh, the other was clutching a razor blade, hovering above her other thigh, which was a mess of bloody slashes. She looked up at me as I came in, but her face was blank. I could see she'd been crying, but all the tears had gone and left this ghost behind. "It's okay," I told her again, and I lowered myself down onto the floor beside her, careful not to make any sudden movements, and took the blade from between her thumb and finger. It was at that point she started to cry again, her whole body collapsing and crumbling into tears. I pulled her to me and held her tight. I'd never felt anything like the force of her emotion before, and all I could do was sit there and hold her. As she sobbed, I couldn't help looking at her leg. The cuts were deep and bloody. I didn't know much first aid, but it looked as if they needed stitches. And there were other cuts on her legs in different stages of healing. I nearly cried just looking at them. How hadn't I noticed this?

"It's alright," I told her. "I'm gonna get some help for you, okay?"

"No!" she snapped and sat up suddenly then pulled her dressing gown over the legs. "It's nothing. I just need to get some sleep."

"You need a hospital, Sheila. They look nasty."

"No!" This time she said it so I understood, but that didn't mean I couldn't do something to help her myself. I got up, ran to the bathroom and grabbed anything I could find that might help. When I came back in, she was sobbing again, her arms hanging limp beside her like dead weights, defeated.

"Let me see," I said, and when she didn't put up a fight, I pulled her dressing gown open and sat on the carpet beside her. As gently as I could, I put a wet flannel over the cut. Although they were bloody, they'd stopped bleeding, which was something I suppose. When I wiped them over and looked again, I could see just how deep they were. She wasn't messing around. I pressed the flannel down again and sat back against the bed. I'd bought in steri-strips, plasters, anti-bacterial cream, but there was time enough to patch her up. I don't think either of us had the energy, and we both just sat there, watching Jeremey Kyle silently shout down some poor mug who'd gone on TV to air his dirty laundry. We couldn't take our eyes off it, but I don't think either of us were taking it in. Then I finally said, "Does it help?" It probably wasn't the right thing to say, but I had no idea what was.

She turned and looked at me, tears still heavy in her eyes. I don't think it was the question she expected me to ask, and I was surprised she even answered. "It does," she said, and looked away again.

"Doesn't it hurt?"

She laughed at that. I hadn't meant to say anything funny, but I was pleased she was still able to. "That's the point, Degsy."

"Are you punishing yourself?"

She let out a sigh and narrowed her eyes, staring straight back to Jeremy, as if deciding how to answer that, then said, "No … It just … I don't know. When this hurts, nothing else does."

"Like when you've got a headache and then you stub your toe?"

She laughed again – sad, little laughter. "Something like that."

"How long?"

"As long as I can remember," she said then added, "On and off. More on lately."

"Why? We're here for you, Sheila. You can talk to us. We can take on the world together. You know that."

She sighed deeply again. "Some things can't be fixed, Degsy."

"Like what?"

"Can you change the past?"

"No one can change the past, but I can help you deal with

it."

"With what? Counselling? I've got counselling coming out of my ears, Degsy. It doesn't change anything."

"Okay, what do you wanna change?"

Now she looked at me as if I was thick, but I didn't let it put me off. "I'm serious. And I'm talking practically. What do you wanna change, Sheila? I'm your fairy godmother. What can we do to make things better?"

"The world doesn't work like that, Degs. You can't just wave a magic wand and make things better. I know it's your approach to life. You run in, see a problem, change it, but you know what happened to me. You can't make it not have happened."

"Alright, I can't change the past, but we've gotta try and make things better for you – nar'mean? Let me ask you something; did you ever report those blokes at the church?" I half-wished I hadn't asked because she crumbled into tears again, but I had to.

"That's half of it, Degs. I know they're still out there. They could be doing it to some other kid. They probably have, and it's my fault for not speaking up. God knows how many kids have gone through what I went through because I've been too weak to speak to the police."

"Let's do that, then," I said.

Again, she went from crying to laughing in a matter of seconds. Again, I hadn't meant to say anything funny.

"Life's just black and white to you, isn't it, Degsy?"

I nodded and smiled. I don't know if she meant it as a compliment, but this wasn't about me. "You're not on your own anymore, you know," I said. "I'll go with you. Hold your hand. We can do it together. It won't be easy, but you're right. It is the way I do things, and it works. Not all the time, but it works. If you're drowning, it ain't the time to give your arms a rest. Going to the police ain't gonna change what happened to you, but you're right: it might save some other little kids.

You ain't to blame for what those pricks have done to anyone else, but getting them off the street has gotta be a good thing. It might even make you feel a bit better. It has to be better than cutting yourself up."

"And how can I feel better about Michael?" she said, fresh tears crawling down her cheeks. "He was sixteen, Degsy. He was so full of life and energy. I've never met anyone like him before. They've caught his murderer, and that didn't make me feel any better. How can I ever feel better about seeing him …" She couldn't say the words. "He looked after me when no one else would, when I didn't have a friend in the world. He kept me safe and looked out for me like a brother, and then he was gone. Just like that. How can I feel better about that? I didn't even get to say goodbye to him, to tell him how much he meant to me, how he had changed my world and been the first person ever to show me kindness. I miss him so much, Degsy."

I held her again as she sobbed. I'd never seen her like this before. As she cried now, Mya appeared in the doorway and I nodded for her to leave. I'd take care of things here. But Sheila was right, and I knew it deep down. There was nothing to take away the pain she felt, and I wondered why I was surprised she was cutting herself. I shouldn't have talked her into sharing her story in schools and prisons. It'd been a sort of healing experience for me and Mya, and Winston said he found it empowering to use what he'd been through to help others. We should've seen that the opposite was happening to Sheila.

As it turned out, though, just talking to me was a bit of a turning point, I think. She was pale, quiet, broken and cut, but she came downstairs and had Chinese with us that night for the first night in a long time. She didn't say much at all, but I could see she trusted us not to make her feel worse about what she'd done, and she wanted to be around us, which was a huge step in the right direction. Don't get me wrong; I knew we hadn't fixed anything, but things were out in the open. We knew what was going on, we knew she was gonna need a lot of support, and me and Mya were gonna give it to her.

The next morning, she was up before both of us and she'd made breakfast. She still looked terrible, but I thought it best to keep that to myself, especially since she was managing to smile.

"You didn't have to do this," I said, but I wasn't gonna turn away a full English. It smelt amazing, better than that from Turkish Beryl's cafe and I sat myself down at the table while she finished off frying the bacon. Mya was still in the shower.

"I wanted to thank you, Degsy, and apologise. I didn't want you to see me like that."

"Seriously, you've got nothing to thank me or apologise for. You're one of my favourite people, Sheila. And I hope you know I love you."

I was doing my best to make her feel loved, and what did I get for my trouble? A clout round the head with a newspaper. When I looked up, I could see she was touched by my words; she just wanted to put it all behind us, and a clonk on the head with a newspaper always lightened the mood.

"Page twelve," she said, and then I realised there was more to her bashing me around the head than common assault.

I opened the paper. *The Great Firebug of London* was the headline, and there were pictures of loads of fires that'd been set in the last few weeks, including Unit 16-21 and our gaff. They were linking them all together, but they had no leads. It couldn't have been too interesting, though, or it would've been on the front page.

"You could go to the police, Degsy."

"We've been through this," I said as she set a plate down in front of me. It smelt like heaven. "This lot's too big. Take out X and someone else would fill his shoes. Anyway, I don't wanna think of any of that right now. How you doing?"

"I'm okay," she said and took the seat opposite. She was

eating cereal and a banana. It was sweet that she'd cooked just for Mya and me.

"And the leg?"

Her face reddened, but she managed to say, "I've done worse, Degsy. It will heal."

"So what you gonna do then?"

"I've already done it."

"Eh?"

"I've already done it, Degsy. I called a helpline in the middle of the night. They said they can help me speak to the police and support me through the process. They said historical abuse like this is taken more seriously than ever before these days, and there's a good chance of prosecution. You're right, I can't be a victim anymore. I have to stand up and make things right." Her voice was soft and gentle, as it always was, but there was more power in it than I'd heard for ages. Maybe this was a new beginning, but it wouldn't be an easy path. That much, I knew.

"He'd be proud of you," I said.

"Who?"

"Michael," I answered, but as soon as I said it, I wished I hadn't because her face changed, but she managed to hold back the tears. She wasn't gonna hang around, though, and pushed her half-finished cereal away from her.

"I need to get ready," she said and managed a weak smile before getting up to leave.

"Do you want me to come with you?" I asked, and she shook her head. "Thanks again for the breakfast," I called after her, but she was in a hurry now, and I didn't get an answer. I couldn't get it right all the time, I suppose.

A few minutes later, I was joined by Mya in her Sponge Bob PJ bottoms and vest with a towel wound up and balancing on her head.

"I made you breakfast," I said.

"Nice try. I passed Sheila in the hallway."

She sat down and tucked in just as I was finishing mine, so I just sat back and watched her eat. She didn't notice at first. Then she clocked me.

"Any reason you're eyeballing me having my breakfast?" she asked.

"Can't a man watch his beautiful girlfriend go to work on her bacon and egg?"

"Pervert!" she giggled, but I was kinda serious. Since we'd got together, I could happily watch her do just about anything. It was all full of new revelations: the way her body or face moved, the way she shifted her hands, her breathing; I loved it all.

"Look, I've been thinking," she said.

"I thought I heard noises this morning."

"Very funny. It's about your boy Slope."

"What about him?"

"Well, don't you find it a bit strange, Degsy? He didn't wanna have anything to do with you or the project one minute, and then he has this sudden change of heart. Next thing we know, things are going down that we can't explain. A fire starts at Unit 16-21 when security's tighter than a nun's watsit. And this X geez knows exactly what school Asha and Ray go to. They know all about Nosit and Ivan."

"Hang on! Loads of people know about my brother and sister. And I ain't exactly made a secret of going over to see Nosit and Ivan."

"And the codes on the gates at Unit 16-21?"

"Loads of people know the code too. Hang about! What you got against Slope?"

"Me? Why would I have anything against the kid? The timings don't lie, though, Degsy."

"He's a good kid, Mya. He wouldn't pull something like this. He's starting to trust me. I can see it in him."

We could both see this was escalating, and Mya was the one to stop, take a deep breath and steer us away from our first argument. "I know you like him, Degsy," she started up again, lowering her voice. "I know you see yourself in him, but I'm just trying to make sure your eyes are open. If you think he's on the level, then I trust your judgement, but I need you to think about it."

"He ain't a mole, Mya," I said. I was calmer now too, but I needed her to know how I felt. "But you're right. Something doesn't add up. X has to be getting his info from somewhere."

"Well, I'll leave you with that thought," she said and walked round to kiss me on the head. It bothered me that it wasn't on the lips. Maybe I'd pissed her off by not believing her about Slope. It was bullshit, though. She didn't even know him. He wouldn't do something like that.

I grabbed my laptop off the side and set it up on the table in front of me. I'd wash up in a bit, and do the hundred and one other things I needed to get sorted before leaving for work, but I allowed myself a few minutes first of social media. I was new to Facebook and Twitter and slowly getting the hang of it, but I couldn't see how people spent 24/7 staring down into their screens. I lasted ten minutes before I got bored. Then I went to Google Images and typed *South Sudan Mountains*. Mya had set me off thinking about Slope and how he missed the mountains. The only mountains I'd ever seen were in movies, and I suppose I envied Slope his past. It was stupid because his life had been shit, but being out in the mountains sounded like the most exciting thing a kid could ever do, and the pictures that came up left me breathless. I pictured myself trekking up them, hiking down. I could almost feel the fresh air in my lungs. Then I read a bit.

The highest mountain in Sudan is Mt Kinyeti

Shit! I nearly jumped out of my seat. I'd ballsed up the name when I'd been searching cafes before. It wasn't Kinseti; it was Kinyeti! I opened a new window and typed *Café Kinyeti*. My heart was pounding now. This was it. I was closing in on him. I could feel it. But within seconds, my hopes were shite. Nothing. Café Kinyeti didn't exist, but then I got excited again. I don't know why I didn't see it sooner; the answer to it all was the mountains. Mountain slopes, Mount Everest, Kinyeti – Slope had told me himself how precious the mountains had been to him. I started to research other South Sudanese mountains and look for cafes named after them – little cafés by the coast, just like the geezer in Australia had told us. I found two. Iro Patisserie on the French Riviera and a little place that was just called IRO in Brighton, both named after Iro Mountain in Imatong, South Sudan. There was nothing in Africa or Australia, but we already knew the geezer got around.

I got on the blower and dialled up France first. I spoke no French whatsoever, so I only hoped whoever answered spoke English.

"Bonjour!"

This wasn't a good start.

"Bonjour!" I said, murdering it with my cockney accent.

"Parlay Englishland … erm … Do you the English … Erm?"

There was a giggle on the line and a young woman said, "What can I do for you?" in a thick French accent.

"Blinding! Look, I just wondered who owned your gaff, love? Can you tell me?"

"What is this 'gaff'?"

"Sorry, your café. Who owns it?"

She thought for a moment then said, "My mother and father, Monsieur Frank Dubois and Madam Isa Dubois."

"Oh."

"Is everything okay, sir?"

"Err, yeah. Thanks for your time," I told her and hung up. I didn't mean to be rude, but I still had that other place to call, knowing I was fresh out of ideas if this led me nowhere.

When I dialled the number, IRO in Brighton took a little longer to answer, but when they did, I nearly burst with excitement.

"IRO. How can we help?"

I knew that accent. Slope had tried to lose it, talking Cockney to fit in, but he couldn't get rid of it completely.

"Alright, geez," I said. "I'm looking for Malik Wardi. That wouldn't be you, would it, bruv?"

I didn't even get to the end of the sentence before he hung up.

This was it. I had him.

13 I FORGIVE YOU

I called that little café again and wasn't surprised when no one answered. I waited, listening to the ringing, and then that posh woman from O2 was giving it all, "Sorry, the caller is unavailable. Please leave your message after the tone."

"This is Degsy Hay," I said. "I'm a youth liaison working in London. I ain't working for police or immigration, bruv. I'm calling about Slope, Sadiq Wardi. That's your brother, right? We've been working with him, and if anyone needs a brother, it's this kid. Call me back," I added and hung up, feeling like Sherlock Holmes or something. I couldn't believe I'd tracked the geezer down, all the way from Australia. Who knew he'd end up back in the UK? And Brighton of all places, just an hour down the road. I was busy patting myself on the back and not more than a minute later, my phone rang.

"He's alive?" a tearful voice shouted in my ear. It was him, Malik.

"He's alive," I told him. "He's got a mouth on him like a docker and doesn't know how to stay out of trouble, but he's alive."

There was silence and then the muffled sound of crying in the distance. I pictured him with his hand over the receiver in his little dream café on the coast, sobbing over family he never knew he had. I knew how he felt.

"Is he with you?" he managed to say.

"Nah, he doesn't know I've been looking for you. I didn't wanna disappoint him. You're a hard man to find."

"I like it that way. How did you find me?"

"Well, let's just say it was a proper game of global cat and mouse, and I'm glad it's over. How soon can you get here?"

"I am leaving now. I will be there in one hour."

"Bloody hell, mate. Don't kill yourself on the motorway.

The little geezer ain't going nowhere. I'll get him in the office," I said and told him the address. And that was that. Malik was coming to get his brother, and I couldn't wait to see the look on Slope's face. I was fit to burst as I found his number in my phone and called him up. It rang for ages, and I thought he wasn't gonna pickup, and then, finally, there was movement.

"Hmmmm?" he grunted as he answered.

"Did I wake you up, Slope?"

By the grunting and groaning that followed, I guessed I did.

"Look, get yourself down to our offices. I got something to show you, bruv."

"Huh! S'early."

"You're gonna wanna see this, geez, I swear."

More groaning and stretching.

"One hour. Be there," I said and hung up.

I had a few things to sort before I got to the office. I stopped by the community centre to make sure Katya, Ibrahim and the others would have that mural finished by Sunday and to finalise a few other details for the fundraiser. The mural looked great. Katya had designed it, and it was a bit off the wall, but it showed people of all different shapes, sizes, colours and abilities all walking and wheeling together. It was so bright and colourful that I was looking forward to unveiling it. Ibrahim was still messing about the place, making life difficult, but Katya had it in hand. I'd planned to go straight to the office after that, but then I got a strange call. It was a withheld number, and I didn't know who it was at first. It sounded like someone was messing about.

"Who's this?"

It was like someone was heavy breathing down the handset, and I was about to start shouting, tell them where to go, but then I heard a little voice.

"Degsy?"

"Who's this?" I repeated, more gently this time. Whoever

it was, they sounded old.

"It's me, Degsy, Mrs Bukhari."

I sat up straight. Why would X's nan be calling me? But then I remembered I'd told her to call me if there was an emergency. "You alright, Mrs B? You sound terrible."

"I didn't know where else to turn, Degsy. I've tried the police."

"What is it?"

She hesitated again and stumbled on her words. Sounded like she was in a terrible state. Then she managed to say,

"It's the kids outside. They've put my window through again. They've spray-painted the house. I need to go out, Degsy, get some shopping, but they're there. They pushed me over last year, and I broke my bloody hip. I can't go through that again," she sobbed.

"Alright, look, just stay where you are and I'll be right there," I told her and hung up. I had about forty minutes left, and it was close enough to get over there, take care of business, then get back over to the office. On the way, I called Three Pies and Han and asked if they wouldn't mind going over. They'd been popping in on her, and I couldn't hang around, although I needed to know the old dear was alright.

I parked up outside her flats, knowing my car was too much of a banger for the thieves to bother with. If it was anything worth having, I might have stashed it a few streets out the way, but I was in such a hurry to make sure Mrs B was okay, I almost ran off with the window open and the door unlocked. As I ran towards her block, I couldn't believe what I was seeing. There were three of them, all old enough to know better, maybe even older than I was, hanging around on the wall close to her door as if they had nowhere better to be, blasting music, off their heads on cheap cider and glue. If they'd washed or changed their clothes in the last year, I'd be surprised. Poor old Mrs B's window was smashed in and, as she said, they'd sprayed some kind of symbol that didn't make any sense on her flat. Maybe they were just trying out the can, because it looked like a dirty splodge to me.

"Oi!" I shouted, running up, and was soon in their face, seriously pissed off. My mug wasn't a pretty sight when I was this pissed off, but they were so off their nuts that they didn't even flinch. I'd make them pay attention, though. I knocked the two-litre bottle of toxic cider out of this ugly-looking geezer's hand and it went off like a rocket, spraying the whole balcony and flying around until it was empty.

"What the fuck?" he slurred. This dude didn't look like he had the energy to be angry, but his mate was straight off that wall, fronting up to me as if he thought he was the shit. He wasn't quite as tall as me, but that didn't stop him, and then the third guy got in on the act too, backing him up, edging towards me.

"What the fuck?" I asked. "I should be asking you that. D'ya get off on scaring old ladies, do ya?"

The guy at the front shrugged and said, "Look, mate, I don't know who you are, but I'm gonna give you three seconds to get out of here then I'm gonna make you pay for knocking over my friend here's cider. You get me?"

He thought he was all that until I stepped closer to him, so close that I could smell his filthy breath, and said, "I'll give you three seconds to fuck off out of here or you'll be paying for it for the rest of your life."

He hadn't expected that. He looked round to his mate, who shrugged and worked on opening another piss-coloured bottle of rocket fuel.

"Hang on!" the third guy said, looking nervous. "You ain't Degsy Hay, are ya?"

"I don't give a shit who he is," Ugly spat. "I'm gonna give him—"

"You ain't giving me nothing." I laughed, and just as his mate managed to open the next bottle of cider, I kicked that out of his hands too. I knew it was all gonna kick off, but these idiots were small fry. I'd see off ten geezers like this before breakfast when I was inside, and I ain't gone soft.

The second bottle sprayed the walls and flew around even more spectacularly, and this mouthy guy wasn't having it anymore. He lunged forward, but I caught hold of his wrist, flipped him forward and held his hand behind his back. I pushed his head so close to the ground that he'd be able to smell the dog shit in the cracks in the pavement. I know I was showing off, but as I held him there with one hand and while he was screaming, begging me to let go of him, telling me I was breaking his arm, I laid down the law to his mates. I had their attention now.

"I'll tell you what's gonna happen here. The three of you are gonna pack up your shit show and take it on the road. You get me? If I see your faces around my nan's house again, I'll have ya."

"She's your nan?" one of them dared to ask. "But she's a paki!"

I twisted the ugly dude's hand, using two hands now, making him pay for what his friend had said. His scream tore through us all, but I didn't think I'd broken his arm.

"She's a what?" I shouted as I twisted, and this geezer's wingman threw his hands up in the air and said, "Nothing. She's nothing. We got it wrong. You won't see us here again, mate. I swear it."

I gave that arm a last twist then threw the ringleader down on the ground. No damage done, but when he looked back at me there was terror in his eyes. The three of them were just looking at me after that, like dogs waiting for a command, and I shouted, "Get lost!" so loud that they almost fell over each other to get away from me.

Then I ran over to Mrs B's door and knocked.

"Mrs B? It's me, Degsy. You alright in there, love?"

She opened the door before I finished, and her face was flushed and smiling. "You were great, Degsy!" she was beaming, and then the old girl started throwing punches in the air, showing me her fight. "I knew you'd see 'em off!" she laughed.

"Bastards!"

I laughed too. I loved how much fight she had in her, and I hated the idea that scumbags like those three could make her a prisoner in her own home. It took me back to Gladys from when I was a kid, and how the local boys did all sorts to her until I stepped in. I just didn't get it; just because you're stronger than someone, you ain't gotta show it every five minutes. Just makes these idiots look like they ain't got nothing in their lives except pushing other people around. When it comes to a real fight, with someone like me, they run a mile. I wondered if X was like that deep down. I didn't think so. The Notorious was a big outfit, and it took balls to rise to the top of a crew like that. He hadn't got there by swigging cider outside little old ladies' houses. And if he was anything like his old nan, then he was a fighter. She really made me smile, standing there, growling, swinging her fists.

"Teach me that move you did, Degsy," she was saying.

"Next time, Mrs B," I told her.

"You ain't coming in then?"

"I can't, but …" I looked down the street and saw Three Pie's car roll up. He pulled over, and he and Han came strolling out. They were both big boys, but they were two of the gentlest lads I'd ever met. I could see them becoming carers or nurses – even doctors – and Hay Assist was great experience for them. "I'll leave you in the care of these two," I told her, and I was about to make off, but she stopped me.

"Hang about, Degsy," she said, and dodged back inside. She was rooting around in her handbag, and when she came back to the door, she had a 50p piece in her hand. "Buy yourself some sweets, son," she said.

"I can't take your money, Mrs B."

"Go on. Take it. I used to give my 50ps to Aziz, but he ain't nowhere to be seen. Go on, take it."

What could I do? I pocketed the money and thanked her. I'd put it in our charity pot later. "You're a diamond, Mrs B," I was telling her as I moved away from the door. "We'll be seeing you on Sunday at the fundraiser, won't we?"

"Looking forward to it, Degsy."

I was really in a hurry now, but as I passed Three Pies and Han, I made the time to tell them what had happened and asked them to stay in touch. Anything they needed to help fix the window, get rid of the graffiti or keep Mrs B safe, they had it. I thought of asking Three Pies why he was called Three Pies, but I was in too much of a hurry and ran down to my car then drove off. With minutes to spare, I made it to the office. As it turned out, Slope got there first, which would've been a good thing if he hadn't run into Mya. They were in the snug together, and I heard raised voices before I even got there.

"He might not be able to see through you, but I know your game, Slope!"

"What? I ain't done nothing!"

Shit! I dumped my bag on my desk and legged it over there. Just as I burst through the door, Mya was saying, "Don't give me that shit! I know you're working for X, and I'm gonna prove it!" She was terrifying when she was angry, and poor old Slope had backed right away from her. Any further away and he'd fall out the window.

"What the hell's going on in here?" I said. I couldn't believe what I was seeing.

"Good, you're here," Mya said. I'd never seen her looking this mad. "I caught him snooping around in here." She pushed her hands on her hips and her flushed face towards him, accusing him of all sorts. "Go on, ask him."

"I told him to meet me here," I snapped and moved to stand beside Slope. The poor little geezer needed backup.

"Oh," Mya said, and her face fell, but she was soon on it again. "That don't mean he ain't spying, Degsy. Why can't you see it?"

"Because there ain't nothing to see."

"If you're blind there ain't."

"Slope's in our care," I snapped at her, surprised at how angry I sounded, but she was really starting to wound me up now. I loved her and all, of course I did, but she had no right to do this. "This is unprofessional—"

"Unprofessional?" she interrupted, fuming every bit as hard as I was, and took a step towards us. I thought she was gonna explode, but she didn't say anything. She looked down at Slope and then at me and then between the two of us again and rolled her eyes. "I ain't got time for this," she eventually said and charged out.

I was so wound up that all I could do was watch her go, and then I turned to Slope.

"Women, eh!" he said, folding his arms and rolling his eyes like a man of the world.

"Don't push it, little man," I said. "I find out you got anything to do with the shit that's gone down around here, then we're done, d'ya hear me? And I'll drag you down to the police station myself. Am I getting through?"

He was listening at first, I know he was, and then he looked like he was on another planet. Instead of looking at me, he was looking over my shoulder. At first his face was blank, and then his eyes and mouth got wide, his face flushed, and I wondered what the bloody hell had gotten into him ... until I turned around.

"Sadiq? Is that really you?"

A tall man was standing behind me in an apron decorated with mountains that he hadn't bothered to tear off before jumping in his car and driving to London. He was as big as me and looked the way I was sure Slope would after a growth spurt and a lot of maturing.

Slope tried to speak, but the words caught in his throat. He swallowed hard, not taking his eyes off his brother, and tried again. "*Lanceukna? Éta bener anjeun?*"

"Yes, it's me, Sadiq. You are alive, and—" he began to say, but Slope launched himself across the room, and Malik caught him and dragged him in close. I'd never seen such raw emotion in anyone's face as I saw in Malik's as he held his brother to his chest, fixing his hand on the back of the young boy's head, drawing him closer still, his eyes to the sky, tears and emotional Sudanese words flowing freely, his whole body heaving with sobs. And Slope stayed nestled there, in the arms of his brother, as if this was where he belonged. This was his home.

"I thought you were dead," Malik sobbed.

Then Slope found his voice and sighed, "I thought I'd never find you," just loud enough for his brother to hear.

I'd cry too if I stayed any longer, so I crept out of the room and left them to their reunion, which made all thoughts of Mya and spies disappear. I walked out of there on air, like anything was possible. Finding Malik was like tracking down a bleeding needle in a haystack, and I'd managed to pull it off. If I could do that, then anything was possible. It was a good omen. Everything was gonna be okay.

They stayed in the snug together for about an hour, chatting and hugging, making up for lost time and just silently enjoying being in the same room as each other. When they came out, Slope looked like a different boy, years younger and smiling like I'd never seen before. He couldn't totally let go of his hard man act, though; he put that wasp right back in his mouth when he saw me and started chewing.

"This is my brother, innit," he said, pushing his hands deep into his pockets. "Malik."

"Yeah, I know," I told him.

Then Malik said, "I do not know what I can do to repay you, Degsy. I thought I was the only one left alive, and you have delivered my brother safely back to me. Anything you need, just name it."

Me being me, I took him at his word. "Well, there is something. We're having a bit of a shindig on Sunday. You couldn't put together a few sandwiches or something, could you? Maybe a cake we could raffle?"

This made him laugh. "I like you, Degsy. Of course I can."

"I'm moving to Brighton," Slope added, and it almost looked as if he was smiling. It wasn't up on his face for all to see, but I knew it was there.

"Is that so?"

He gave a solid, single nod and a shrug. Perhaps his brother could give him some lessons in communication when he got him down south.

"That's great, geez," I said. "Happy for you."

Then he surprised me by sticking his hand out for me to shake. He kept his eyes fixed on me the whole time, and when I took it and shook it, although no words passed between the two of us, I knew he was thanking me, in his own special, Slopey way.

I spent the rest of the day organising the fundraiser and trying to smooth things over with Mya. Don't get me wrong; she was one hundred percent in the wrong, but I shouldn't have gone off the way I did, and I know she was only looking out for me. And it was like I was walking a path that could crumble under me at any minute – nar'mean? I just wanted things to be good between us. Life was too short. Just ask Winston. So I tracked her down and gave her my word I'd taken it all on board. I still didn't think it was Slope, but maybe spies weren't just for the flicks. If X wanted to get near me, then a spy was a pretty good way of doing it. So I told her I'd watch my back, sent her a dozen red rose emojis, and then I told her about Malik, which helped a bit, mostly because it meant Slope would be off the scene. If he wasn't around, at least we wouldn't be arguing about him.

Tensions were still high that night, though. Not just because of Slope and the fact that I'd be committing a robbery the next day, but because we were going over to Mya's mum's place for dinner, and it was hard to play nice when we'd been arguing. Mya had invited us over to dinner herself, and her mum didn't know much about it, but her support workers said it was a good idea. She still had no idea who we were, but she was always welcoming, and we could be a family for her. Although it looked like she was in her own little world, they said making happy times like this helped her and could even keep her well.

We turned up at her little flat at five. A couple of the Hay Assist volunteers had been over to clean that afternoon, so it was looking neat and tidy. We'd taken a Chinese over, so no one had to cook. Mya knew her mum loved her Chinese from when she was a kid. They couldn't afford takeaways often, and Mrs Garcia smiled now, sitting up the table with me, as Mya served it up, as if she really did remember it was a treat.

We ate with the TV on because Mrs G was calmest when there was someone babbling in the background about antiques or cookery. Just before Mya sat down, I watched how delicately and lovingly she placed her hand on her mother's back and kissed her thin, white hair. I don't know if she noticed, but her mum closed her eyes as she did it, soaking up the attention her daughter was giving her. I loved Mya more in that moment than I ever had before.

"I'm sorry," I told her, while Mrs G stared at the TV. "I know you're looking out for me with Slope. I love you for it."

She reached out and took my hand, brushing her thumb over my fingers, then brought them to her lips, kissed them and said, "I love you too."

"You heard that, Mrs G," I joked. "You're a witness. She loves me, and she can't ever take it back."

I expected Mrs G to ignore me, as she always had, but she surprised us both by turning to look at Mya. There was something in her face I'd never seen before. It's hard to explain. It was like she was normally just a body or a house with the lights off and no one in, but someone had flicked a switch. She was younger. She was there.

"I love her, too," she said, turning to me. Even her voice was different.

Mya was swept away with emotion. Her hand leapt up and covered her mouth. Her eyes closed and tears leaked from the slits. I took her other hand and squeezed it.

"I always have. Will you tell her that, Degsy?" her mother said, talking to me as if Mya wasn't there. "All that stuff; it's in the past. Does she know that, Degsy? I'm her mum. I'm here for her. And I'm sorry." She stopped and looked over at the TV, and then her eyes found me again. "Tell her I forgive her, Degsy. Will you do that, son?" I reached out with my other hand and held hers, almost linking us in a circle. Her skin was soft, like tissue paper, and I was afraid it'd tear if I was too rough. And then the moment was over. Mrs G took her hand away and looked down at it then back at the TV. Her face was childlike again, innocently gawping at her programs with a smile on her face, like they were the only thing that existed. I turned to Mya. Both hands were covering her face and her shoulders were juddering. I got up, put my arms around her, and now her emotion flooded out of her. This had been one of the most emotional weeks of my whole life, and I had to swallow hard to stop myself crying with her. It had been a privilege to witness this moment, though.

A few minutes later, Mya pulled away from my arms, and although her face was flushed and teary, she was smiling. She looked across at the old woman at the table with such love and relief. "I love you too, Mum," she said, and as we ate the rest of the Chinese, she told me stories from her childhood, adding, "Do ya remember, Mum, do ya?" and "Ain't that so, Mum?" every couple of minutes. Her mum had nothing to add and wasn't even paying attention, but Mya was happy to be doing it, and I loved hearing more about her and her life. We stayed that way – our little happy family – until Poppy, the night care lady, arrived to help Mrs G wash, change and slip into bed. Mya had told me there seemed to be a different face coming through the flat every day, but they all seemed professional, and Mrs G was always happy to see them.

"Do you mind if I help?" Mya asked as this Poppy moved towards her old lady.

"Of course," Poppy beamed. "That'll be nice won't it, Maria, for your daughter to help you?"

Mrs G didn't agree with Poppy, but she didn't complain either. She was like a little girl who wanted five more minutes in front of the TV, but as soon as it went off, it was like it had never been on, and she was happy to get ready for bed.

"I'll wait out in the car," I told Mya, and I left them to it, but not before I gave her old lady a kiss. "Be good, Mrs G," I told her, and I felt so much love for her. I loved her more and more every time I saw her. She was family – nar'mean?

Alone in the car, the moment we'd all shared in the house was a lifetime away, and all I could think about was the Unit 16-21 project and the robbery. In less than twenty-four hours, I'd be turning over a bleeding security van and running down the street with five mil – if I even got that far. Robbery was always more Winston's bag than mine. How I wished he was around to help me out. As I sat there, I wondered where I'd be this time tomorrow night. Celebrating with Mya? I hoped so, but my brain put prison bars in front of any picture I thought of, and my stomach lurched at the thought of going back inside. I'd lied to Slope about prison rice pudding; there wasn't a single thing I missed about doing time. And then there was the very real possibility that this time tomorrow I'd be lying beside Winston in a hospital bed, shot down by the police, torched by X, or worse. I didn't even wanna think about it and was grateful when the door opened and Mya got in the car, still so happy with what had happened in the flat.

"Thank you so much for coming with me," she beamed as she got in and pulled the seatbelt around her. "It was like we're, you know—"

"A family?" I said as I started the car, and she just smiled. Whatever happened tomorrow, I was grateful for the happiness I was having with Mya. And just having her beside me made all thoughts of prison, fire and hospital wards fall away. We were so strong together that I knew I could do it with her beside me. She gave me confidence I never knew I had. But, as it turned out, I wasn't the only one with the robbery on my mind.

"So, you know what you're doing, yeah?" she said when we were five or ten minutes into the journey. It was a beautiful evening and kind of a relief that we were finally chatting to the elephant in the room.

"Course. I got the codes, the key. I'm gonna do it like we said, so no one gets hurt. I should be in and out in a jiffy. Then back to the church for the drop-off on foot, and we're home and dry."

"Look, Degs, there's still time to pull out. There has to be another way."

"Can you think of one?"

The silence in the car answered that one.

"What if we did run?"

"Are you having a laugh?"

"Just you and me. We could go away and start somewhere new, just the two of us."

"What about Sheila?"

"Alright, just the three of us."

"And Winston?"

"Alright, so it's not a perfect plan. But I'm scared, Degs. I don't wanna lose you. I don't wanna lose what we've found together."

"I ain't going nowhere, Mya. In and out, that'll be me tomorrow, and then we've got the rest of our lives together." I even managed to smile as I said it, but that pit was back in my stomach like a manhole.

When we got in, Sheila was sitting on the sofa with her legs curled up under her, watching *Beaches*. It was her favourite film, and although it made her cry, it was a good sign. I plonked myself down beside her while Mya went and put the kettle on.

"How you doing?" I asked.

"Seriously, Degsy, we can't spend the rest of our lives with you tiptoeing around me and asking me if I'm alright every five minutes."

"Sorry I spoke," I smiled. This was more like the old Sheila I knew and loved.

Mya came in, balancing three steaming mugs in her hands, then joined us, and Sheila started talking again.

"I spent the day with the police," she said.

"Holy shit! Why didn't you tell us? We would have come with you."

"I had to do it on my own."

"And?" Mya asked.

"And I told them everything, all the gory details. I was in there for hours."

"Are you okay?"

She turned sharply in my direction. "What did I just tell you, Degsy?" she said, and then her face softened. "Yes, I'm okay. And there's other news – news that's good and bad." She played with the tie of her pyjamas as she spoke, hesitating. "I'm not the first to come forward, but with my testimony, they can start making arrests."

"Sheila, that's …" I said and stopped. I didn't know what to say about it, and then I moved more decisively, knowing what needed to be said and throwing my arm around her. "That's great news."

"Is it? It means that there were other kids, Degsy. I could have put a stop to it and I didn't."

"Hang on," Mya cut in. "Are you out of your mind? You telling me you're feeling guilty for what those twisted scumbags have done after everything you've been through. You've had enough on your plate just staying alive, and you've been a little busy changing the lives of others with us."

Sheila smiled. "I appreciate that, and I know deep down that this is a good result. It's just gonna take time, I guess," she said. I knew what she was saying was right. I also knew that she looked a million times better than she had the night before. She'd started to chip away at one of the weights around her neck; getting closure over her friend's death would be trickier, but she'd done well for today. Life was like the bloody London Eye, though – round and round you go, passing the bits that hurt over and over again, but you manage to smile and have a good time too, if you're lucky, or at least you try. Sheila wasn't fixed, but none of us were. Not really. We were all broken in one way or another, but we had each other to hold the pieces together.

That night in bed, Mya held my pieces together more passionately than she ever had before, and as we made love, it was with the urgency of a couple who feared it might be their last time. I reassured her that it wouldn't, that I'd get away with the robbery, and X would be out of our lives for good, that we'd make love in every room in the house after, and the garden and out in the middle of the road if she fancied it. Now I just had to convince myself.

14 THE ROBBERY

The sun wasn't shining the following morning, and as I lay in bed, looking at the gloom beyond the curtains, I tried not to see it as an omen. It was harder when I got up, looked out the window and saw it was pissing it down. It wasn't wimpy, weedy rain either; this stuff wasn't messing about; it was on steroids, coming from all angles, whipping down onto the road, trying to take out the cars, with wind raging like a flipping tsunami was just around the corner.

"You seeing this?" I said to Mya, but she didn't stir. The day before had been emotional for her, and I let her sleep. Truth be told, I wanted to be on my own. I couldn't face what she might be feeling this morning. I had to focus on getting through it, keep my mind on the plan, so I showered, made a quick breakfast and was out the door. I wished I was still in bed as soon as I set foot into what felt like a bleeding tropical rainstorm, though; I was drenched before I got to my car. I was wearing a black jacket and balaclava for the job, but that was in the boot with everything else I needed. For now, all I had was a Hay Patrollers tracksuit top, which was a much use in the rain as a lacey umbrella. It wasn't the start I was hoping for, but I had to get on with it.

I went over to see Nosit and Ivan first. This wasn't part of the plan, but I knew what I was risking, and I wanted to see them. They were surprised to see me so early, but welcomed me in as they always did.

"You're drenched, Degsy! Don't go dripping rain into the flat. Com'on," Nosit fussed. "Get dry." Then she said, "Why ain't you off to work?" thrusting biscuits under my nose. I'd miss that, I started to think, and then I shot myself down. *Stay positive, Degsy,* I was telling myself. *Just stay positive.*

"I'm gonna see Winston then go later," I told her. "Can't a

boy just come over and see his favourite Nosit in the morning?"

"Your favourite Nosit?" she smiled. "Know many Nosits, do you?" The rain was still thrashing outside. Then all I could hear was lumping down the stairs. "Here comes your favourite Ivan," she said, rolling her eyes, and then Ivan came in in his old-man pyjamas.

"What's that?" he said, yawning. "What did I miss?"

"Well, Degsy here's in some kind of trouble, but he's keeping mum about it."

Man, she was good. "I ain't in trouble," I lied.

"Pull the other one, Degsy," Nosit said, looking me square in the eyes. "Your nan told me to look out for you, so out with it."

"It's nothing, Nosit. I just wanted to see you both."

"Is it the Unit 16-21 project is it? I am sure you can get it started again."

"It's a part of it, but not all of it."

"Com'on dear, you can tell me."

"Leave the boy, alone," Ivan told her as he lumped down into his armchair. "If he says there's nothing going on, then there's nothing going on."

Man, they were both good. They were tag-teaming me now – good cop, bad cop – and I couldn't let them get a foothold.

"Both of you, please. There ain't nothing going on. I just wanted to invite you to this fundraiser at the community centre on Sunday, that's all. We're unveiling the mural and promoting the new Hay Assist thing I was talking about. You guys had better support it. Won't be long till we'll be Hay Assisting you."

"Oooh! You cheeky bleeder!" Nosit said and clipped me around the ear. Then we drank our cups of tea with all talk of trouble forgotten, and I couldn't help making a note to myself that I had to work on being a bit less suspicious. If I couldn't get past these two with a guilty conscience, what chance would I have against the police if it came to that?

"Course we'll be there, Degsy," Ivan said. "And we will get the Unit 16-21 project restarted, soon as the police have finished their investigation. Thank god we were insured.""Insured were we," I said smiling.

"Yep, fully, to the hilt and once the police have finished the insurers will pay out a large amount up front to get started."

Hearing that had made me feel so happy and relaxed, but what if I did get caught and banged up for a long spell. It wouldn't be good for the project nor for the team.

"Let us know if you need a hand with anything for Sunday, Ivan said. "You are a good lad Degsy, like a son I never had."

"We're pretty set, I think, Ivan. Thanks."

After more chatting, tea and biscuits, Nan's name came into the conversation.

"I spoke to her last night," Nosit told me.

"Oh yeah, how is she?" I asked, and now I felt guilty because I hadn't spoken to her since before the bleeding fire.

"You know she's nearly got the money to launch the Hay Patrollers over there in the States now?"

"You serious? Last time I spoke to her it was all still pie in the sky."

"Looks like she's got some backing from somewhere. Anyway, if you play your cards right, son, she'll want you over there before you know it."

"Alright for some," Ivan added. "Australia one minute, the States the next."

I was smiling, but I had too much on my mind to take it all in. I didn't think Nosit and Ivan had noticed – I thought they'd let all this talk of trouble go – but as I was leaving, after I'd hugged them both and said my goodbyes, Ivan collared me on the doorstep.

"Degsy, whatever's going on," he said, "I want you to think about everything you've built up here."

"Course," I said, giving him the brush off, trying to get

away, but he wasn't done.

"Do you know how proud we are of you? Me, Nosit, your nan? We can't believe how far you've come. Most blokes would have stayed in the gutter, Degsy. You've been inside and on the streets, caught up in all sorts, but you've come through it. Whatever's going on, just remember that, will you, son, how proud we are of how far you've come?"

Every word was a dagger. Some of the kids I've worked with used to tell me the worst thing their folks could ever say was they were disappointed in them. They could rant and rave and shout and throw things, but it was telling their kid how disappointed they were that got to them. I didn't really understand that before, but I guess all my mum ever did was put cigarettes out on me and throw me around our prison cell and then that little flat on the Addie. She hated me from the moment I popped out into the world; what did I care if she said she was disappointed in me? I saw it now, though. This was kind of what Ivan was saying – we're proud of you; don't disappoint us, and don't disappoint yourself. I wish I could have told him what was going on. I wish I could have asked him if he could see another way out of it, but I didn't wanna drag them into it, and, I suppose, I really didn't wanna disappoint them. I wanted them to always think of me as Degsy the geezer who makes things happen and looks out for the young and old alike, not Degsy the thief who held up a security van to get himself out of trouble.

"Thanks, Ivan, I appreciate that," I finally said, and then I was away, pulling my top up over my head to fend off the rain, feeling shitty now, but I had to put that behind me. There was one hour until the robbery; time to start putting the plan into action.

So here was how it was gonna go. First, I needed an alibi. Cue Winston. The geezer would be happy to help, that much I knew, so I thought I'd take advantage of his ground-floor room, go visiting, leg it out, pull the job off, and then get back there before anyone got wise. The job and the church were close enough that half an hour would do it. The nurses came in to check on Winston every hour. It was the perfect alibi. *Me, officer? Couldn't have been me, officer. I was visiting my sick friend the whole time.*

So, when I went in, I made a point of chatting to the nurses, making them laugh a bit, being a bit of a lad. It helped that I was wet through and dripping everywhere. It made me more memorable. I had the rucksack on me by this point, with everything I'd need inside, but I often had a bag, so it wasn't unusual. Then I wandered through to Winston's room, my heart pounding already. I swear, if the police or X didn't get me, I'd be lucky to end the day without having a bleeding heart attack – nar'mean?

"Alright, geez?" I said as I walked in. "Today's the day, Winston."

Of course he didn't answer, but there was a change in him. The bandages were off. I moved in closer to get a good look. I'd been fearing this moment. I didn't wanna face the fact that he'd have to walk around like the flipping Elephant Man for the rest of his life, but it wasn't too bad. I know there were worse burns on his body, but only a few bubbly, red wounds were visible on his hairline.

"I thought I'd seen the last of that mug!" I beamed at him.

"Don't know if I like you more with or without the bandages."

I imagined his reply, "You ain't no Ryan Gosling yourself, mon!" But there was only silence, so I took a seat, and I didn't say anything either, but my mood fell. I took my phone out of my pocket and checked the time. I had a few minutes before it was time to go. "Look after this for me, mate, would ya?" I told him and slipped my phone under his pillow with the sound switched off. I'd never had to worry about being tracked with a phone before, but I knew a bit about GPS now, and I wasn't taking any chances. As far as anyone else was concerned, neither me nor my phone left this room for the next half hour. After I did that, I moved right up close to Winston's ear.

"I know nothing ain't gonna go wrong, Winston, but supposing it does, supposing I don't make it back today, I wanna know you got Mya and Sheila's back. It's all very well dossing around here all day, but we can't both be missing in action. Anything happens to me, I need you up and active. Do you get me?"

No answer.

"Shit, you're infuriating, geez. If you can hear me, just give me a sign."

Nothing.

"I ain't messing around, Winston. Show me you understand."

Now, I ain't sure if I imagined it or not, or if I just saw what I wanted to see, but the geezer's thumb twitched. I swear it.

"Winston!" I was shouting now. "You in there, geez? Did you mean to do that? Do it again." There was no movement, but it wasn't stopping me. I ran to the hallway and called for the nurse, Jane. "He moved his thumb," I told her when she appeared.

"Is that so?" she said, but she didn't seem too interested.

"What does it mean? Don't you need to call a doctor?"

"Now don't get your hopes up, Degsy. It's not unusual for muscles to twitch."

My face fell.

"I'll let the doctor know when he does his rounds in a few hours, though," she said, more brightly. "The best thing to do is stay with him, talk to him, let him know you're there," she said and left me to it, but I know what I saw. I asked for a sign, and he moved his thumb. I asked him to look after things if anything happened to me, and he told me he would. If there was nothing else to celebrate that day, at least I knew Winston would be there to pick up the pieces for me. I snuck a peek under his pillow at my phone again. It was time.

"That's me then, geez," I told him and moved over to the window. "Don't go shouting and giving me away or anything," I joked, but neither of us was laughing as the window swung open, and the gale and rain took my breath away. It was easily wide enough for me to step through, but I couldn't open it too wide or the floor would be soaked. I was used to the idea that I'd spend the day drenched and no longer cared; as long as I got there and back without being seen or getting hurt, I didn't care if I spent the day covered in squirty cream and baked beans. I just wanted it done.

When I stepped through and landed on the flooded grass outside, I made a point of covering my tracks, wiping the window, shutting it a bit and making sure my boot prints were nowhere to be seen. The rain made it harder than I hoped, but I was still winning. Me and Mya had worked out all the CCTV blind spots, but we knew I wouldn't be able to get my car out without being seen, so it was all on foot from this point, which meant a run to the high street, along back roads and then into and out of crowds, giving any kind of surveillance the run around. By the time I got to the van, I was coming from the other direction, so the hospital would be the last place they'd track me back too. And, anyway, there was nothing to link me to the job. I was an upstanding member of society these days. I had a cup of tea with a few of London's finest a few weeks ago to talk about crime prevention; I went into prisons and schools to talk about making life changes; I ran the Hay Patrollers; why would anyone suspect me? I was golden, but it didn't stop my heart beating like a jackhammer as I got into position near the Cliff Vault, hidden behind the wall, two eyes poking out of a balaclava, and waited for the van. Me and Mya had worked out the safest way to take the guard down was with chloroform. I had a cloth in a bag all ready to take him down. He'd be awake again in a few minutes and wouldn't know what hit him. I'd tell him I was sorry while I was doing it and hope he wasn't too traumatised. Then I had the key and codes, and I was ready to make off back behind the wall after, where I'd pile the money in my rucksack, take off the balaclava and coat and blend back in with the Thursday morning shoppers. I'd head away from the church, U-turn back, drop off the money and that would be that.

I watched.

I waited.

The rain drenched the wool of my balaclava, and I couldn't breathe, so I lifted it up to free my mouth, struggling to see, too. I thought about taking it off, but that would've been madness. I didn't have to be comfortable. I just had to survive, but all sorts were going through my head as I squatted there waiting. I was starting to worry that I'd missed it, that I'd taken too long hiking through town and getting into position. Then a whole load of other worries powered down on me. What if the rain drenched the chloroform rag and it didn't work? What if the guard was built like a brick shithouse and I couldn't even get close to him? What if there were two of them? What if? What if?

Then the scene began before I was ready, like I was an actor in a play that was going on without me, but I don't think I'd ever really be ready. I took some deep breaths, willing myself into action, and watched as this massive, reinforced van rolled up outside the vault. I hadn't paid these vans much attention before, but now it looked a lot like those vans that pick convicts up from court and take them to prison. I'd been in enough of those to know, and the thought was not a happy one.

There were two guards, but one was the driver and, as I'd hoped, he stayed in the van while his mate opened the door and dropped down onto the street in steel-capped boots that could end a guy with a single kick. Again, it wasn't a thought I fancied, so I took my brain back to the plan: stay calm, stay patient, wait for the guy to do his pick-up, come out then pounce.

He went in. He looked even bigger than I thought as he passed by, and his visor was down, so I'd have to work out a way of getting the rag close to his mouth and nose. I wasn't exactly a small geezer, so I'd work it out. I didn't stand a chance taking him on in a fight, though, especially with all the body armour he was wearing, and for a split second, I thought of calling the whole thing off and just staying put. I'd let the geezer come out with the cash, unload it into the security deposit on the side of the van, climb back inside and drive off. But what would happen then? How long would it be before X attacked again? How long before Sheila was back in the hospital? Or Mya? Then there were Nosit and Ivan to think about. And don't even get me started on Asha and Ray. These people were my whole life. They were the reason I was crouched there getting drenched on a Thursday morning, and each of their faces popping into my head gave me strength and courage. So when that great big fella came marching out of the Cliff Vault, I jumped up, ready to pounce. Only, before I could take a step forward, I was pulled back.

"What the—?"

I dragged my arm away, terrified I'd blow it and miss the moment, and then I turned and looked behind me, still determined to free myself and run at that flipping guard, but then I didn't know what to do. I wasn't alone. This little drowned rat had hold of my jacket and wasn't about to let it go.

"Get off me!" I snarled. "I have to—!"

"Don't do it!" he shouted, struggling to make his voice heard over the rain. "Don't do it!"

"Slope? What the—?" The window of opportunity was slowly closing, and I had to make my move, so I easily shook him off. There was too much at stake to let him stand in my way.

"Don't do it!" he was shouting, but I couldn't listen. The guard had the cash and had moved to the side of the van.

I had seconds now rather than minutes. If I didn't make a move, the money would be out of reach forever. I lunged forward, determined, but Slope must have been just as determined as I was because he was on my back now, and my forward momentum threw us both off balance. That little shit might have been smaller than me, but the shock of his attack took me straight down to my knees. Then all I could do was watch as the finale of the play went on without me. The guard dropped the money into the van, all smiles, and then he got back in beside his mate and closed the door behind him. I pulled Slope's arms off me and shoved him down into the mud. We were both already slathered in the stuff by this point, so a little more made no difference. Then I turned on him, sharp. I couldn't believe what I was seeing and had to stop myself from laying the little shit out.

"What the fuck?" I shouted instead. "Do you have any idea what you've done?" I grabbed him by the collar, pulled him up to my face, and then threw him down. He didn't look scared, but he wasn't that kind of lad, just like I hadn't been. I didn't wanna scare him anyway; I just wanted to make sense of what had happened. After everything I'd done for him, after reuniting him with his brother and kickstarting a new life for him, he repays me by trashing my chance of sorting this shit out, getting X off my back, keeping my family and friends safe. "Just what the fuck?" I screamed again. And then my eyes and ears were dragged back to the road. The van hadn't moved, but there was movement all around it: chaos, lights, sirens, police cars, shouting. I threw myself down into the mud beside Slope and watched. Three police cars had skidded to the front and side of the van and a small army of armed officers had leapt out with guns ready to blow someone's head off. The security guards must have shit themselves. I saw their arms go up in the air, and then they both climbed out into the road, keeping their hands held high. I couldn't hear what was said, but I could see the disappointment as the cops lowered their guns and shrugged their shoulders, looking around them and scoping out the van. They'd come for a fight and found no one home. I turned to see Slope's muddy face beside me.

"I told you not to do it," he said. "They're setting you up, bruv."

15 A CHURCH SERVICE

I couldn't believe what I was hearing, but those police sirens were showing me the truth, and me and Slope just stayed where we were, down in the mud, like quicksand in the rain, watching as the lights went off, and the armed coppers took a last look around before getting back in their cars and pulling out. Then the van reversed, did a turn, and that drove off too, leaving us watching the deserted vault building, as if nothing had ever happened. I pulled the balaclava off and wiped my face in my arm; I couldn't have been wetter if someone had thrown a bucket of water over me. Then I pulled myself up and just sat there in the mud, staring over at where it all kicked off. My jeans were brown with mud by this point and when I turned to look at Slope, I almost laughed at how covered he was – like a little mud wrestler. But I didn't laugh. I didn't know if I'd ever laugh again. Things had got real a lot quicker than I wanted.

I pulled myself up to my feet and gave Slope a hand. He slipped and skidded, but then we were both on the move. He tried to talk, but I couldn't hear him over the rain that just wouldn't give us a break. "Not here!" I shouted. I didn't know if the police still had eyes and ears on the place, and although there was no crime to answer to, I didn't want any fingers pointing in my direction. Then I pulled him into an alleyway just past the shops. The deeper we walked into it, the quieter the rain got and the more echoey our voices sounded. We were both shivering, but I didn't care. I wanted answers.

"You need to start talking," I told him.

"I told you, it was a set up."

"Yeah, I got that. What I don't understand is how you knew and how you were there to do your Sudanese Superman bit – nar'mean?"

He rubbed his head then folded his arms. He hadn't come out prepared for the weather either, but I couldn't take pity on him. He looked as if he had an answer, but then he turned away and said nothing.

"Slope," I said, a little softer now. "Just tell me what you know."

"Your missus was right," he said, and he couldn't meet my eye now.

I took a deep breath, trying to keep my calm, trying to act like this wasn't a surprise and I could deal with it, but I felt like I'd been clobbered round the head. "And?" I said.

"And I didn't want anything to do with your crappy kids' club, with their stupid uniforms and painting shit!"

I took a step closer. "Are you really gonna stand there and insult me after all this, Slope?"

"Nah!" he said, and held his hands up to me. "It ain't like that, bruv. I'm just telling it like it is. It ain't for me."

"So?"

"So, your gang ain't for me, Degsy, but The Notorious is. Have you seen their church, all their kit? I want people to look at me, Degsy – nar'mean? I want them to know I'm coming before they see me and fall down at my feet. I don't wanna be seen with a fucking feather duster in my hand. I wanna be like X."

"No you don't."

"I do, and he gave me a shot. Get in with you, tell him all about what matters – that Ivan and Nosit, your brother and sister – tell him where you're hanging out, what you're doing, how to break through your security. And I was doing a good job. I was inches away."

"You don't wanna be in a gang like The Notorious, Slope."

"No? You don't know me, Degsy. You think you do, but I'm not you. I'm not even like you."

"So why'd you pull me out of there? I'd be banged up right now if it weren't for you. Why did you do that if you're so much like X?"

He looked down at his feet then back up at me for the first time, meeting my eye now. "Because I was in your debt, Degsy. You found my brother, and I'm grateful. But now we're quits." His eyes were locked onto mine, and I saw something there I hadn't seen before when he'd been throwing himself at the bigger boys, trying to take control of his life but being too small to get anywhere, trying to be the gaffer. I saw something powerful. Maybe it'd been there all along, and I'd felt too sorry for the little geezer to see it, or maybe it was a new thing. Maybe he was growing all the time, right in front of my eyes, making up his own code. I didn't like where he was heading, but at least he was honourable. It was a trait that went a long way in my book. Right now, though, I didn't know whether to hug or slap him. All that turning up at the offices and wanting to work with me? Without him, Unit 16-21 and Asha and Ray's school would still be standing, but because of him I was standing in an alleyway freezing my arse off rather than getting a strip search and mugshot done. So we didn't say anything to each other. He'd called it: we *were* quits. There was nothing left to say, and he gave me a final nod then made off out the alley. He moved at his own pace, as if he was a foot taller than he'd been before, and then disappeared into the light at the end of the tunnel. I wondered if his brother had any idea what he was taking on, but then Malik was no angel himself, was he? He'd made a break and was living his dream now, so I could only hope some of him rubbed off on Slope and not the other way round. Anyway, with Slope gone, reality hit me all at once. I'd been saved from the slammer by Slope, but now my anger was rising. This was X's plan all along. If he couldn't get me to leave his manor, then he'd set me up and get the police to drag me off. Unlike Slope, here was a man with no honour whatsoever.

Seconds after Slope left me standing there, I was off, marching out, back into the torrential downpour, but I wasn't even noticing it anymore. The rain thrashed at my face, dripped from my nose and sprayed off my lips as I walked faster and faster, gathering momentum, almost running now, getting my thoughts together as I passed all the normal people, doing their shopping, pushing their kids in pushchairs, pulling their elderly parents out of my way before I ran them over. Every footstep thudded down, smashed a puddle to bits and cleared the path in front of me, every stride taking me closer and closer to that bloody church, thoughts of what I'd do to X growing in my head with every stride. "I'll kill him!" I was mumbling to myself over and over again now the truth had sunk in. That bastard wanted me to fry one way or the other, and now I had nothing to lose. "I'll kill him!" But deep down, I knew it was only words. Yes, I was furious, but another part of my brain was counting up my chips and seeing that I had the advantage now. X had played his hand and come up short.

It didn't take long to reach the church, and this time, I didn't have a steel door and stone wall to deal with. Not only was the place wide open, but X was outside with a couple of ugly-looking geezers and a girl who looked like the back end of a bus, shouting right up in their faces. I'd only ever seen him looking cool and in charge, so I loved the sight of him losing it. Three guesses what had rattled him?

"Not your day, is it?" I shouted as I marched up, and his mates took a step back. They could see I wasn't messing.

X totally ignored me and took care of business. "Just find him!" he was shouting at his worker ants, and then they made off into a car and drove away. They could only be talking about Slope. I still didn't know what side I came down with that little shit, but I wasn't gonna drop him in it. He'd be safe enough in Brighton, and his brother knew how to keep a low profile, so there was no problem there.

With business taken care of, X turned to me. The look on his face just made me smile – I loved seeing him on the ropes – and suddenly I was loving every minute of this, but I knew I hadn't won, not yet anyway. And he was quick to get himself together. He was still dry under the arched doorway, and he looked as pristine as ever in his package-fresh tracksuit and white trainers that had never felt the grime of the streets on their tread. I felt like dragging him out into the mud, but that wasn't how I wanted this to go. He didn't need to know that, though.

"Give me one reason why I shouldn't take your head off!" I shouted.

He smiled at this, and I became that bit more aware of our positions – me, out in the cold, drenched; him, cosy, dry, safe.

"I'll give you ten reasons," he smiled, "and they're all in there." He nodded behind him, into the church. "I'll give you twenty reasons if you throw their blades into the mix, bruv. I take it you ain't got the five mil."

"Are you taking the piss?"

He laughed again. "Yes, Degsy. I'm taking the piss. Looks like we underestimated you a bit, though. And your boy, Slope."

"Looks like you did, and I ain't your bruv. See, we need to talk. You torched my house, put my best mate in hospital, burnt down my business, my brother and sister's school, beat up my friend, and now you try to get me banged up. I'm sick of playing things your way. You don't even look after your nan, *Aziz*. And that's the biggest crime in my book."

"What the fuck do you know about my nanny?" he shouted. He'd gone from calm to nearly blowing his top in a second. I'd obviously touched a nerve, and I liked it. "You go near her, and I'll do ya. You get me?"

"Me? You can't even find five minutes to visit the old dear," I shouted, turning the knife.

"Shut your mouth, Degsy. I love my nanny, you fucker."

I was starting to enjoy myself, I liked seeing him on the ropes, and I was gonna say more,

but then my mouth jammed shut.

The bastard pulled a gun on me.

It wasn't the first time a geezer had pointed a gun at me, but it'd been a long time, and I knew what a nutcase X was.

"Sorry, what was that?" he said. "What you talking about, Degsy? Don't stop. What's a little shooter between friends?"

The rain was fiercer than it had been all day, falling in on us from a dark, concrete sky, pasting my hair flat against my forehead and forcing me to squint out at him, but I could see that shooter clear as day. I could see the tension in the hand that held it and the white knuckles. He was so unpredictable that it could go off any second.

I put my hands up. It seemed like the right thing to do, showing him I saw what he was doing and I wasn't putting up a fight, and I said, "Alright! You win. We'll go. Give us a few days to pack up and take care of business then you'll never see us again."

"Now you're talking my language, Degsy, but I've got some bad news for you. The rules have changed a little bit."

I kept my eye on that gun, and I could see the change; his arm was straightening, he was gripping it even tighter as he spoke to me. I had to act, so I didn't give him a chance to finish whatever shit he was gonna say. And I called it right. I dodged out of sight and mud-slid down behind a headstone just as the gun went off. A second later and I'd have been dead. And I didn't wait for him to regroup. I was off behind the church when the next two deafening shots cracked through the air, sending bits of stone flying everywhere. When I got around the back, I kept going, and like something out of a flipping cartoon, I'd run all the way around while he was taking his first steps out of the shelter of the arch to follow me. A gun might make a man powerful, but it can also make him lazy. Maybe he thought he could just stand there and shoot, but I wasn't gonna make it easy, and now I watched as he tried to protect his tracksuit and trainers from the rain, walking as if the ground was lava, shouting his mouth off about what he was gonna do when he found me. Now I really did have the advantage, and I know I should've run – every part of me was screaming, "Run, Degsy! He's a lunatic with a gun," – but what would that solve? We'd be back to square one, with X wanting Hay Patrollers' blood and us doing anything we can to stay alive. We were better than that, and we deserved more than that. Winston deserved more than that, lying half dead in that bloody hospital room. So I crept past that massive arched doorway and followed him around the back. I expected a whole load of guys to come running out at the sound of gunshots, but it was quiet, save for the birds that had legged it out of the trees, squawking all the way. This could only mean he'd lied; he was on his own, and he wasn't too smart sending the last of his guys to search for Slope. That was the arrogance of the man, though. He had no idea what he was dealing with.

I hung back, keeping my back to the stone wall, edging forwards every time X made a move, but staying patient. I only had one shot at this, and if I got it wrong, there'd be a headstone here with my name on it. He was moving slowly, flicking his drenched hair off his face and moving his gun from side to side. I couldn't see his face, but I didn't think he was smiling anymore. His outfit was ruined.

Then I made my move. With no warning, I ran at him from behind, gripped my arms around him and slammed him down to the ground, sending the gun flying. But he wasn't an easy target. He was quickly up on his knees and swivelled his fist into my face, throwing me down onto the swampy grass. Then he was on top of me, landing one punch after another into my face with fists like boulders. Each one shook my brain as my nose crunched, and I nearly choked on a tooth as it was smashed out of my gum into my throat. I guess I'd underestimated him. The dude knew how to fight, but so did I, and a couple of punches weren't gonna keep me down. I reached out to the side and my hand found something hard. I hoped it was the gun, but when I pounded it into the side of X's head, I saw it was just a mad-looking rock. It did the job, though, and toppled him off me. I lay there getting my breath back for a few seconds then sat up and started to scan the grass for that gun, but it was too muddy and wet. I couldn't see a thing. I didn't even see X getting up and launching his boot into my face until it was too late, and I was on my back again. I had no time to get myself together now. He was dragging me by the foot. I had no idea why until he slammed me into the side of the church, breaking me against those sharp rocks. I spat blood and knew I was close to passing out, but I had to get myself together. I managed to turn my body and saw X close by, bent over, eyeballing the grass as if he was looking for lost treasure, trying to find that shooter.

"Com'on, Degsy!" I told myself. "Get up, geez!" My body wasn't listening at first, but I forced it to pay attention, and I was soon back up on my feet. I was so off balance, though, that all I could do was run at X like a loose cannonball and hope to take him down. Thankfully, I hit my target, and as we both went down, I heard a crack. And then nothing. I lay there. It was silent. I didn't even dare look over at X. There was only one thing made a crack like that, and that was a skull. I'd killed him. I'd bloody killed him. All I wanted to do was save myself and my friends and family, and here I was killing a man and getting my robbery charges jacked up to murder. I just couldn't look. And I shouldn't have, because the moment I managed to pull myself up onto my elbows, I got another boot in the face, knocking me down again. At least he wasn't dead, but I'd be dead soon if I wasn't careful. And then he was on top of me again. He wasn't punching this time, but slamming my head down into the muddy grass. If it'd been concrete, then one blow would've been enough to finish me off, but all I was getting was a headache. And then I saw it. The gun had flown out of his hand and gotten lodged in a bush just next to us. We'd both been looking too low. I managed to twist out of his grip and hoist myself up enough to throw him off. Then I made a run for it, which was a mistake because he saw it too now and was climbing over me to get there first. We were scrambling over each other, powering forward and dragging each other back, both desperate to get there first, and all I knew was I couldn't let him get there. I had to do something and make it count, so when I dragged him back this time, I pushed my fingers into his soft, fleshy eye sockets. He was throwing himself all over the place to get out of my grip and when I dropped him, he was rolling around on the grass, a mess in his shit-brown tracksuit, clawing at his face while I launched myself over to that hedge and snatched the gun. He was quick to find his feet, but when he did, he was face to face with me, and his little friend was in my hand, barrel pointing at his head. I spat blood and pushed my hair back, preparing to shout at him, telling him that it ends here, but that boot swung into the air once again, hammered my fist and sending the gun flying again. I just couldn't catch a flipping break. But, as he spun, I manged to get my arm around his neck and crush it with a headlock that must have hurt like fuck because his legs gave way. I squeezed tighter, but this guy's strength surprised me again, and he was on his feet, lifting me off the ground, still hanging onto his neck with the headlock, and then he ran backwards towards the church, slamming me into it, throwing my lungs up into my throat. I slumped to the ground, hardly able to breathe, but I had to think quick. He was away, and he quickly found the gun, and then he started shooting without giving it a second of thought. You couldn't argue with how crazy and powerful he was, but his aim was shit, and I managed to get up to my feet and leg it. He fired three shots, and I knew the third was millimetres from my head as I burst through the church doors into their den. Thankfully, there was no one home, although it looked like the place had been vacated in a hurry; games had been abandoned halfway, drinks left undrunk, and even a few coats, phones and keys had been left behind. As glad as I was to be alone, I was far from safe and had less than seconds to find a hiding place or a weapon. I grabbed at a PlayStation. The moment he came running through the door, I launched it at him, knocking him off his feet, and I ran to pick up anything else I could get my hands on and threw that too – a mug, an ashtray, a battered *Grand Theft Auto* case. "This has to stop!" I was shouting, and my voice sounded mad with blood gurgling, a fat lip and less teeth than I started off with. But he was the one with the gun. He was the one who made the rules, and nothing I threw at him was stopping him, so I threw a half-full bottle of Bud, forcing the geezer to turn and duck, and then I made off where the choir used to sing, and slid myself in between the fridge and microwave. I crouched there, panting, hearing my heart beat in my ear so loud I thought it'd give my hiding place away. Then it sounded like the fridge had exploded, and I pulled my head into my hands. He'd shot at it, and the door flung open. More shots fired – a TV smashed, something heavy crashed down from the ceiling. The lunatic was just firing randomly in all directions. If I stayed where I was, he'd find me and shoot without a second's thought. I had to move.

"Stop messing about and come here, Degs!" he was saying. "I ain't gonna hurt ya." His voice sounded more twisted than ever, but I was glad he'd spoken because I knew he was over the other side of the church, where I'd seen the dancefloor. I took my chance and crept out of my hiding place, moving noiselessly over to where the geezers in here got themselves spruced up. I couldn't even look at the mash-up of my face in the mirror and just grabbed a couple of bottles of the Lynx they kept there and crept away, keeping low. It wasn't long before I found a lighter, and now I'd just wait while X wore himself out over on the dancefloor, ranting and raving about what he'd do to me when he got his hands on me. I snuck down behind one of the leather sofas, and as soon as he was on the move, I got ready, with the aerosol in one hand and the lighter in the other. Then, just as he backed past me, saying, "I know where you're hiding, Degsy, innit, and you're dead when I get my hands on ya," I flicked the lighter, sprayed the Lynx, and felt the power straight away as the whole room was lit up by my flamethrower. And X didn't know what hit him as I set the roaring flame on those ugly, dirty trainers of his, sending them up like lumps of coal, giving him the full Joan of Arc treatment. And I watched him dance as he tried to put them out, screaming down at the flames, shouting at them, shouting at me, the gun going flying. And then I saw my chance and ran at him, taking him down onto his back, all the way back to the dance floor, where a mirror ball spun above us, reflecting those foot flames all around the gaff. He tried to move, but I kept him pinned, screaming like a little girl as his trainers burned and he couldn't do a flipping' thing about it.

"Those are some pricey kicks, but I don't know if Adidas make them fireproof," I smiled down at him.

"Please, Degsy! Get 'em off! Get 'em off!"

"What's the matter, X? I thought you loved fire?"

"Ah! Get 'em off!"

I turned to look at his feet. The trainers were taking their time to burn, but it wouldn't be long until there was serious damage to the geezer's feet.

"I'll get them off when you tell me enough's enough. You're gonna leave us alone to do our work, stay away from my friends, stay away from my family! This has to stop!"

"Anything you say, Degsy! Just put them out!"

His body was flapping as he kicked his legs, desperate to put out the flames, but powerless, and I held him down easily.

"How do I know you won't change your mind as soon as I get off you?"

"I swear it, Degsy! Just put out my fucking shoes, man! I'll do anything you say!"

I took a stupid-long time making a show of thinking, and then I got off him, ran over to the fridge and looked inside for something to put the flames out. All I found in there were cans of Red Bull and bottles of Bud, so I grabbed a few Red Bulls and ran back to him. By the time I got back over there, the bottom of his tracksuit had caught and he was screaming and crying. Now, I didn't mean to be a shit about it, and I know I should've just put him out, but I didn't trust the gee-zer to back off. The moment I put him out, I knew he'd be on the hunt for that gun again, and I knew he'd never let us walk free, so I grabbed a phone I'd seen near a PlayStation. Mine was still under Winston's pillow. I swiped the screen, found the camera and took a video of this geezer on fire, crying like a baby, begging me to put it out. "You go back on your word and everyone sees what the leader of The Notorious looks like crying for mercy, do ya get me?" I shouted, and then I slipped it into my pocket and started opening cans of Red Bull. I doused him in a couple, and he was already wet from the rain, so he wasn't ever gonna go up like Guy Fawkes, but the cans were too small and the flames weren't budging. Then I went at him with a couple of sofa cushions, suffocating the fire, stamping it out until he started to sizzle and hiss. We were both so warn out after that, we just lay there together, side by side, the battle fought, but we were both so messed up, it was hard to see who the winner was until I started to get up and he stayed down, whimpering over his crispy bits. I couldn't feel sorry for the geezer; he wasn't lying in a coma like Winston. I couldn't forget that. And then I just left him there, limped out of the home of The Notorious, and didn't look back.

 # THE FUNDRAISER

I didn't need to go back to the hospital after that, but it was like I'd programmed myself, and that was my next move, so I limped all the way there, with people jumping out of my way because I looked like a bloody monster, and then I climbed back in through Winston's window. I didn't need to do that either. I didn't need an alibi anymore, but I suppose I wasn't thinking straight, and all I had was my plan. It was like I was on rails, and if I didn't keep going, if I didn't keep one foot moving in front of the other, I'd fall down, and that'd be the end of me. It'd been easy to climb through that window on the way out, but now it was like climbing a wall at the end of a marathon, and I barely made it through. And when I did manage to drag myself into the room, I thudded down onto the floor and just stayed there. I don't know if I passed out or fell asleep, but the next thing I remember is seeing a couple of legs in tights and squinting my swollen eyes to see what was at the top of them. It was Jane, the nurse, and I don't think she knew what to make of me. She'd left me sitting with Winston an hour or so earlier, in one piece, my normal happy self, and now she'd come back in to check, and I looked like I'd gone ten rounds with Tyson Fury. She didn't move to start off with. She was looking all around as if the monster who did this might still be in the room, and then I started to sit up.

"My God, Degsy! What the—? I mean, how—? What happened?"

"Never mind that," I answered. "You got any paracetamol?"

"I think you need a bit more than that. Let me take you down to A and E."

"No!" I snapped and then spoke a bit more gently. "Thanks, but can't you help me a bit?" To be honest, I didn't think I'd make it over to A and E. If I did, there'd be too many questions asked.

She looked over to the door and wrung her hands. "I shouldn't really. Insurance," she said. "But I do have a duty," she added. "Just stay there." And she left me alone with Winston.

I got up onto the chair, reached under his pillow for my phone and put it in the bag. Then I took that other geezer's mobile out and found that video I'd taken. "Check this out, geez," I said, and pressed play. There was X, jumping around the place, feet on fire, crying like a baby, begging me to put him out. I tried to smile, but my face hurt too much. "Not the day I was expecting," I said and slipped it back into my pocket. "We've done it, though, Winston. It wasn't the way I thought it'd go, but that nutcase is out of the picture. You just need to wake up and we can carry on with the plan – getting young people out of gangs, off the streets and into the Hay Patrollers, employed, educated, helping the elderly and disabled. There's nothing to stand in our way now, bruv. So if you wanna give me another sign, now's the time."

I waited, but he didn't move this time. I didn't let it get me down, though. I know I saw him do it before, and in my mind, that meant he was slowly coming back to us.

Jane came back a few minutes later and started to patch me up. She told me I should probably get myself down to x-ray, but all I wanted was to go home. So I promised I'd come back if I had any problems and limped out of there.

Mya was waiting on the doorstep for me when I got home. I'd never been happier to see anyone in my entire life, and I almost cried as she hugged me. But my body was doing all sorts of crazy things, and I needed to get out of my wet clothes and into the bath. Mya ran it for me while I told her everything that had happened and showed her the film.

"So I was right, then?" she said, as she pulled my shirt off me, which was caked with mud and blood.

"About what?"

"You know what," she smiled.

I did know what, but I wasn't gonna let her win that easily. "About Slope."

"Nah! You said he was spying from the beginning. He wasn't when I first met him, and he came good in the end."

"Seriously!" she joked. "Just admit it, Degsy. You were wrong and I was right."

"Okay. You were wrong and I was right."

"Very funny!" she said without laughing and helped me off with my T-shirt. She winced as she saw my skin, so I knew it was bad. I didn't bother looking in the mirror. I could already feel how bad it was. I'd taken some beatings in my life, and this one was up there. It hurt, but I was still smiling. I was lucky to be alive. I felt less lucky when I got in the bath and the water stung me all over, but I settled into it, and it was just what I needed. Mya brought me a cup of tea and some paracetamol, and I stayed in there more than an hour, topping up the water every now and then so it was boiling, until I finally fell asleep in there.

"Degsy?"

I knew that voice. I hadn't heard it for a while, but I'd recognise it anywhere. It was a voice that reached inside my chest and held my heart, tenderly. It was a voice that was songbirds flying through my body, resting in my soul. It was a voice that I'd heard every day until it was taken away, and all I had left was silence.

I turned my head. I wasn't even aware of my body until I did that, and then it just appeared below me, as if I'd been invisible before or hadn't even existed. I was still naked but for this tiny pair of swimming trunks. Nothing hurt anymore. I reached up to touch my face. All the swelling had gone down, and I could breathe easily. She was there beside me, Gabby and her son, lying on that flipping sun lounger again with Sadface jumping around her. I lowered myself onto the other sunbed and that little fella jumped up on my chest and licked my face all over.

"Alright, boy! I've missed you so much."

He jumped off and darted back over to Gabby, lounging there on her sunbed in a gold two-piece, looking like something out of a celebrity magazine. God, she was beautiful. I wanted to reach out and touch her, hold her, love her, but I didn't. I stayed on the sunbed and took in my surroundings. We were on a beach again, maybe in the Caribbean, with sand as golden as her bikini and a gentle, calm, turquoise sea. We were completely alone. All I could see was miles and miles of that sand and sea.

"What's been keeping you, Degsy?" Gabby asked. She didn't look happy, and I couldn't bear it, but I didn't go over to her. It didn't seem like the right thing to do. Instead, I reached out my hand to her. She reached out and took it, and we lay together on our sunbeds, holding hands. Her hand in mine was like a key in a lock, neither mattering without the other.

"I'm sorry," I told her. "I should've come back."

"What's she like then?"

I dropped her hand. I didn't mean to, but the question shocked me. I sat up and turned to face her.

"What's who like?"

"You know who," she said, and I calmed down a bit when I saw she was smiling. She was so beautiful.

"She's …" I stopped for a moment to think of how I should answer. What was Mya like? She was amazing and beautiful and caring and strong. I couldn't tell Gabby that, though. That was the last thing she wanted to hear.

"I'm waiting, Degsy," she said, still smiling, and I found myself being honest.

"I'm sorry, Gabby. I didn't mean to fall in love. I didn't think I could fall in love again. It just happened. Do you want me to break up with her? I will. I loved you first, and I'll love you forever."

Now Gabby sat up too and leaned over to me, laying her hands on my thighs then taking my hands in hers.

"I want you to know, Degsy," she began and paused until she had full eye contact with me, "it's okay. I want you to be happy. I want you to be with someone who looks after you and is good for you. If it can't be me, then I'm glad it's someone like Mya."

And then all the emotions I was feeling were too strong to keep a lid on. "But I want you, Gabby," I said, trying to hold back my tears. "I'd give up everything I have for you to come back to me. It's you I want. I love you, Gabby. I love you."

"I love you, too, Degsy, but this is goodbye."

"No!"

"Yes! Come here."

I shuffled over to her, kneeling through the sand to reach her, and she wrapped her arms around me. The smell of her took me back to every moment we'd shared when she was still alive.

"You love her, Degsy, don't you?"

I nodded my head in her hair and closed my eyes.

"Then I'm happy for you, Degsy, and you have to let me go."

As I knelt there, nestled into her hair, holding her in my arms, the desire to shout and cry for her to stay drifted away, and I was left with this one perfect moment. I guess it was the goodbye we couldn't have in real life. I wished it could go on forever, but goodbyes don't work like that.

"Degsy!" she was saying.

"I love you," I mumbled.

"Degsy!" louder now.

"Hmmm!"

"Degsy!!"

My eyes snapped open.

Mya was standing there with her hands on her hips, looking over my bubble bath as if I was in big trouble.

"You can't fall asleep in the bath, Degsy!" she said, and I couldn't help laughing. She looked so furious.

"I'm serious, Degsy!" she shouted.

"Come 'ere!" I laughed, and I dragged her into the bath with me. She was fighting me off, telling me to get off, and then she was laughing as hard as I was. We soon worked on getting her clothes off, and then it was our perfect moment in the bath together, soaking, kissing, being with each other, and I don't think I'd ever felt as content in my life.

That night, we had Ivan and Nosit over and finally filled them in on what had been going down. Sheila cooked, and we even got Nan, Jarra and Darel on Skype, so the whole family were there. We'd won. We were almost all in one piece, and we'd live to fight another day.

I spent the next day in bed. I was lucky nothing was broken, but I needed a good rest to kickstart the healing. Everything hurt still. By Saturday, I was up and moving slowly. I couldn't lounge about; I still had a whole bundle of things to organise for the fundraiser. Just as we said, we were celebrating the Hay Assist project, launching the mural, but, more importantly, we were putting a message out there. There's no taking us down. We're here to stay. You can throw what you like at us, but we ain't going nowhere. I'd already shown X what happens when someone tries to take us over, and now we'd show the world just how little damage he'd done.

When Sunday came, it was a beautiful day. I have no idea where that torrential rain had come from, but it'd disappeared without a trace, and the sun was shining down on us as we arrived at the community centre. The decorations were just as we wanted them, and we'd set up different stalls in the centre and out on the field to raise funds, with games, food and drink (including plates of food donated by Malik, who, I imagine, still had no idea what a toe-rag Slope was), things for sale, that kind of thing. I suppose it was a bit like a fayre, but with a Hay Patroller twist. Hundreds of people turned up and, I swear, I couldn't stop smiling as I greeted them. We had loads of publicity, which was great, but it was the familiar faces that made me smile: Ivan and Nosit, the Hay Patrollers I'd invited to represent us: Katya and Ibrahim (I just hoped she could keep him in line), and Han and Three Pies (I still didn't know where he got that nickname), a few of the young people working and patrolling in The Grove. Mya came along with her mum and one of her carers, and some of the other Hay Assist old dears turned up, including X's nan, Mrs B.

"Degsy!" she shouted when she saw me with my face all mashed up. "What the hell happened to you? I've seen you fight, lad. The only thing that could do that to you's a bus."

I didn't have the heart to tell her that her grandson was behind it, so I just laughed and shrugged it off. "You should see the other guy," I told her. "Been no sign of those idiots round your place again, has there?"

She shook her head. "You put the shits right up them," she giggled. "I was thinking; you could teach us some of your self-defence moves? You could do a class, give us oldens a bit of confidence, you know."

She made me laugh. I loved her fight. "I'll think about it, Mrs B," I told her. Then she was off. She was a wild one, that one, and she'd seen some friends she wanted to talk to or some game she wanted to play. I was just so happy to see her looking so much happier than the last time I'd seen her. The thought of her being scared in her own home broke my heart, even if X didn't give a shit about her. I should've let his trainers burn right through for neglecting such a sweet nan like Mrs B.

At about two, it was time to unveil the mural. It'd been taped up with plastic and sheets, so no one could peek at it and spoil the surprise, and I couldn't wait to see it. A massive group obviously felt the same and had gathered around outside, and Katya and Ibrahim were beside me. He was wearing a hat that said *I'm with stupid*, with an arrow pointing to the side, but he was standing in the wrong place and the arrow didn't point to anyone. Katya just rolled her eyes whenever she looked at him, and I wondered if maybe there'd be romance between them one day. Hate and love are so close together that maybe Katya's irritation and frustration with the geezer would switch over to affection. On second thoughts, looking at them, hell would freeze over before those two got it together.

"Thanks for coming, ladies and gentlemen!" I announced, and everyone shut up so they could hear me. "It's been a proper good afternoon, and thank you all for turning out to support us and all the good work we've been doing. As you know, the money raised today will help get Unit 16-21 back up and running after the fire. No one deserves to be homeless, and we, the Hay Patrollers, will keep on fighting until the streets are clear and everyone is housed." A cheer went up. It was a bold claim, but it got them going, and that's what we needed. "Now," I began again, turning to Katya. "I'll hand you over to Katya for the unveiling of her masterpiece."

I handed the mic down to Katya, and when the applause died down, she said, "I can't begin to tell you what the Hay Patrollers have done for me. Being a part of this amazing crew has changed my life and changed who I am, and I'm excited to be able to give something back with this mural."

She spoke so confidently, and I couldn't believe she was the same young woman who'd come to us barely able to hold her head up around other people, worn down by life and the fact that she was stuck in a wheelchair. None of that had changed, but now she had support, and her outlook on life, thankfully, was completely different.

"At different times, eighteen of us worked over three weeks to get the mural finished. To me, it represents togetherness, unity, harmony and diversity – all the things that make the Hay Patrollers so important."

"Shall we?" I smiled over to them both when she'd finished

her speech, and the crowd erupted again as we set about unveiling it, pulling off the sheets and attacking the plastic with scissors. It was a real ta-da moment – Nar'mean? And then the crowd went silent. I'd been so busy fighting the plastic that I hadn't even looked at what was underneath, and now, as I stood back, I could see why they'd stopped cheering. The mural that had taken eighteen people three weeks to paint – the colourful portrait of a happy community – was now a mess of blacks, reds, oranges and dirty yellows, thick angry brushstrokes that had trashed through the hard work in minutes, leaving something that looked like a filthy paint fire. And I knew straight away who was responsible, but I couldn't let it show, so I started clapping. "Ain't it amazing, everyone!" I was shouting, and heads started tilting, looking the bloody thing up and down, and a lukewarm applause started up again. "Modern art," I said down the mic, and a few more people joined in the clapping. I could see Katya was about to explode, and I tried to calm her down with just my eyes while I smiled at the crowds as if everything was going exactly as we'd planned.

"Thank you! Thank you!" I said. "Please hang around, play some games, eat some grub, spend some more money and help support the great work we're doing."

People were already starting to move away from the eyesore mural, and I moved over the Katya, who'd grabbed Ibrahim by the balls. It was the first time I'd seen that smile of his drop.

"If I find out you're behind this …" she was threatening.

"Nah! Nah! It weren't me."

"Let him go, Kats," I said. "I know who did this. I'm so sorry it's happened, but it's got nothing to do with him."

She almost looked disappointed that she couldn't bust his balls any longer. It was definitely love. She even apologised to him after, but I didn't hang around to hear it. I was straight back in the community centre, rounding up my troops, my blood pressure sky high.

"I thought this was all over, son," Ivan was saying when we all got into the back office.

I couldn't even answer him. I was just pacing. I thought it was over too, but we were right back at the beginning again. I should've known a pair of torched kicks and a video wouldn't be enough to keep X down. He was the craziest guy I'd ever met. He'd probably enjoy watching a film of himself on fire – twisted nut.

"Calm down, Degsy," Mya was saying, but I couldn't stop moving, strutting up and down, my brain on overdrive.

"We need to shut this down," I eventually said. "It's a warning. It ain't safe here."

"But the fundraiser, Degs." This was Nosit.

"We've already raised …?"

"About fifteen hundred," Sheila told me. "And there's the online page. Not a bad day's work."

"Alright. Shut it down. We'll do it slowly. Tell 'em it's licencing or something. Just get everyone out, and then we can try and sort out what to do about all this shit, but I tell ya, I'm out of ideas. This geezer's a worm; you cut him in two and he just keeps on wiggling."

"But we're stronger than that," Mya said gently into my ear and squeezed my arm. "We've got each other."

So we went around, clearing out the punters, shutting down the stalls, packing up for the day and making our excuses. The crowds had started to thin after the ugly mural spoilt the afternoon anyway, but some people still needed a push.

And then, finally, we were alone, just friends and family: Ivan and Nosit, me, Mya and Sheila. The carer had taken her old lady home, and it looked like she'd had a lovely afternoon out. Katya, Ibrahim, Three Pies and Han had stuck around to help us tidy things up, but it was starting to get late.

"You guys should get going," I told them, and thanked

them for all their hard work. They headed off, chatting together, even Katya and Ibrahim, and now it was time for the business in hand. Something serious had to be done about X and The Notorious, and I'd decided we weren't leaving the community centre until we came up with something, but before we could start throwing ideas around, Ibrahim came running back into the office.

"You got the key, Degs?" he asked.

"It's open," I told him and turned back to the others, expecting him to leave us alone.

"It ain't."

I sighed louder than I meant to. I didn't mean to sound frustrated, but it was hard to hide it. I just wanted to get some ideas together and find a solution to this mess. I missed Winston. He'd know what to do, and my painkillers were wearing off. Everything was starting to hurt again.

"Go and show him how to use a door, would ya?" I told Sheila.

She smiled to cover up how grumpy I looked and make it look like a joke, and then she was off with him, but they were back minutes later, and I didn't wanna hear what they had to say.

"*Is* there a key?" Sheila asked.

Me being me, I jumped up and stomped over there, mumbling that if you wanna job doing right you gotta do it yourself. I tried the door, expecting it to open, but they were right; it was locked.

"See! Told ya! Prick!" Ibrahim said.

"Watch your mouth," I said and started shaking that handle, putting my weight behind it, because I had the key in my pocket, and there was no way it could be locked, but the bloody thing wouldn't move. I crouched down and looked through the keyhole; I could see right through to outside. Then I looked at the crack between the door and the frame. There was something there, and when I shook the door, it rattled.

"It's chained up," I said. "The caretaker must have thought no one was here and chained the place up. We'll just …" I said and left it hanging in the air as I swept across the hall, through the office and out to the back door. I grabbed the handle and pushed it down, but this one wouldn't even budge. There was something heavy wedged against it outside. Suddenly, I had a bad feeling about all this. Then I heard a smash and a scream from the main hall.

"Degs!"

I ran back in to see what all the fuss was about, but I didn't need telling. I could smell it and feel it before I even got there. The place was on fire. Mya, Sheila and the others were pressed up against the wall while tables began to burn. I'd been a bleeding Molotov. I could smell it.

"Just keep back!" I was shouting, and ran over to grab the fire extinguisher. I wish I'd paid more attention to these things now, but I managed to work it out. I pulled the pin, pointed and sprayed at the flames, feeling the heat on my face, until it was empty and all that was left was black, sizzling wood. "Everyone alright?" I asked when it was out and wandering back over. Everyone was shaken, but there were no casualties. I moved over to Mya and discretely said, "There's no way out."

"Just stay calm," she said. "We'll think of something."

And then my phone rang. The number was withheld, but I didn't need caller ID to know who was calling.

"You've had your fun, X!" I snapped into the phone. "Let us out of here!"

There was no answer to this, and then all I could hear was sinister laughter. The geezer was insane.

"You better hope I don't ever get out of here," I was raging, and he still hadn't said a word.

Then he said, "You ready for another one?" More laughter, and then the line went dead.

"Shit! Everyone back against the wall!" I shouted, and

herded them over. "Cover your faces." Then I was over by that door, kicking and shouldering it, trying anything I could to get it open, but he'd really done a number on it. I raced over to the empty fire extinguisher, wishing I hadn't used it all now, and used it as a battering ram, but that door was going nowhere. Then – whoosh! – more fire through that broken window, sending the tea and coffee section up in a second and the curtains with it. "Cover your faces!" I repeated, and I was breathing into my arm now as I moved across the hall, trying to think of a plan. The windows were too high and too small to help us out, but there were bigger windows in the office. It was our only chance.

"Call the fire brigade!" I shouted, and legged it to the office with that empty fire extinguisher. The fire was bad, but only about a quarter of the hall had gone up, so I knew everyone would be safe for a minute or two. I hadn't realised how smoky the hall had been until I got into the office and could breathe a little easier. I half expected X to have boarded up the window, but he obviously hadn't thought of that, and I started ramming it. Bloody thing was like concrete, but I wasn't about to give in. I pounded it and rammed it, and I could've cried when I finally saw the crack. Then I got my boot in there. I kicked the flipping thing in, and I can't even tell you how good the fresh air felt as I cleared the glass, before running back into the hall to get the others. Even in the short time I'd been out of the hall, the fire had grown into something I no longer recognised, raging across the ceiling with its fistfuls of black smoke and fury. The others had edged closer and closer to the office and didn't need telling twice when I shouted, "Quick! This way!"

There was coughing and retching, but no one was hurt, and the youngsters lifted Katya out before springing straight out the window themselves and flopping down onto the grass beyond. I stayed back and gave Ivan and Nosit a hand. She was coughing like mad.

"You alright, Nosit?"

She gave the thumbs up, but I'd be a lot happier when she was outside, breathing fresh air. I held onto her arm as she stepped out, and I watched as she lay back on the grass outside. Ivan followed her, then me. I dropped down onto the grass beside Nosit and looked back into the building, feeling the relief flow out of me, although now all we could do was watch as the building slowly burned. All that work we'd put into the place: painting, mending, fundraising, and it was all going up in smoke, but at least we were safe. At least we'd all got out.

Or so I thought.

"Who the fuck's that?" Three Pies was shouting, and I followed his line of vision to a tiny frosted window next to the office. It had to be the toilet. A hand was waving out of it, desperately trying to get someone to see it. I raced over there.

"Hello! Who's in there?"

"Help! Help!"

She didn't need to tell me who she was. I recognised that crackly old voice, and I wondered what X would think if he knew the only person trapped in his fire now was his old nan.

"Just try and stay calm, Mrs B! We'll have you out in no time," I shouted, and then I turned to Three Pies. I didn't mean to shout, but I was getting heated. "What the hell's she still doing in the karzy? Weren't you supposed to be looking after her?"

"I thought Han took her home," he said, and I thought he was gonna cry.

I turned to Han.

"I thought Three Pies had taken her," he said.

"You were supposed to do it."

"No, you!"

"No, you!"

I put my hands in the air to stop the arguing. As furious as I felt, it wasn't gonna get us anywhere. "You two, stay here and keep her calm. How long for the fire brigade?"

"They said they'd be here as soon as. Dunno!" Mya told me. And I was pacing now, looking at my watch, listening out for the sirens. "You're not going in there," Mya told me, but I wasn't listening. If I had to, I would. I couldn't let a sweet old dear like Mrs B burn.

Then my phone rang again. That same withheld number. I snatched up my phone and answered it. I was about to shout at the geezer, but he spoke first this time.

"You disappoint me, Degsy, spoiling my fun so soon."

I was turning on the spot, looking around. "Can you see us, X?"

He was laughing again, but I'd soon knock it out of him.

"Can you see the frosted karzy window with the hand sticking out of it?"

He was still laughing.

"That's your nan, X." Last time I'd mentioned his beloved nanny to him, he'd pulled a gun on me, so I was glad this was a phone call.

The laughter stopped.

"You're lying."

"Am I?" I said and hung up. There was no more time for games. We couldn't hear sirens, and the fire was raging now. If I left it any longer, Mrs B wouldn't make it. If only that bathroom window was big enough to fit through, but there was only one way she was getting out of there, and that was if I went in after her.

"Give it five more minutes," Mya shouted, holding onto my arm.

"She hasn't got five more minutes," I told her, and we both knew it was true. We could hear the roar of those flames in the hall now. They'd soon close in on the office, and then there'd be no way in.

Mya was still shouting, at the fire and the hopelessness of the situation now rather than at me, and I gripped the window frame, feeling the broken glass pressing into my palms. I brought my leg up and pushed my boot onto the windowsill, but then I stopped. All I could think about was Winston. The last time I was in this situation I ran in without a thought, up the stairs, into Winston's room, and the geezer ended up in a coma trying to get me out of there. I wanted to fling myself into the office, run through and grab Mrs B, but my body wouldn't let me. Then I thought of Winston again, and what he'd do in this situation. If that geezer was here, he'd be in there already, no questions asked, and out by now. I knew I had to do the same, and I took a long, deep breath. It was like I had Winston with me now, pushing me on, telling me I'd got this, giving me his bravery as I pulled myself up onto the windowsill and finally stepped inside.

The office was a little smoky, so I pulled my shirt up over my nose and moved as quickly as I could. I couldn't believe my eyes when I opened the door. Hell itself wasn't as hot as this. Part of the ceiling had collapsed and half the room was a bonfire of floor- and plaster boards. It stank of some kind of chemical too, which worried me.

I looked back to the window, to where there was cool, breathable air, and thought of turning back, but then that little voice I'd heard at the window kept me going. "Help! Help!" I hadn't known her long, but I'd become fond of Mrs B. She was an adventurer, but this was probably a little too much adventure for the old dear.

Every part of me was screaming out, telling me to turn back, but I did the opposite and stepped into the inferno that had once been a community centre. I moved as quickly as I could, but the smoke and heat were slowing me down, and that familiar feeling was starting to come down around my head again. I wasn't built for fire, and I knew I couldn't take much of this without passing out like I did before, but my goal was in sight and I kept going. I edged around to the lavs, opened the door and threw myself in like my life depended on it. Then I slammed it shut behind me and threw my back against it, coughing out my soul but safe for the moment at least.

"Degsy!" a tearful Mrs B was shouting.

"Mrs B. What you doing here? The fundraiser ended ages ago."

"I must have dropped off," she said sadly, and I ran over to the sinks and doused my face. The cool was like nothing I'd felt before. Then I stood up onto the sinks, stuck my face out the window and sucked in a lungful of clean, crisp air. I could feel it giving me life, and I was gonna need it if I was gonna get out alive with Mrs B. I breathed in and out, in and out, then I got a surprise.

"Degsy! You better get my nanny out of there in one piece, bruv. Do you get me?"

I turned my head and was face to face with X.

"Aziz!" Mrs B was shouting. "That you, boy?"

"It's me, Nanny. Just do what Degsy says. He'll get you out," he shouted. I couldn't believe the change in him. I could see traces of the boy in that school photo I'd seen at Mrs B's house. I could almost forget he was the geezer who'd set the fire in the first place, but when he spoke again, just to me now, he showed me his true colours. "And if he don't get you out, I'll end him," he growled. "You get me, Degsy?" With that tinge of insanity back in his eyes, I believed him, but he didn't scare me.

"How are your feet?" I asked, and then I jumped down off the sink and left him there, raging. Threats from X were the least of my problem. We still had to get out, although Mrs B was smiling now as if everything was fine.

"Are you working with him now, Degsy? Helping him turn his life around like you said?"

"Something like that. Look, we need to move, and we need to move now."

Her face changed as I started to move towards the door. "I

can't, Degsy. Don't make me. Leave me here. I'm too scared."

"I ain't leaving you anywhere. And there's nothing to be scared of. Just take my hand, and we'll go together."

"I can't! I can't!" She was in tears again now.

"Mrs B! We ain't got time for this. Take my hand." I was trying to stay calm, but she wasn't moving, and all the time I could hear more of the hall falling in on itself and burning. I didn't even know if there'd be a clear path through, and I was losing my nerve again. It'd taken everything I had to climb through that window and move through the flames. The thought of doing it again made my stomach lurch. What other choice was there, though?

"Okay, get on my back," I told her and skidded over, dropping down in front of her. She was about half my height, so I doubted I'd even notice her on my back. Then we could just get going.

"I can't!" she was still crying.

"Just trust me, Mrs B. That's it. Just grip round there and hold on tight." Finally, she'd got on my back and now I was back at the door. I could feel her trembling as she gripped as hard as she could. I opened it just a touch, and the heat nearly took my head off. I felt Mrs B wince, and I tried to reassure her, but I didn't know how we were gonna make it out, and there was still no sign of a siren. I closed the door again and tried to set her down.

"We gotta go low, Mrs B," I said. "It's the only way." I hoped she'd get off and start getting low, but instead she held on even tighter and didn't even answer me. "Mrs B!" I tried again, but she was going nowhere. The only way she was gonna get down low was if I crawled through with her on my back, like a flipping snail. So I started to crouch, and then I opened that door again. It was a world of raging reds and black and oranges, screaming in my face, roaring its thousand-degree breath. "Hold on!" I shouted, and I don't know if she could hear me over the furnace, but I dropped as low as I could now. There was still space between the bathroom door and the office, but it was a low tunnel and I'd have to lie flat and claw my way across the floor if I wanted to get there without scorching Mrs B's head off. I could feel her making herself smaller on top of me, tucking her head into my shoulder, but I still couldn't take any chances. I reached out for the wall and dragged us half a metre. The strain, with the smoke and heat, was unbelievable, and I was already coughing and finding it hard to breathe. I reached out again and didn't even manage to clear a half metre this time. My lungs were about to explode, and it felt like my boots were melting on my feet. All I wanted to do was sleep, and I could feel my eyes getting heavy, but then I saw Winston's face again, and Mya's and Gabby's, and I felt my strength growing, not to any great level, but I reached out again and managed to drag us a little further. That was is, though. There were maybe five metres left, but it could have been five miles. My arms were drained, my lungs had turned to stone, it was the end.

"Degsy! Degsy! Reach out!"

My eyes must have almost been shutting, because it felt like the voices woke me up. I looked up and that office door was open. Mya and Sheila were crouched in the doorway holding their hands out to me.

"Take my hand! Reach out!"

I didn't think I had the power to do it, but I reached out, hacking my guts up, and felt the tip of Mya's fingers. Then Sheila gripped my wrist, and we were on the move, reeled out of hell and dragged back to safety. When we were safely in the office, I felt the massive weight of Mrs B lift off me. She hadn't seemed heavy in the beginning, but now it was like I'd had a tonne sitting on my back. Then I felt pressure on my feet and managed to turn around to see Mya and Sheila throwing their jackets over my flaming boots. The sight made me sick, and I wanted to sleep again.

"Com'on!" Mya screamed and hoisted my arm up over her

shoulder. I was in another world by this point, in a fog of smoke and flames, but I still managed to get up onto my burning feet, with Sheila supporting my other side. Then Ibrahim, Three Pies and Han were in there too, and they must have lifted me out, because the sudden rush of air was a heaven I never thought I'd feel again. They lowered me down onto the grass, and I thought I was gonna pass out, but the more I breathed, the more I started to feel a little better, although everything hurt, inside and out.

"How's … Mrs B?" I managed to splutter to Mya.

"Have a look yourself," she said.

I managed to lift my head, and saw her hugging her grandson. She was crying and laughing at the same time, and it was almost a beautiful reunion – except her grandson was a right nasty piece of work and had caused all this in the first place. They turned, and now it was his face that I could see. It looked like he was crying too, and when he met my eye, he nodded, and I knew it was over. He may not have known how to look after his own nan; turns out he was pretty grateful that I did. The next thing I knew, sirens blasted as the emergency services finally decided to join us, the geezer legged it, and it was the last time we ever saw him.

"You look like shit," Mya said, sitting beside me as I lay there in the grass.

"Thanks."

"No problem."

"No, I mean really thanks," I said. "I'd be dead without you and Sheila."

"Well, maybe we'd be dead without you too," she said and kissed my forehead.

"Mya," I said when I could see her beautiful face again. "Will you marry me?"

17 WINSTON'S STORY

No surprise that I needed a hospital after all that. The ambulance geezer took one look at me and bundled me into the back, patching me up as we went. Turns out, I was okay. A few burns, a bit of smoke inhalation, and my feet weren't as bad as they looked, but they kept me in anyway. You know me, though. I ain't one to stay put, so as soon as it looked like the nurses were gonna leave me alone for the night, I slipped out of bed, crept past the nurse's station and went down to visit Winston. I heard them chatting about some geezer they'd both got off with at a party the night before and what a scumbag he was, so they weren't about to notice me creeping past. Once I was out the door, I walked like I meant business. I'd learnt the best way to hide was in plain sight, so I walked like I owned the place, and no one I passed gave a shit about who I was or where I should be. When I got to Winston's room, that same nurse, Jane, nearly fainted when she saw me.

"Bloody hell, Degs! Can't you stay safe for a single day. You look like you fell out of the sky without a parachute."

"I feel like it an' all. Is it alright if I go in?"

She looked at me as if I was really pushing it now, but she nodded towards his door anyway. She must have felt sorry for what a state I looked with my busted face, limping around the hospital at night in my pyjamas. I felt sorry for her, though. Didn't she ever go off shift?

"Alright, geez," I said when I was through the door. The sight of him didn't shock me anymore. I sort of wished it did because it meant I was getting used to seeing him like this. The last thing I wanted to do was get used to seeing him in this state, but I didn't let that get me down.

"It's over, Winston, really this time." I told him. "I know

I said it before, but X ain't gonna be touching us again, and we ain't going nowhere neither. All we need's for you to wake up now and everything will be back to normal," I told him, trying to smile. "Com'on, mate. It ain't hard. Just open your eyes." But he didn't even flinch. I reached out and took his hand. It was warm, which was a relief. "Com'on, mate, just your thumb, like you did before. Just move your thumb." But the geezer obviously wasn't in the mood for dancing and didn't even twitch. "Have it your way," I told him. So then I told him everything that had happened at the community centre in graphic detail and how I'd asked Mya to marry me. I couldn't quite believe it myself as I was saying the words, but nothing about my life had ever been straightforward, so why should it start now? Then I chatted some more shit to him, including how the Unit 16-21 project was fully insured. I told him all about the new projects I was thinking of, how excited I was to go over to the States and set up the Hay Pa-trollers there, told him more stories about Jarra and Darel in Oz, and about how I knew I could clear things with Asha and Ray's foster parents now that X was off the scene and start a proper relationship with them. Mostly I talked to him about how relieved I was that it was all over. I'd really thought I was gonna die, that we all were, and now I was dancing on air.

After chatting like this most of the night, I could feel my eyelids getting heavy. They were already heavy enough with swelling, but now I could feel the tiredness creeping in. I needed to find a bed. Luckily, the hospital was full of them.

"I'll pop back in tomorrow, geez," I told him. Then I took a final look at him and pushed through the door. I was happy to see a different nurse, so maybe Jane wasn't here 24/7 after all. I nodded to this replacement nurse, and she looked like she was gonna start shouting at me, but I kept on moving, so she didn't have the chance. As I limped off, I was still thinking about Jane, wondering if maybe she had a husband at home. Kids? Perhaps she lived in a cabin in the woods or a tepee.

She was that proper hippy type. Anyway, I was just grateful she'd been around. I carried on thinking about her, but then my thoughts were interrupted when all these white coats started rushing by me, one after the other, as if the place was on fire, and I'd seen enough of that to last a lifetime. I was so tired, I almost carried on walking, but I couldn't help looking back. They were going into Winston's intensive care unit. There were a few patients in different rooms in there, but my stomach started to roll. I knew they were going in there for him. Don't ask me why. I just knew it.

"Winston!" I shouted, and then I ran back in, burst through the door, past the nurse and back into his room. I was right. They'd been running to get to him, and the closer I got, the more ear-splitting the bleep from his machine became. He'd arrested again, and the bed was surrounded by worried faces and busy hands, all fighting to keep the geezer alive. Again, I was pushed back out of the room, and just as I had before, I stood there watching through the glass, holding my breath as they shocked him, and his whole body spasmed, jerking him forward, but there was no life in his face or body, and that long, high bleep was tearing through my brain.

"Again!" one of the doctors shouted, and they prepared to shock him again. "Back!" Winston's body jerked, and everyone stopped and looked at the monitors, and then they burst into action again. It wasn't working. It wasn't bloody working. It wasn't working. Come on, Winston! Come on, geez! But it wasn't working. And that bleep was an ice pick through my ear and a dagger in my heart. And I couldn't watch anymore. I threw my palms on the glass, but I closed my eyes. It wasn't working. I closed my eyes. I just couldn't watch anymore. It wasn't working …

We had the memorial service a week later. He was never a black suit kind of bloke, so Sheila suggested we wear our most colourful clothes to celebrate what a colourful character he'd been. I still didn't have much to wear since everything had burned in the fire, so I ended up buying this rainbow-striped t-shirt. I wouldn't wear it again after today, but it was a fitting tribute. He also wasn't much of a church kind of geezer, so our memorial service for him was held in the park. I thought it'd be a small, low-key event, but Sheila was having none of that. She'd invited all our friends and every Hay Patroller we'd ever worked with, so when we walked in through the gates, we were met by a sea of multi-coloured mourners who'd come out to pay their respects. It made goose bumps break out on my arms and a lump rise in my throat. I don't think I'd ever seen anything so touching.

Sheila had set things out so we'd stand at the front, with Nosit and Ivan, and even Asha and Ray were there, with the multi-coloured mourners behind, and she'd lead the service, standing in front of a picture of him, looking handsome, cheeky and far too young to have died. Mya took my hand in hers as Sheila started to speak.

"Thank you for coming here today to celebrate the life of my dear friend, which ended far too soon."

Then Winston put his hand on my shoulder and whispered, "I hope this helps her, mon!"

"Me too, bruv," I answered.

Oh, didn't I mention? I might not've been able to watch, but they managed to stabilise Winston that night, and it's like the geezer has nine lives. Just three days later, he started to move and stir, and then he came out of it. Just like that! Lucky bugger didn't have brain damage or anything. He was still pretty weak, and it'd take a while for him to get back to his old self, but he'd thrown on his colourful Rasta cap for the service and a pink t-shirt with sequins on it that really made Sheila laugh. It was gonna be a long road to recovery, but we had him back.

"When I met Michael," Sheila said, turning to the photo of her dear friend. "I didn't have a friend in the world. I was totally alone, and I didn't even know I could have friends. I didn't know it was possible for anyone to like me – or even love me. But Michael was made of love, and there was always enough to go around. He showed me how easy it was to love and be loved when I thought it was impossible. He showed me how to be a friend, how to be loyal, how to stay safe, but, more importantly, how to live knowing that tomorrow isn't guaranteed. Sometimes I wonder if he knew what was coming because there wasn't a single day he didn't live as if it were his last, and we can all learn from that. Don't wait. Go on that trip, eat that cake, jump out of that plane, dance, skip, live, love, because you can never know when it's too late to live your dreams until the time has passed. So do it now. Do it for Michael."

The multi-coloured congregation cheered as Sheila said this, and cheered again when she blasted Michael's favourite Kylie Minogue track across the park. Suddenly, this wasn't a memorial service, it was a party. And the music might not have been to my taste, but I was tapping my feet as the whole park broke into dance. Sheila danced her way over and threw her arms around me.

"He would have loved this," she whispered into my ear, and I could feel the relief in her body and hear it in her voice.

"Feel better?" I asked.

"I'm getting there," she said and kissed my cheek.

When we broke away, we saw Mya and Winston dancing in their multi-coloured clothes, spinning each other around to Kylie Minogue, laughing, joking. Ivan was doing something that looked a little like dancing with Nosit, and Asha and Ray were running around together. I grabbed Sheila and started spinning her around. I hadn't seen that smile on her face for months. I hadn't felt this happy for months either. I took a deep breath, looked around at the happy, dancing faces around me, at Sheila, at my best friend and my beautiful fiancée, and realised I might just have been the luckiest man alive.